Grigori
Returned

The Atlas Series
Book 2

BECCA C. SMITH

Published by Red Frog Publishing, a division of Red Frog Media

First published in 2014

The characters and events portrayed in this book are fictitious. Any similarity to real persons, living or dead, is coincidental and not intended by the author.

ISBN 978-0990565000

Printed in the United States of America

Dedicated to my sister Julie for being the best darn big sis on the planet! Love you :-)

DAY ONE

Chapter One

Kala watched Jack's body drop to the floor with a small thud.

She was frozen in place.

Her mind completely comatose.

She stared at the pool of blood forming on the ground from the hole in Jack's head.

He was gone.

Forever.

And she had been the one who did it.

Kala killed the only man she ever loved.

The gun dropped from her hand.

The gun that had killed Jack.

Jack.

Her eyes couldn't look away. The blood crept across the wood floor and surrounded Kala's feet. Jack's face was slack, empty of all life. No more smiles. No more sparkling eyes. No more kisses.

Dead.

Kala felt like if she moved, her whole brain would crack. She'd end up curled in a ball sobbing until her body would give up and die.

If she hadn't been so still, Kala probably wouldn't have felt the slight brushing of a hand on her arm.

"We need to go." Penny's voice sounded small in the silence.

Kala still couldn't move. She continued to stare at Jack laying at her feet.

"I can't," Kala managed to say.

"You have to," Penny said with some urgency. "It'll be harder to kill you now, but you can definitely be tortured and imprisoned. Asmodeus will be here any second. I won't be able to protect you."

"My dad banished him to the 5th Level of Hell. He and Talan both seem to think Asmodeus will be there for a while." Kala's brain started to feel like it was thawing. Talking about two very powerful Grigori angels: her foster father, Owen, and her stalker, Talan, began to bring her back into reality. Using the word *reality* in the same sentence as angels still made her feel nuts, but the last four days had been a crash course on what was *real* in the world she lived in.

Besides, seeing Penny's face at the mention of Talan, and now her dad, was all worth it. The supernatural world had no idea the Grigori were back and it scared them to pieces. Though Penny claimed to be on Kala's side now, she had been a royal pain in her butt since the beginning of the *Atlas* ride. Making her squirm gave Kala a small surge of happiness in this darkest moment of her life.

"Impossible." Penny sounded terrified.

Good.

"You keep saying that," Kala pointed out with a little bit of snark. Right now, panicking Penny helped her break out of the shock-coma she was in.

"Because it is!" Penny exclaimed.

"Relax," Kala scolded, finally looking away from Jack's body to stare down Penny. "Why is it so *impossible* that the Grigori are back? Asmodeus was just as freaked. Are they really that powerful?" At this point Kala was fishing. She didn't know much about the Grigori except that there were only a handful of them that had escaped some kind of "Heaven prison." She *did*, however, have a firsthand account at some of their tricks. Talan had made a Malak explode with the touch of his hand, and had taught her a pretty nifty fire trick that allowed her to set Malaks and Demons into a fiery blaze. But her foster dad, Owen, had never revealed his true nature, so aside from banishing the king of Demons to the 5th Level of Hell, she had no idea the extent of his power.

Penny shook her head. "It's too much to explain. Please. I can't bear to see him like that." Her voice broke.

It brought tears to Kala's eyes. Hearing Penny so hurt at Jack's death only reminded her that she was the one who had killed him. Kala felt a surge of overwhelming emotion. She didn't think she could contain it much longer.

So she nodded.

Penny left first.

Kala forced herself to look at Jack one more time, knowing this was the last time she'd ever see him. Watching him lying there, the pool of blood now a lake surrounding his body, Kala hoped that Jack was in a place like the heaven Talan had shown her. It may have been a prison to the Grigori, but it was the most beautiful place Kala had ever seen. Jack was the best person she had ever known and if anyone deserved to be in an eternal paradise it was him.

Tearing her eyes away, Kala followed Penny out of the building.

As she walked through the exit door, Kala fell to her knees.

A flash of light and she was suddenly in a gigantic chamber. There was a throne the size of a large house at the end of the enormous space. Pillars lined the walls on both sides. A man sat on the throne, surrounded by five men on his right and six women on his left. They were huge! Well over twenty feet tall.

Kala looked down at her body and noticed that she wasn't in *her body*. She was in a man's body.

As she viewed the giants more carefully, Kala realized that she actually knew them.

With a certainty that fascinated her more than scared her, Kala realized that she was seeing one of Atlas's memories. Somehow when she had swallowed the Titan whole, she had apparently swallowed his memories as well.

It was Cronus sitting on the throne, with his sisters and brothers beside him.

Kala immediately recognized Atlas's father, Iapetus, by his disapproving glare. Then Kala cringed as she sorted out Atlas's lineage in her head. All the Titans that stood in front of her were brothers and sisters. But this was where Kala's disgusted-bell went off. Iapetus's brother and sister, Oceanus and Tethys, had a daughter, Asia, and Atlas was the offspring of Iapetus and Asia. So Atlas was the product of some serious inbreeding. Kala shuddered. There were only twelve of them around back then and the pickings were slim, but still.

Asia was nowhere to be found, but Grandma and Grandpa were scowling at Atlas/Kala in the same way that Pops was.

At first glance Kala had registered the twelve figures as human, but the more she looked at them, the more otherworldly they seemed. Aside from their size, they had a deep blue glow around them as if they were outlined in light. Their faces looked like they were carved in stone, they were so symmetrical. Their presence was intimidating for Kala, but she could feel it even more so for Atlas. In this memory, he was downright terrified.

Kala took a deep breath.

This was who she was now.

Atlas's past was her past.

This must be a part of the integration process, she rationalized. *But why this memory?*

Kala had the sneaking suspicion she was about to be scolded by some serious mojo-toting gods. She tried to remember the rest of it so she wouldn't have to go through it in real-time, but it wasn't working. She even tried calling out for Penny, hoping she could pull her out of this dream-state. Kala probably still stood in the doorway to Jack's hideout, drooling in the sun, or collapsed on the front porch.

But nothing worked. She was there to stay.

Kala shrugged.

It looked like she'd have to take her licks. She just hoped it wouldn't last long.

Then Kala spoke, or at least, Atlas spoke. Kala was just along for the ride in this flashback.

"They threatened me! I didn't have a choice!" Atlas whined like a baby. Kala wished she could change the memory and say what was really on Atlas's mind. He was furious that his plan hadn't worked. Apparently, there had been another war between the Titans and the Olympians and Atlas had picked the wrong side.

Again.

Kala was really starting to hate the fact that she had to share any part of herself with Atlas. To her, he was a coward. A guy who picked the team he thought would win with no loyalty. And when he inevitably lost, he groveled. Kala despised people who did that. She had seen enough soldiers like Atlas to make her skin crawl.

Cronus, apparently, felt the same way as Kala, because he leaned forward in his throne. "You are pathetic, Atlas. A sniveling rat who begs for his life after betraying your father."

Kala wished she could shut Atlas up, but as this wasn't her memory, she cringed when he yelled, "*You* castrated your father to take over the world!" Kala felt Atlas calming himself. "I just sided with your son. Is that really a crime?"

The other Titans stayed silent, waiting for Cronus to speak on their behalf. "Yes, Atlas, it *is* a crime."

"May I remind you that I have to do my job or you won't have a world to rule." Kala could tell Atlas was trying to remind the Titans that he had some value.

Cronus nodded and laughed. "That was your punishment for siding with us, your true family. If you had stayed loyal, we could have made Zeus lift this burden from you."

Atlas must have seen something in Cronus's eyes that Kala couldn't, because his fear level jumped drastically. "It's fine, really. I like my burden. Just doing my part to keep the earth spinning and such…" Atlas started to back away.

Kala began to see what Atlas saw. Cronus's smile turned into a wickedly cruel snarl, as if he had just swallowed a canary. "Atlas!" Cronus announced as if he were making a decree. "The next time you complete the cycle, you will be stripped of all your protections, and we'll see how you fare against everyone you've wronged. The four-day curse is still your burden, and after this cycle we will no longer hide you from the ones who want to stop you."

Kala searched her brain for any kind of thought or memory as to what happened to Atlas after he completed his next cycle, but she came up with nothing.

She could feel Atlas in a complete panic. "But if I fail, you lose everything! Why would you risk that?" Atlas couldn't fathom why the Titans would drop their protections over him when it could mean the end of the world.

"Making you live in constant fear and shame over what you did is worth the risk. We can always find another if you fail. We'll have to force my son Zeus to comply since he is the one who created the curse, but torturing him will be extremely satisfying." Cronus stopped smiling as if he were now officially bored with this conversation. He leaned back in his throne. "Go. Do whatever it is you're supposed to do."

Cronus snapped his fingers.

Kala's eyes opened and she found herself sitting on the front steps of Jack's hideout, leaning against the iron railing.

Penny was next to her. "What happened?" she asked, more curious than concerned.

"Memories," Kala grumbled. "So am I going to pass out every time I have a new flashback of Atlas's?" Kala stood up, annoyed.

Penny joined her and motioned for Kala to walk with her. "Something like this has never happened before, so I have no idea. What did you see?"

Kala followed Penny's lead as they walked down the street toward the train station.

"Some big-ass Titans scolding Atlas for switching sides. They said they were going to take away his 'protections' as punishment. What happened to Atlas after that? Please tell me he got his butt kicked." Even though Kala was officially the same person, she still despised him. He represented the complete opposite of who she was.

Penny was silent for a few moments, then she spoke quietly. "That's when I took him into hiding and showed him how to trick the first human. He never lost his protections from the Titans because he never completed the next cycle on his own, his surrogates did."

Kala rolled her eyes. "Of course he didn't. What a dick."

"You're missing the point here, Kala. *You're* Atlas now." Penny stared at her knowingly.

But Kala didn't understand what Penny was trying to imply. "Yeah, so?"

"So, *this* is the next cycle. After it's over, it'll be *you* that loses those 'protections'."

Kala groaned.

Chapter Two

Kala didn't say a word after that information bomb. She had too many other things to think about anyway. First off, the most important piece of knowledge she gained from her trip down memory lane was the fact that Zeus had created the four-day curse and was the only one who could break it. It literally tore her insides to shreds to think that there might have been a way to stop killing Jack. She blamed herself for not finding out about Zeus and the curse earlier. It had never occurred to her that Zeus even existed let alone was hanging around somewhere and she could have forced him into taking Atlas's curse away. Of course, that probably would have required handing over Atlas as opposed to what she had done when she swallowed him whole.

Thinking about that moment brought a chill to her bones. Kala hadn't had any idea what she was saying when she confronted Atlas. It was as if someone else had been speaking, like she was a puppet on strings. Kala started to remember the words of the prophecy Penny had been so sure was about Jack, but ultimately had been about Kala. *One cannot live while the other one exists. A new Atlas shall reign; and the potential must die. A beginning to the end; and an end to the beginning. A new paradise shall be born. The Fated One will be the last.*

Kala felt a surge of hope. If she was the Fated One and the Fated One would be the last, then maybe that meant she'd talk Zeus into letting her out of this four-day contract. The prophecy did mention paradise being born, that had to be good, right? Kala's head started hurting. Her whole life was making her sick.

"In here." Penny nodded towards a small brick building.

It was nondescript and blended into the blocks and blocks of brick row housing. If Penny hadn't stopped, Kala wouldn't have even noticed it had been there. Penny opened the door. Inside was completely empty except for a twin mattress on the floor and a small desk in the corner with papers stacked on top.

"Is this yours?" Kala asked with curiosity. Somehow, she had imagined Penny living in some plush, fancy penthouse somewhere in the swanky part of D.C., not this grungy heap of squalor in Alexandria.

"What did you expect?" Penny walked over to the desk and started shuffling through the papers looking for something.

"Not this." Kala shrugged. "What are you looking for?"

"I have a copy of the Ancient Texts. Now that we know you're the Fated One, we need to know everything we can about the rest of the prophecy," Penny said as she continued her search.

"Wait. There's more to the prophecy?" Kala would have gulped if she had it in her. But Kala still grasped onto the words *paradise* and *the last*. Maybe the rest was just details on how to corner Zeus and make him lift the curse.

"Of course there's more," Penny snapped. "We need details." Penny didn't even look up.

Kala could see that Penny was frantic, as in, something personal was at stake. There was no way Penny was this concerned about Kala, of that she was certain. Kala gathered that her being the Fated One meant something more to Penny, more than she was letting on anyway.

Kala walked over to Penny and grabbed her arm. "Hey, what's all this about?"

Penny shrugged her off and practically scowled. "I thought *you* of all people would want to know what your destiny is?"

"At this point, I'm thinking I find Zeus and beat the crap out of him until he breaks the curse. I was hoping you'd point me in the right direction seeing as you're his... what... niece or something?" Kala's grasp of Greek mythology was still lacking, but from the family chart in Kala's brain from her brief encounter with the Titan memory, it was a safe bet that Penny or Pandora... Pandora...

Penny had confirmed that she was the one and only Pandora to Kala before she had to kill Jack. Kala's brain hadn't had time to process what that meant or if it was of any importance to her at all. But her curiosity got the best of her. "Was there ever a box?" Kala asked referring to the one legend she *did* know. Pandora was given a box and opened it, despite being told not to and that was how all the evils of the universe were released. Supposedly, Pandora closed the box before it all leaked out and hope was still contained inside.

"No. Like most of your human histories, it's more of a symbolic version of the truth. The box or jar, whichever legend you go by, was my part in helping Atlas trick the humans into taking his job. So, in a sense, I did release all the evils of the world onto humanity, by making people responsible for keeping the balance of good and evil in check," Penny said as if she had prepared to answer that question a long time ago. "And, no, I'm not Zeus's niece. I'm his granddaughter. Hephaestus is Zeus's son and Hephaestus is my father, and if we don't figure this out, he is going to die." Then Penny looked at Kala like she was a nut job. "And even with Atlas's super strength, Zeus could crush you, so I wouldn't be too keen on picking a fight with the guy. Besides, the Titans keep him locked up in the 5th, so good luck trying to get to him."

"Wait a minute. The 5th? As in the 5th Level of Hell? That place my dad sent Asmodeus? Isn't that where the Elders or whatever are?" All these new places and vocabulary were making Kala's head spin.

Penny stared at Kala as if she were an irritating gnat. "Who do you think the Elders are?"

"Some kind of old super Demons or something?" Kala had figured that, since Asmodeus was the king of Demons, he answered to… other Demons. She hadn't given it much thought.

"The Elders are Titans, Kala, as in Elder gods. It's in your human history books." Penny went back to searching the papers. "Your daddy and grandparents waged war against the entire supernatural existence and won. They rule from the 5th to protect themselves from rebellion. If they find out the Grigori are back after all the energy they spent banishing them, they're going to be furious. And you don't want to see Cronus furious."

Kala remembered Atlas's memory. "Yeah, he seemed like a dick."

Penny briefly glanced up at Kala and a hint of a smile showed on her face, then she shook her head. "He is. A dangerous one." Penny grabbed a piece of paper with triumph. "Here it is."

Kala fought the urge to grab it out of Penny's hand. It was about her after all, but she let Penny scan through it first.

"So the Titans banished the Grigori? How'd they manage that?" Kala wondered.

Penny focused on the paper and it took a moment for her to respond. "The Olympians had a weapon that drained the Grigori of their powers, but the Titans secretly spelled the weapon to drain the Olympians too. The Olympians didn't even know what hit them. But even then, it wasn't enough. You asked how powerful the Grigori are? It took the combined strength of the Olympians and the Titans to banish them. Now that the Titans have the Demons on their side, they may be able to fight back the Grigori, but I'm just not sure." Penny gave Kala an exasperated groan. "Can't you access Atlas's memories so I don't have to be your walking encyclopedia?"

Kala tried to take as much sarcasm out of her voice as she could. "Well, I'd love to, but it's not exactly something I can control…"

***

Great.

Kala had no idea where she was, but it wasn't like any

place she'd ever been to on earth. She could be anywhere really, considering this was Atlas's past she was visiting. It looked like she was in the center of a nebula with purple and blue gasses swirling around her. It was a strange sensation being inside someone else's body, and frankly, Kala hated it. Being knocked unconscious just to have a flashback was extremely dangerous in Kala's position. The soldier in her despised that. She was trained to always have an exit, but Kala had no control over her own brain. That left her vulnerable. The only plus side: now Kala was an actual Titan. She couldn't be killed that easily or even at all (she still wasn't convinced of that one). It was a mental adjustment she hadn't quite accepted yet. She still thought of herself as human. And as a human, her body could easily be killed. But as a Titan, she was… less killable.

The first thing Kala noticed in this blast from the past was that she was not alone. She was standing next to…

Asmodeus.

Could she ever get away from this guy?

At least he wasn't lusting after her Atlas form. Kala was spared that. Not that she minded necessarily, the Demon was definitely a hottie, but he was such a jerk about it. In this memory, Asmodeus wore all black and his sandy brown hair wasn't in the modern day swoop cut that Kala was used to. It was longer and pulled back, which only made his chiseled face all the more chiseled. With his straight nose, slightly full lips, and completely ripped physique, the guy looked like he had just walked off a romance novel cover.

Currently, Asmodeus looked at Atlas as if he were a leper. "Are you sure about this Atlas? If you're lying, you know what I'll do to you."

Kala felt herself speak. "I'm a Titan. I can squash you, Demon King."

Asmodeus yawned. "Please. You're a second generation Titan. And I'm more than willing to see who would win the fight. How about you?"

Kala experienced a thrill of fear run through Atlas. He may be threatening Asmodeus, but even he didn't believe he could best the Demon King. Kala inwardly moaned. Atlas was such a wuss! "I'm telling the truth. The Olympians will take down the Titans once and for all."

"I'd like to hear that from someone besides the weasel that switches sides like he's a hot potato." Asmodeus crossed his arms. He looked like he was about to leave if Atlas didn't say something convincing enough for him to stay.

"Listen, Zeus is gathering his army against Cronus. It's only the Grigori that stand in their way. I made the mistake of siding with my father in the last war and look where it got me. With the Demons on our side, we'll crush Cronus and the Titans once and for all." Kala could sense the determination in Atlas. He really thought the Olympians would win.

Asmodeus spat. "The Grigori? They can't be defeated. Not even the Olympians can hurt them."

"They can, I swear on my life." Atlas tried to convince Asmodeus.

"What's in this for you?" Asmodeus eyed Atlas carefully.

It took a few moments before Atlas finally responded, "Zeus promises to relieve me of my curse if I help him."

But Kala knew Asmodeus better than Atlas because she could read that snarky look on his face. Asmodeus was simply gathering information. He had no intention of helping Atlas or Zeus, and Atlas was clueless. He was spilling state secrets like a fool.

"You and that curse." Asmodeus chuckled. "Zeus's biggest mistake. Tearing out the balance of the universe as if it were made of fabric and turning it into a neat little curse. Now that's abusing power. He's my kind of god."

Kala felt the hope rise in Atlas at Asmodeus's words. Kala waited for the inevitable letdown that was about to come.

Asmodeus shook his head as if he felt sorry for Atlas. "Thanks for being an idiot. You never disappoint, Atlas. While we stand here, the battle has already begun. It's too late for you to warn them. It's too late for anything. You gods love your double-crosses. I'll be sure to tell your daddy you said hello."

Kala woke up in Penny's dingy apartment. She lay on the twin mattress while Penny sat on the edge of the bed, completely engrossed in reading the prophecy and ignoring Kala entirely.

"I'm back," Kala announced. Not that Penny cared.

Penny turned to Kala with a frustrated expression on her face. "Good. Read this. See if it makes any sense to you."

Kala took the proffered paper from Penny. Though the actual paper itself came from the nearest office supply store, the copy of the text on the page was obviously from a really old document. It was handwritten in calligraphy, making it very difficult for Kala to decipher. Kala grew up with computer keyboards, not handwriting, let alone the fancy kind. The text took up half the page, making Kala's heart sink. If this was all they had to go on, it wasn't much.

After a few moments of squinting and rotating the paper

every which way, Kala finally sighed, "You might have to help me with this."

Penny snatched the document back with a roll of her eyes and pointed to a specific sentence. "This top part you already know, but this is the rest of it." Penny read out loud, "*The cost will be great, and the immortals will reign. The one that knows death will release the curse of balance.*"

WTF? "What does that mean?" Kala asked aloud more gracefully than what she had thought in her head.

"I don't know," Penny answered honestly. "Does anything resonate with you? I think we've established that you're the Fated One at this point. I thought you'd be able to translate."

"Not a clue. Sorry." Kala tried to read the prophecy herself. Now that she knew what it said, it was a little easier to navigate through the calligraphy. "*The one that knows death will release the curse of balance.* In my memory flashback, Asmodeus said that Zeus created Atlas's curse by ripping out the balance of the universe. Is this talking about that same curse or are there other crazy-ass curses you haven't told me about? Do you think *the one that knows death* will break *my* curse? Cronus seemed to think Zeus was the only one who could undo it, maybe Zeus is *the one that knows death?*" Kala brainstormed more to herself than expecting any real answers from Penny.

Penny had a kind of helpless expression on her face that said it all to Kala. Penny was as confused as she was, but more apparent was the fact that Penny looked defeated. "I'm never going to find him."

The tone in Penny's voice made Kala's heart squeeze. "Your dad?"

Penny nodded and turned away just as her eyes welled up, not wanting Kala to see.

And even though she mostly hated Penny, Kala found herself saying, "Look, I'll help you find your dad. Maybe he's being held with Zeus or something." It took a few seconds to register in Kala's brain what she had just said aloud. Granted, everything that had happened to her in the last four days left little room for doubt of the supernatural, but it still wasn't normal for her to have a conversation about Greek gods in a serious way.

"We can't go to the 5th Level of Hell!" Penny exclaimed in fear and shock. "We'd be killed or tortured for eternity!"

"I can take you there."

Kala and Penny whirled around to see who spoke.

Standing in the doorway was Talan.

Chapter Three

Kala didn't know if she wanted to run into his arms or kick him in the groin. Both options seemed satisfying at the moment. Instead, she chose to stay where she was on the mattress. Kala wasn't mad at Talan; in fact, he had been the perfect gentlemen in the most difficult moment of her life. It was the fact that he thought they were destined to be together and wasn't shy about telling her. Talan's admission made her angry, like he was belittling how she felt about Jack. And now, by looking at her with nothing but love, it felt like he was disrespecting the dead. Kala had killed her one true love and Talan stared at her as if *he* were her one true love. She wanted to punch him in the throat, and now that she had Atlas's strength, she was seriously considering it.

Penny stood up, terror in her eyes. "Talan."

Talan nodded kindly. "Hello, Pandora."

It wasn't hard for Kala to figure out that the two of them had a history. "You two know each other?"

Penny gave Kala a look of annoyed disgust. "Mind your own business."

Kala took that as a yes. She stood up and walked over to Talan. "How can you get us to the 5th Level of Hell?"

Talan's eyes bored into Kala with so much concern she had to turn away. He started to reach out to touch her arm, but stopped himself. "Are you okay?"

The way he asked made Kala's heart squeeze, but she didn't want to cry, not in front of him and definitely not in front of Penny. "I'm fine. Can you get us there or not?"

Penny apparently had felt like she needed more answers. "Talan. How are you back? And how long has it been?"

Talan kept his eyes on Kala as if waiting to make sure she was all right before he talked to Penny. Kala didn't like his intensity, she wasn't ready for it, but she nodded nevertheless. "Go ahead. I'll back your play," Kala said to Talan, letting him know that if he chose to lie about how many Grigori had escaped their prison, she'd go along with it. As far as Kala knew only a handful of the Grigori made it through, but she wasn't sure if Talan wanted Penny to know that. If her dad was the Olympian god Hepha-something, that may put Penny on the ally-at-a-distance list. Penny had tried to make Jack kill her for the last four days, and Kala was a grudge-holder.

And friends? Seriously? Talan and Penny? She couldn't imagine it. Did they *hang* out? It was hard for Kala to picture the two of them doing anything casual. What the heck was Penny anyway? A god? Demi-god? Thinking of them together annoyed Kala even though every fiber of her body didn't want to care either way.

Talan spoke to Penny. "You should have known that the prison wouldn't be strong enough to hold the Grigori. Haven't you wondered why technology has grown exponentially in the last century? The Elders imprisoned the Grigori for involving ourselves with humans, but they were just scared that the humans would surpass them. And trust me, Pandora, they *will*," he said passionately. Kala could tell Talan was angry and he took it all out on Penny.

Penny yelled back just as vehemently. "Don't kid yourself. The Titans banished you because they were afraid of the Grigori. You're stronger than they are. Stronger than the Olympians. And, Talan, you *were* making humans too powerful. You had to be stopped! If you hadn't..."

Kala answered for her, "Then *humans* would be able to kick the gods' collective asses."

"It doesn't matter." Penny crossed her arms defensively. "The prophecy says very clearly that *the immortals will reign*. So teach away. The humans will always be weak no matter how many weapons you show them how to create."

"We'll see." Talan eyed Penny as if he would smite her where she stood.

It gave Kala a perverse satisfaction, and she understood his sentiment. Kala had, after all, done her fair share of *smiting* Penny. From shooting her to snapping her neck to lighting her on fire, Penny's immortality had protected her from any real harm, but Kala hated to admit that it had helped get out all her aggression toward the girl.

22

Instead of attacking Penny, Talan focused all his attention on Kala. "How are you integrating?"

Penny felt the need to chime in snootily, "If you mean she keeps passing out every five minutes from memory flashbacks, then the girl is doing fantastic."

Talan's eyes never left Kala's. "Is that true?"

Kala nodded, a little embarrassed at her obvious lack of control over her own consciousness. "I can handle it," Kala lied. The truth was, the blackouts were becoming more than she could manage. What if she blacked out in the 5th? It was a level of Hell after all. Kala took another second to re-live *that* sentence, then turned to Talan. "How long do you think it will keep happening?"

Talan finally moved from the doorway and led Kala back to the mattress. He acted as if Penny wasn't even in the room with them. Penny didn't seem to want to force the issue of her presence either, so she stayed planted where she was with her arms still crossed.

"Lie down," Talan instructed Kala. "I'm going to need to touch your forehead." He awaited her approval.

Kala nodded. She had made Talan promise not to touch her, and he had held true to his word. When his hand pressed down on her forehead, Kala felt her whole body shiver. It was *the* reason why she didn't want him to touch her. Chemistry. They had it. Kala didn't like it. It made her feel guilty about Jack. End of story.

The shiver turned into something more physical, as in actual heat. Talan was doing something to Kala, something *Grigori*.

Kala suddenly cried out in pain as a flood of images rushed before her eyes. They were moving so fast she couldn't focus on any single one. It was the same as when Talan had shown

23

her memories of his past. And also when he had shown Kala her possible future if she didn't kill Jack. But unlike both those instances, there were too many images flying past her to slow it down.

Talan's voice calmed her as he spoke. "Don't try to focus on any of the images. I'm releasing them from where they are stored in your brain. There are too many memories for you to integrate all at once. Atlas is thousands of years old and your mind locked the memories away so you wouldn't go insane."

"My *mind* locked them away or Roberta did?" Kala grunted through clenched teeth. When Kala had consumed Atlas, her human body tried to reject the god's essence. If it hadn't been for her commanding general, Geoffrey Turner and his wife Roberta, Kala would have died soon after. But Roberta had used her own magic–or what she had called astral projection–to help Kala take Atlas in and assimilate him into her body.

"Either way, that's why you lose consciousness when recalling Atlas's memories. They're stored in a spot that takes too much effort to access," Talan explained.

"Aren't you going to kill me by releasing them all?" Kala asked, trying to rein in the throbbing.

"No," Talan replied gently. "I'm putting the memories in your frontal cortex so you can retrieve them at will, but not remember them all at once."

The images stopped and her head no longer hurt. Kala didn't feel any different. She didn't remember anything new. Sitting up, she looked at Talan, confused. "I don't remember any of Atlas's past."

Talan smiled warmly. "You will. It'll be like any of your old memories, you'll see something familiar, and a single recollection will be triggered. No more blackouts."

Kala didn't argue. One thing she knew for certain: she trusted Talan. And if he said she wasn't going to black out anymore, then she believed him. Kala felt an enormous sense of relief. This whole "integration" process was annoying. So far being a god sucked.

Talan rose to his feet, holding his hand out to help Kala stand. She ignored it and stood up herself.

"So are we going to the 5th or what?" Kala said, ready for a fight.

Chapter Four

"What about your mission? Have you seen what you have to do yet?" Talan asked.

"Oh that," Kala complained. "No. I haven't had time. It's been what? An hour since I killed Jack? Relax!" Kala spat in anger. She hoped she could avoid her Atlas duties entirely. Talking about breaking into what equated to a high-security dimension of Hell and possibly fighting Titans sounded like fun to Kala. Being a soldier was everything she had ever known and now that she was a god, she wanted to try out some of her new abilities. So far, Kala only knew she had super strength because of the way she'd tossed Penny across the room the night before, but Kala was eager to see if her Atlas powers could do anything else.

Penny chimed in with an attitude, "Well, you'd better figure out what it is. You saw a glimpse of what will happen if you don't go through with it."

Kala wanted to elbow Penny in the mouth for even speaking. The girl grated on Kala's every nerve. "I have four days," Kala said as if this were a defense.

"It doesn't mean you have to take the full four days," Penny sniped back.

"Listen." Kala stood up and pointed her finger at Penny's chest. "If I have to *commit acts of atrocity* every freaking day I'll go insane. I'm going to take the four days, so get over it." Kala figured that there was a reason four days were given to complete the mission. Even Zeus knew that gods had their limits. Four days wasn't a lot of time to recover from doing the horrible things the Atlas job required, but it was something. And Kala intended on taking full advantage.

Still. A part of Kala was curious as to what insidious thing the universe needed her to do in order to stop the world from ending. Maybe it wouldn't be that bad this time. Nothing could be worse than killing Jack. Nothing. Her stomach turned at the thought of Jack's blood pooling at her feet.

Kala blinked away tears. "I need to see a TV. That's how I see the visions." Kala hid all evidence of her emotions as she stared Penny in the eye. "Let's get this over with."

Talan snapped his fingers and a flat screen television appeared on the wall.

"Does that come with free cable as well?" Kala joked at Talan's ability to make expensive televisions suddenly appear in crappy apartments.

"Whatever you need," Talan answered seriously, "But you probably only need a signal to see the vision."

Kala sighed heavily. "Just turn it on."

The power light went from red to green and the sight made Kala's heart skip a beat.

She wasn't ready to see.

Kala shook out her arms and legs and rolled her neck like she was about to enter a boxing ring. Anything to calm her down. A fight she could handle. She could control. But waiting for a TV to turn on so she could watch some horrendous thing that she'd have to do: nauseating.

The screen on the television finally came into focus. Kala tilted her head to try to figure out what she was seeing. It looked like a close-up of some kind of document.

"Can you turn the station?" Penny asked Talan.

"No. Be quiet." Talan didn't even look at Penny.

If Kala weren't so concentrated on the television, she would have smiled at Talan's dismissiveness toward Penny. It seemed Penny irritated him as much as she irritated Kala.

Kala knew that what the two of them were seeing was completely different from what she was seeing. To them, the television was playing whatever show was currently airing. But to Kala, this was how she saw her Atlas missions. Television screens. From streaming on a phone to the Jumbotron at a football game, the vision of her mission always played on repeat.

Kala fought back tears again as she remembered the last four days and having to re-live the nightmare of killing Jack every time she was near a television. She had thought she could fight it. Stop it somehow…

Shaking off her emotions, Kala focused on the screen.

It was definitely some kind of document. The writing was a series of equations, and that was all Kala could make out. She wasn't great at math, but she had taken enough classes in high school to know that these equations were way over her head. As if a camera was filming the whole event, Kala's view zoomed out to reveal a man that she recognized: John Fortski. The scientist that worked for General Turner. Kala knew almost nothing about the man except for the fact that Turner had a lot of insanely advanced technology and she figured Fortski was probably responsible for inventing a lot of it. On the screen, Fortski was panicked, shaking his head.

Kala cringed. *Please tell me I don't have to kill this guy.* Taking out someone who basically equated to the Albert Einstein of her time made her head hurt. Although a small part of her knew it would be easier than killing Jack. Being a sniper, Kala had killed before, so she knew she could do it again, but she had lost the stomach for it after Jack.

On screen, Kala walked into view. She was holding a gun, but she wasn't pointing it at Fortski. Kala recognized her stance. She wanted Fortski to believe that she'd kill him if necessary, but she could see that the Kala in the vision had zero intentions of hurting him.

They were in some kind of laboratory, filled with metal tables stacked with ongoing experiments. Only Kala and Fortski were in the room.

There were three computers next to Fortski and vision/Kala. All of them were destroyed, their hard drives pulled out and smashed. Apparently, the documents in Fortski's hands were all that was left of whatever was on the computers because the Kala on the TV leapt forward and grabbed the papers from his hand.

Fortski screamed, "Please! You can't! That's the only copy."

"I know. I destroyed all the hard drives." Vision/Kala said somberly. "I have to do this. Trust me. It's for the best."

"No, please!" Fortski pleaded. "Do you know how many lives I can save with that? Thousands! Millions even!"

Vision/Kala shook her head. "I have to."

"Didn't you ever know anyone with cancer? You can save them! You'll be destroying the cure! Do you understand? You're destroying the only copy I have! I can't memorize equations like this! Turner will kill you for this!" Fortski was in a total panic now.

But Vision/Kala looked determined. Calm even. "No, he won't," Vision/Kala said confidently. Then she pulled out the lighter that Talan had given her and set the documents on fire.

Fortski screamed and leapt at her, but Vision/Kala didn't use her gun, she simply shoved him hard. The push from a god made Fortski fly across the room and smash against the back wall. There he slumped to the ground, crying.

When the scene started to repeat, Kala turned the TV off.

"Really?" Kala exclaimed incredulously.

"What did you see?" Penny asked.

The look in Penny's eyes was a little too greedy for Kala's taste.

"I have the mission, that's all you two need to know." Kala decided against telling either one of them. Talan she trusted, but Penny was another story.

Talan didn't seem fazed or offended at all. *Of course!* But Penny… she appeared downright annoyed.

"How can we help you if we don't know what you're supposed to do?" Penny practically harrumphed.

"Just let me handle it," Kala demanded.

Then it truly struck her. She was going to have to *destroy* the cure for cancer. The cure for freaking cancer! Fortski was brilliant enough to discover the cure and the universe wanted Atlas to demolish it? Why? Why would any force of good want something like that to happen? It rocked Kala. Maybe she wasn't a force of good; maybe the job of Atlas was evil. It certainly felt that way. Kala had to remind herself that killing Jack saved billions of lives. But curing cancer? How could destroying something so important be the right thing to do? By not letting Fortski release the cure, it would kill more people than it could possibly save. Wouldn't it?

Glass crashed.

The muted THWAP of a silenced gunshot reached Kala's ears.

She felt the bullet smack her square in the heart.

It took Kala a second to comprehend that a sniper had just shot her! She watched in shock as the bullet popped out of her chest and clattered to the floor.

A rain of muted bullets followed.

Kala screamed over the strange noise. "It's Clifton!"

Before any more bullets could find their way into their bodies, Talan lifted his hand. A clear dome formed over their heads, the ammunitions bouncing harmlessly off its surface.

"I'll get us out of here," Talan reached out to touch both Penny and Kala.

Kala took a step back. "I have to see who it is for sure."

Hundreds of bullets battered the protective dome like metal hail. It even sounded like hail. Kala remembered lying in bed listening to the frozen rain hit the roof when she had first arrived at Owen and Linda's home. She had felt safe for the first time in her life. She was safe now too. If this was Clifton's military team coming to get her, they were way out of their league. General Clifton was Turner's partner, but they didn't share the same opinion of Kala. Turner was on her side and believed in the unexplainable, whereas Clifton was bitter and jealous and wanted Kala dead because he didn't like or trust her. And he had the power to send elite military squads to attempt to take her out.

Through the bouncing bullets, Kala tried to see where the shooters were. She spotted them through the broken window and across the street in the adjacent building. The more she focused the easier it was to see the snipers. It was as if her eyes were binoculars. She almost lost focus it was such a new and strange sensation, but she needed to see who she was up against.

Her view was now close-up, as if she were in the same room with the shooters. There were four. She recognized two, and they were definitely Clifton's guys.

The snipers stopped after seeing Kala's protection. They probably thought she had some state-of-the-art bullet shield. They'd never guess that a Grigori angel was using his powers to protect her.

Within seconds, five soldiers busted down the door and entered the room, guns drawn and pointed at Kala, Penny and...

Where was Talan?

There wasn't a shred of doubt that the angel was still there, it just threw Kala off as to why he'd hide himself.

Teleporting was out of the question. Clifton had already seen Asmodeus *pop* into the Compound. He'd be convinced that some other country owned teleportation technology. And he'd most likely do anything to get it.

"Kala Hicks, you are under arrest by the United States government for treason and the assassination of President Wilkins," the lead soldier shouted. Kala noticed that her head never left his gun site.

Kala knew the five soldiers would bump into an invisible wall in about five feet, or at least she hoped so. A remote part of her kind of wanted to see that happen. It was a surreal moment to hear a fellow soldier accuse her of treason. The one thing Kala had always been proud of was her service to her country. Killing the president had been an extremely difficult decision for her, but when he was threatening to murder thousands, Kala felt she had no choice. Little did she know at the time that President Wilkins had actually been the current Atlas and by killing him, Kala ended up stuck with the job.

"Whose orders?" Kala yelled back.

The lead soldier ignored Kala's question and bellowed, "You're surrounded. Raise your hands and walk over to me."

Kala sighed and noticed that Penny watched the whole situation with mild curiosity as if the soldiers were animals in a zoo. Talan stayed hidden. Kala seriously hoped he was still there and keeping the bullet-barrier up. Not that she could die apparently, but with enough bullets in her, Kala could definitely be put out of commission for a while. Or not. She had no idea. But she didn't want to find out. Somehow being shot in the chest a hundred times didn't appeal to her. The once was enough.

Kala spoke more calmly, "Name and rank."

The lead soldier snarled, "I don't have to answer to you. You are a traitor to this country and I should shoot you where you stand. I could always report that you died while trying to escape." He paused, then smiled. "But who am I to deprive the Compound of a good hanging?" He was genuinely salivating at the thought.

"You talk too much," Kala reprimanded, "And by telling me about the Compound I know Clifton sent you. He put the order out and the public still thinks the president died in an accident." Kala said this with such confidence even she believed it. She was trying to put out feelers as to how often she'd be evading super-soldiers. If it were just Clifton, it would be in small pockets like the men in front of her. But if Turner had decided she was a liability, then Kala would have a lot more to worry about than these guys. Dealing with Clifton was like dealing with a five-year-old bully, whereas dealing with Turner was like dealing with Napoleon, a brilliant military strategist.

Kala could handle Clifton. She wasn't so sure about Turner. He knew too much about her.

The soldier looked miffed at Kala's accusation. "If I have to repeat myself one more time, I'm going to shoot you."

Penny popped out of sight.

The soldiers' training kicked in and a rain of gunfire smacked full force into the invisible wall.

The noise was even louder at this close range.

Kala shouted over the noise. "What are you doing, Penny?" She knew Penny's disappearing trick well. Penny had pulled it on her a few times. Penny's motivation was a mystery to her. They were safely behind the barrier after all, so why disappear? If anything, it would just make the soldiers think she teleported, something Talan had just tried to avoid.

34

Then Kala figured it out. She turned her head away from the soldiers to see the stack of papers and texts that Penny held dear start to disappear from view. Penny was hiding any kind of evidence of who or what they all were. It would be complete mumbo jumbo to someone like Clifton, but Kala didn't want him to be a bigger problem than he already was.

One by one, the soldiers stopped shooting. Kala thought it was because of the futileness of the protective barrier, or maybe they ran out of bullets.

But when she turned to see why, her heart stopped.

Snapping the necks of each soldier daring to try to kill Kala was...

Derek.

Chapter Five

Kala's whole body filled with happiness at the sight of Derek, her one true friend in this world, then she comprehended that three soldiers lay dead at his feet. "Don't kill all of them!" Kala called out.

At that point, Derek couldn't hear. He was in the middle of a fistfight with the last two soldiers, one of which was the lead a-hole.

Kala ran to help him, but slammed up against the barrier. Apparently, it went both ways. She screamed, "Talan! Let me out right now!"

Kala slammed her fist against the barrier and it dissolved.

Derek cold-cocked the soldier next to him with the soldier's own gun. Before Derek could focus the rest of his rage on the lead soldier, Kala grabbed the man first. She lifted the lead soldier up by his neck as if he were a rag doll and tossed him across the room. The man flew fast and hard, slamming against the far wall with enough impact to shake a piece of the ceiling loose. He was out cold.

Derek's eyes were round at seeing Kala's strength, but his expression quickly turned to awe. "Impressive," he smiled.

That smile almost brought tears to her eyes. Kala fell into Derek's open arms and they hugged each other fiercely. "Derek," was all Kala could say.

After a moment, Derek gently pulled out of the embrace and affectionately moved a strand of Kala's auburn hair away from her eye. "So. What's up?"

Kala shook her head and nudged him adoringly. "Nothing much. I'm a god now, so that's new."

"You're not kidding, are you?" Derek's eyes were full of affection, but Kala could see the doubt there as well. She knew there was a part of Derek that couldn't accept what was really going on. She couldn't blame him. If it hadn't happened to her, she wouldn't be able to conceive of it either. But she needed Derek to believe. It hurt too much to have her closest friend think she was looney tunes.

As if in answer to Derek's question, Talan and Penny materialized inside the room.

Derek's gun was leveled and ready, always the soldier.

Kala reached up and lowered Derek's revolver. "They're with me."

"I can tell." Derek gave Talan a disapproving glare.

Talan couldn't seem to hide the way he felt about Kala. She guessed that existing before the age of time took the edge off caring what people thought of you. Kala knew that even though

Derek was staring daggers at Talan, inside he was probably happy that she had some supernatural backup.

Derek turned his focus to Kala. She could sense so many conflicting thoughts racing around in his brain. Kala stared back and admired Derek's flawless features. He was well over six feet with a dark complexion, full lips, and a shaved head. Derek used to be a marine before he joined Kala's elite crew, and he was one of the biggest assets to the team.

A thought suddenly occurred to Kala. "Derek. Why are you killing Clifton's men? Have you gone rogue?" Kala's worst nightmare was coming to fruition: that because of her, Derek's life was ruined. He'd be on the run for the rest of his days. And he wouldn't have superpowers like her to protect himself.

Derek holstered his gun and surveyed the room as if waiting for more soldiers to arrive. He shook his head in the negative. "I'm working for General Turner."

"But Turner and Clifton are on the same team," Kala voiced her confusion. "Isn't Turner going to be pissed that you took out his men?"

Derek smiled. "After Clifton tried to have you killed two days ago, I woke up in Turner's house. He didn't think Clifton would ever trust me again after I went against his orders and clobbered his men."

"Turner's probably right about that." Kala remembered it well. Two days! It felt as if it had been a lifetime ago! When General Clifton had ordered Kala's death, Derek went berserk. He took down Clifton's men in seconds. Asmodeus had almost taken her, but Penny somehow managed to teleport the Demon King out of there. Kala figured she must have used the Demon's own teleportation powers against him, because Kala knew that Penny didn't have the capability herself to teleport. Derek had seen it all, but refused to believe what was happening in front of his own eyes. Kala had even told him that Asmodeus was a Demon and at that point, Derek's alarmed response had prompted Turner to knock him out.

"Turner told me in these exact words, 'protect Kala Hicks by any means necessary. I will back up all collateral damage, just make sure Harry doesn't touch her.'" Derek motioned to the dead and unconscious soldiers. "That's what I did."

Talan stepped forward. "She doesn't need your help." He turned to Kala. "Your friend will die trying to protect you. Is that what you want?"

Derek's eyes never left Kala's. "Do you want me to eliminate this guy?"

Kala raised her eyebrow as if considering the offer, but she shook her head. "He's right, Derek. You'll get yourself killed. Soldiers are one thing, but you have no defense against Demons and Malaks." Kala didn't like Talan's condescending delivery, but his message was true. Though a selfish part of her wanted to keep Derek close, she loved him too much to put him in that kind of danger.

"Turner's wife stocked me up." Derek pulled off his tight fitting backpack and opened it up for Kala to see. Inside was a stack of plastic vials filled with black goop next to a gun that looked like a tranquilizer. Kala recognized the ooze straightaway. It was a concoction made by Roberta that incapacitated Malaks and Demons.

Kala understood at that moment that Derek not only

believed, but he was prepared for battle. She turned to Talan. "This stuff works. He can help."

Talan walked over to Derek and touched him.

Derek disappeared.

"Dick!" Kala spun on Talan with an uncontrollable fury. "What the hell did you just do?"

"You would never have sent him away," Talan stated confidently.

Penny added, "You wouldn't have."

"Shut up, Penny!" But Kala kept her eyes on Talan. "Where is he?!"

Talan stayed calm, which only made Kala angrier. "He's safe. I sent him back to Turner. Roberta and Turner should know you're still alive."

Kala couldn't control her rage. She wanted to lash out and attack Talan. "How could you do that? Derek is the only person I trust! I needed him!"

Penny was livid now herself. "Get over it! Were you planning on taking him to the *5th Level of Hell*? I don't care if those play guns hurt Malaks and Demons, they'll do nothing against the creatures there."

"You know what? Screw you both!" Kala had reached her limit. She stormed toward the door. Talan reached out and touched her arm, but Kala shrugged it off. "Don't touch me!" Kala was out the door before Talan or Penny could stop her.

Kala had no idea where she was going, but she kept walking down the street. Remembering that Clifton had every surveillance camera in existence on the lookout for her, Kala brushed her auburn hair forward lamely. She was a sitting duck out here and she knew it. Not that Clifton's men could kill her, but Kala didn't feel like dealing with bullets. She didn't feel like dealing with anything.

Seeing Derek had given Kala a moment of happiness and peace, and Talan had ripped that from her. Derek was all she had left of her past. Of Jack. The fact that Talan had the nerve to make decisions for her made Kala furious. It was bad enough that her brain was still reeling from Jack's death.

She trusted Derek in a fight much more than stupid-dumb-face Talan.

Kala knew she was overreacting, but it felt good to loathe someone. To have someone to blame for everything. And Talan was an easy target.

Walking by a small electronics store, Kala tried to ignore the televisions replaying the vision of destroying Fortski's cure. She needed to keep it together. The idea of what she had to do was unfathomable to her. Kala had thought that killing Jack would be the worst thing she'd ever have to do. That whatever Atlas task she'd do next would be cake compared to murdering the only man she ever loved. But by destroying that cure, thousands would die. Even though she'd never see their faces, it would still feel like she had pulled the trigger on them all. No matter how much she tried to rationalize what possible benefit destroying the cure for cancer would have for the greater good, Kala came up with zilch. She started to feel like her job was evil and not a *balancer* as everyone claimed it was. Zeus was a genuine jerk for coming up with this punishment.

Kala rounded a corner and smacked right into...
Talan.

Kala didn't even stop, shoving past him. "Go away." She made sure he could hear her.

But instead of having the decency to act human and run to catch up, he materialized in front of her instead. "You're not safe," he replied calmly.

Kala stopped in her tracks. "You think?" she responded sarcastically. "Gee, I'm so glad you popped in to tell me that. I had no idea. I've only been chased by Demons, Malaks, gods, and my own freaking government for the past four days. I'm so glad you warned me. Thank you so much. You're such a savior. What are you Grigori or something?" Kala pushed her way past him again. It felt good to go into a tirade.

But Talan was persistent. He kept teleporting in front of her so she'd almost smack into him every time. So. Annoying.

"Kala, I understand that you're angry, and I'm sorry I didn't give you a choice in the matter of your friend." Talan let the apology sit there for a moment, apparently thinking it would make a difference in Kala's mood, then he continued, "But if the Demons didn't know where you were before that fire fight, they do now. Extracting that bullet from your chest took magic. *Your* magic. Atlas's magic. It was like a beacon."

Kala grudgingly listened, her mood starting to thaw a bit. Just a bit.

Talan seemed to pick up on this. "I know you think Derek can handle himself, and yes, Roberta's magic would give him some protection, but in about five minutes this whole area is going to be crawling with Demons searching for you. He wouldn't have survived. I was trying to save him," Talan pleaded. "I know how much he means to you," he finished softly.

Damn him. Kala softened. But she had to make one thing clear before she let it go. "You could have told me that and let me have the choice. Even if it ends up being the same choice. I need to be the one to decide. Okay?"

Talan nodded solemnly. "Deal."

Kala ran her hand through her hair and sighed heavily. "Where's Penny?"

"I sent her to a safe place. I'll take you there now." Talan started to reach out to touch Kala...

...When his face grimaced in pain. Kala glimpsed the tip of a blade protruding from Talan's stomach, then it was yanked out viciously. Blood poured from the wound causing Talan to stumble slightly.

A man had materialized behind Talan, and he held a gnarly looking knife covered in Talan's blood. Talan grabbed his gut from the newly inflicted gash. The fact that a metal blade could actually hurt Talan momentarily threw Kala off.

Talan turned to face his attacker. "Miss me, *Brother?*" The man smiled wickedly.

Chapter Six

"**R**otoph." Talan looked horrified.

Kala's training kicked in.

She studied Rotoph as an enemy combatant. He referred to Talan as *brother*, so that told her he was Grigori.

A flash in her memory.

Or Atlas's memory...

Atlas knew Rotoph, or at least knew of him. Kala couldn't seem to pull any memories together in the heat of the moment.

The Grigori's expression was cold and calculating, though his bright green eyes twinkled with evil delight at stabbing Talan. Short, brown hair framed his angular face, making his long crooked nose the centerpiece. He was undeniably handsome. Not the ethereal beauty of the Angels and Demons that Kala was used to, but he was definitely easy on the eyes in a rugged kind of way.

Seeing Talan clutching his stomach and Rotoph's triumphant grin made Kala angry beyond belief. She could be mad at Talan all she wanted, but no way was she going to let this jerk hurt him.

She took advantage of the classic mistake Rotoph was making: enjoying the kill.

Before he could respond, Kala snatched the bloody weapon from his hand and slashed Rotoph's throat. Rotoph's hands grabbed futilely at his neck, trying to stem the bleeding, his eyes rounded from the shock of Kala's move.

He dropped to his knees and gargled his own blood. Within seconds, Rotoph was lying face first on the cement, completely still.

Kala pocketed the knife and supported Talan with her weight. "We have to get you someplace safe. Are you okay?"

Talan nodded then pulled away. "I'm okay. Look." Talan pulled away his bloody slashed shirt to reveal smooth skin free of any injury. "That knife doesn't kill. Nothing can kill a Grigori. It does, however, take away my powers."

"For good?" Kala was appalled.

Talan shook his head. "No. At least an hour though." Then he looked over at Rotoph's still form. His face was angry. "You did well. Cutting him like that will make him powerless too."

Rotoph's body stirred. He was healing. Power or not, the guy wasn't someone Kala wanted to have around. "We should get out of here." Kala took Talan's hand and pulled. He didn't budge.

"I have to face him." Talan looked resolute.

"Actually, you don't." Kala yanked harder and Talan reluctantly went with her.

When they were halfway down the street, Kala heard Rotoph's

voice. "Talan!" he screamed. Kala recognized that tone. He was pissed.

Talan let go of Kala's hand and turned to face Rotoph.

Rotoph's throat was bloody, but there was no wound.

With Talan's bloody shirt and Rotoph's horror-movie neck, people were staring. No one seemed to be calling the police though, which wasn't a surprise to Kala. She found that most people didn't believe what was in front of them, as if there were some other explanation for bloody throats and shirts. They would rather look the other way, too scared to get involved. Kala knew it wouldn't last long. Especially since she planned to cause a scene.

As Rotoph neared the two of them, his eyes never left Talan. "So you have a Titan as your bodyguard now?" He nodded to Kala. "Nice move by the way."

Kala leveled the knife at Rotoph. "I can repeat it if you like."

Okay. Kala saw someone dialing their cell phone. It wouldn't be long before another crew of Clifton's men would be on their way. Not to mention real cops.

Rotoph looked like he was a cat about to pounce.

Kala was far too good of a soldier to let some amateur fighter take her weapon from her. The guy may have super Grigori powers but, according to Talan, Rotoph was running on empty. That made it an even playing field to her human self. But she was a god now so Kala could do some real damage.

Rotoph leapt forward to grab the knife.

Idiot. Kala wanted to roll her eyes, but she went into fighter-mode instead.

As Rotoph's hand grabbed at the blade, Kala swung her body to the side: now she could use Rotoph's momentum to her benefit. When his hand didn't grab onto the intended target, Rotoph had nothing but air for support. He stumbled forward. Kala took advantage of the opening, used her Atlas-strength, and elbowed Rotoph hard in the small of his back.

He screamed in anguish as he collapsed to the ground.

"You Grigori are babies without your powers." Kala rested her foot on Rotoph's back to keep him down. "I'm keeping this knife. So stop trying to take it back."

It was mayhem now. People were screaming and running away. Sirens echoed in the distance.

Kala viewed the knife more closely. Every part of its surface was covered in strange runic markings. It was a stunning piece of work. The blade itself was slightly curved with a jagged edge on the outside and a smooth sharpness on the inside. The handle was made of bone. "How can this knife take your powers away?" Kala asked Talan as if Rotoph weren't there.

"There used to be twelve of them. One for each Olympian. How do you think the Grigori were banished? The gods needed help, so the Titans had Hephaestus forge them," Talan shared.

Kala remembered now Penny mentioning a weapon that drained both the Grigori and the Olympians of their powers. This blade must be it.

Talan nodded toward the screaming pedestrians. "I'd teleport us out of here…"

"But you can't. Right. What about him? Do we take him with us?" Kala asked.

Rotoph responded. "This wasn't how I planned my morning."

Kala dug her foot in harder into his back, making Rotoph groan. "Did I say you could talk?" She turned to Talan. "Well?

He's your family. What would Owen do with him?" Kala asked of her foster father.

Talan didn't even blink. "He'd kill him if he could."

"Right." That was all Kala needed to hear. She leaned down to Rotoph's ear and whispered. "This is for my dad."

"Dad?"

But before Rotoph could utter another word, Kala slit his throat again. She knew it wouldn't kill him, but the mayhem of her stabbing him so publicly would give her and Talan enough time to escape.

The area was filling up with quite a crowd. The audible screams and gasps when Kala cut Rotoph made her feel as if she was a gladiator in some kind of ancient Roman stadium.

Talan grabbed Kala's hand and they were off down the first alley they ran past. Before long, they had twisted and turned so many times Kala wouldn't have been surprised if they had made a giant circle. But Talan knew his way around and he led her into a small hole-in-the-wall bar at least a mile away.

It was still morning, so there were only a few patrons inside. The place was darkly lit and barely fit six small tables. There was a seven-foot bar on the left where a plump, balding bartender served his only customers. He nodded at Talan as if they knew one another. Talan gave a friendly wave back and the two of them sat at the table farthest from the door.

Always the soldier, Kala sat facing the entrance so she could see whoever entered the establishment.

She knew they were hiding out, but she felt she could really use a drink. "I'm ordering, so get over it."

As if on cue, a waitress arrived at their table.

Kala got right to it. "Glenlivet on the rocks and some fries. You serve fries, right?" The waitress nodded. "Make it a double order then."

"Coming right up," the waitress chirped warmly.

"You're paying," Kala replied pointedly.

"With what? My good looks?" Talan said with an ample amount of sarcasm.

Kala was impressed. "You have a sense of humor. Noted." She patted her pockets looking for money. "I'm not into dining and dashing so if I don't have cash I'm cancelling my order." Being a foster kid, Kala had lived in some pretty sketchy homes. Some of the other foster kids would make a habit out of going to seedy diners, eating, and then taking off without paying the bill before anyone could stop them. Kala always cringed when a new set of kids *dined and dashed*. When she refused to go along with it, Kala ended up washing dishes or cleaning toilets for a week as a result. It just wasn't in her to do something like that.

A few seconds later, Kala pulled out a fifty-dollar bill from her back pocket. She couldn't remember how it got there, but she was happy she found it. Fries and scotch sounded like the perfect breakfast. Kala wondered if her constitution would be much different as a god. Maybe horribly unhealthy foods wouldn't give her indigestion. At least she knew she wouldn't die from it. Kala didn't think Titans had to worry about cholesterol much.

Kala waved the fifty bucks triumphantly, then asked, "Did you want anything?" She paused. "Do angels eat?"

Talan replied, "We don't have to, but we like to. I'm sure you saw Owen eating once or twice."

"True," Kala acknowledged. Mentioning Owen brought her

back to reality. "Who was that guy? I gathered that he's Grigori, but I thought all of you were best pals or something."

"Like you're *best pals* with General Clifton? Grigori are no different than any other species. We don't all get along. Rotoph betrayed the Grigori and will never be forgiven, nor does he want to be," Talan stated as if he were an offended child.

Kala raised her eyebrow in fascination. She wasn't used to seeing Talan in this light. He was normally so calm, cool, and collected. To see him almost human was actually quite comforting. "Where'd he get the knife? You said Penny's dad made them. Was that the weapon that the Titan's spelled?"

Before Talan could answer, a memory took shape before Kala's eyes. She was relieved that she was still conscious, but it was still more jarring that a normal *human* memory. It was as if she was in two places at once. A part of her sat in front of Talan in a bar, while another part of her was Atlas standing in front of Hephaestus on a beach overlooking the ocean. Hephaestus was both familiar and new to Kala. Logically, this was because Atlas knew Hephaestus, but it still tripped her out. He was tall, but not like Cronus and the other Titans. Kala guessed that the Olympian gods, being the next round of offspring, were smaller. His hair was black, long, and curly and there was a lot of it. Even his beard went down to his flat belly. The Olympian was in shape, Kala gave him that. Her Atlas memory bank told her it was because he was the god of fire and spent most of his time blacksmithing. His arms were like tree trunks he was so built. Derek had nothing on this guy and Derek was seriously cut. Atlas/Kala was eye-to-eye with Hephaestus and she could sense that Atlas was excited by the meeting.

"I'm here," a familiar voice called out.

Kala recognized Rotoph as he walked up to Atlas and Hephaestus.

From thin air, Hephaestus produced a long ebony box. He opened it in front of Atlas and Rotoph.

Inside, resting on black satin, were twelve knives identical to the one Kala had stolen from Rotoph.

Except one thing: there were no runic markings.

The blades were a beauty to behold without the engravings, but the more Kala watched the more she understood why Owen and Talan hated Rotoph.

Hephaestus handed the box to Rotoph. "Your turn," he said. Though Atlas couldn't see it, Kala could – Hephaestus didn't trust Rotoph.

Poor, pathetic Atlas did, of course. He really believed that the Olympians were going to double-cross the Titans after they took down the Grigori, and that Rotoph was like him: willing to turn on his own kind to save his skin.

Kala watched as Rotoph took the box and recited an ancient spell. As each word fell out of his mouth, a new rune would appear on all twelve knives until they looked like the blade Kala currently had stashed in her jacket.

"It's done." Rotoph nodded. "One cut to a Grigori and they are powerless for a time. Make sure it's enough to banish them or, god or not, they will destroy you."

Hephaestus looked worried. He definitely feared the Grigori. "Are you sure the blades will work?"

"They'll work," Rotoph replied flatly. "Just make sure you're ready."

The memory faded. Kala came back into focus. Fries and a glass of scotch had been placed in front of her.

Talan watched her carefully. "A memory?"

Kala nodded. "Atlas knew Rotoph."

"Rotoph betrayed Atlas and the Olympians worse than any of us. The whole time he was really working for Cronus. He made them believe that he engraved the knives to help the Olympians take down the Grigori and then in turn kill the Titans once and for all.

"Zeus fell right into Cronus's hands. He was so focused on double-crossing his father, he didn't see Cronus's true plan coming until it was too late.

"Cronus had convinced Zeus that the Titans were still weak from their last war, that the Olympians needed to take down the Grigori because they were stronger. Zeus suspected his father was up to something, but he didn't know what. He thought having Hephaestus make the blades would protect them. He never suspected Rotoph would be working for Cronus." Talan motioned for Kala to pull out the knife. "Let me show you something."

Kala took out the knife and placed it on the table. Talan pointed to a small rune in the shape of a slanted "F," on the bone handle. "See that there? Rotoph seared it into every handle so that it would drain the power from the user. The more the Olympians used the blades, the weaker they became." Talan sat back as he stole a fry from Kala's plate. "Weakening the Olympians worked too quickly and the Grigori almost escaped banishment, but the Titans stepped in and used their combined powers to capture and torture the Olympians and seal us into the 5th Heaven."

"A lot of fives going on: 5th Heaven, 5th Level of Hell.

What about one through four? Aren't they any good?" Kala didn't bother hiding the snark from her voice. She sipped her scotch and sighed in bliss. Just what she needed.

"Five is a powerful number. Look at your human religions. The Torah contains five books, Jesus had five wounds, there are five pillars of Islam, the five sacred Sikh symbols. I could go on, but I can see the drool forming around your mouth." Talan stole another fry.

Kala liked this side of her stalker angel. Attitude and sarcasm went a long way with her. "Cute." She grabbed some fries herself and began eating. They were greasy and scrumptious. Kala added thoughtfully, "Let me get this straight, the Titans spent too much energy destroying the Olympians and banishing you guys, so they hid in the 5th Level of Hell? Couldn't the Demons or Malaks take them down at that point?"

"A weakened Titan is still more powerful than any Demon or Malak," Talan stated frankly.

"What about a second generation Titan?" Kala asked of herself.

"Thousands of years later? Yes, there *are* some Demons and Malaks who could challenge you, but you still have the advantage. Plus, you have two Grigori on your side. Not to mention Turner's toys if you need them." Talan finished off her fries.

Talk of Turner reminded Kala of her Atlas task. She could tell Talan. "Turner may hate me after I complete my mission."

"You don't have to kill Roberta, do you?" Talan's face paled.

"No. No killings..." But Kala didn't get to finish her sentence.

Through the door walked Rotoph, but this time he had company. Though they looked human, Kala knew that they were Demons. Three of them. Kala was surprised that she could now tell the difference between humans and Demons. It wasn't anything she could put her finger on. She simply looked at them and knew what they were. She wondered if it would be the same for Malaks.

After Rotoph and the three Demons entered the bar, she got her answer.

Behind them, entered two Malaks.

"It's about to get ugly," she muttered under her breath.

Kala was on her feet, holding the Grigori blade. She knew she couldn't rely on it too much though. If it could drain the power of an Olympian, it could most certainly drain the power of a baby Titan.

Talan took her lead and stood beside her.

"Power?" she asked.

"I'd say I'm up to half strength," Talan answered.

"It'll have to do. And, by the way, this situation right here is why I wanted Derek with me. No one can win a bar fight like that man," Kala reprimanded. Derek had always been her back up and she'd pretty much needed it on a daily basis. Bar fights were what Kala did best. She just felt sorry for the handful of people that were still in this joint. They were about to see quite a show.

Kala watched the group of six make their way toward her. It was an intimidating sight for all the patrons to watch.

The bartender stuttered weakly, "I don't want any trouble."

One of the Demons waved his hand in the general direction

of the barkeep and the poor man flew into the air, smashing against the wall of bottled alcohol behind him. Glass and liquid shattered and poured over his unconscious body.

That was enough for the rest of the people in the bar. They took their cue and ran out the front door.

Kala eyed the Malaks behind Rotoph and the Demons. She hadn't had much luck with Malaks, seeing as the only one she ever met tried to kill her... twice. But these two stared at Rotoph with pure hatred.

"Oh, don't think these two will help you. They're under my complete control." Rotoph smiled.

The Malaks looked positively enraged but didn't say or do anything to contradict Rotoph's words.

Kala did the math in her head. If Talan was only at half strength, then Rotoph should be even less since she'd stabbed him later. Nevertheless, the fact that he could control two Malaks testified as to how powerful the Grigori really were.

"What's your deal, Dude? Why are you even here?" Kala gave him a look that diminished most men where they stood. But to Rotoph, Kala was simply irritating.

"I'm here for *him*." Rotoph pointed at Talan.

Kala was surprised by that. "Talan? You seriously aren't after *me*?" She looked at Talan and shrugged. "That's surprisingly refreshing."

"Why me?" Talan asked Rotoph.

Kala knew Talan's curiosity was his Achilles heel. A part of being Grigori she guessed. She just wished he could focus on taking these beasts down as opposed to having a conversation with them. But Kala could use it to her advantage. As long as they were talking, they were off guard. And from the steaming piles of hatred radiating off the Malaks, Kala knew she'd have allies if she could break Rotoph's hold over them.

"Simple, Brother. I want you to help me free the Grigori from their prison."

Chapter Seven

"**W**ait. What?" Kala felt the need to join in this conversation. "You were the one to trap the Grigori in the first place." She turned to Talan. "Don't trust this guy."

"I don't plan to." Talan kept his eyes on Rotoph.

Kala felt the need to drive her point home despite Talan's agreement. "And! You stabbed him in the back. Not really a way to show you're a good guy."

"I don't need to explain myself to a reject Titan who has a nasty habit of picking the losing team," Rotoph snarled.

Kala decided to try a little bluff. "Atlas *was* weak, and this *lowly* human consumed him. I might just do the same to you." She didn't think she could perform a repeat of the act. Nor did she want to. Having to integrate with one schmuck was difficult enough. But she needed to make Rotoph believe it. And from the look on his face, it worked.

Kala decided to hammer the last nail in the coffin. "Being raised by a Grigori gave me everything I needed."

That did it.

Rotoph took a step back.

The three Demons didn't like the way this confrontation was going. *They* obviously wanted a fight.

More importantly, they wanted to fight Kala.

The Demon on Rotoph's right leapt at Kala full force.

Kala was prepared. She shifted her weight to the side and avoided impact. As the Demon flew by her, she grabbed the back of his shirt and threw him against the wall. Dust and plaster fell in chunks to the floor where his body made contact.

Rotoph ordered, "Attack her!"

The remaining four Demons and Malaks came at Kala in a pack. Kala knelt down and tucked herself into a ball as their groping hands reached for her. She rolled away, causing them to smash against each other.

Rotoph used the distraction to reach for his brother. He was about to teleport Talan, Kala knew with certainty. She couldn't let that happen. The little angel had grown on her, doe-eyed and all.

The Demons and Malaks didn't take long to regroup. The Demon closest to Kala grabbed for her throat. She used an Aikido move by rotating her arm to deflect the blow. Being fast kept her out of their grasp.

Kala spun and jumped toward Rotoph before he could touch Talan.

But Talan was on it.

He threw his hand out: Rotoph grabbed his own throat,

writhing, as if he were choking from invisible hands.

Within seconds, Rotoph shook off the attack. Being Grigori himself, he knew all the tricks and how to counter them. Even at half power.

Half power. Kala let the words roll in her head. She looked at the blade she was holding and immediately felt foolish.

Vaulting onto a table, Kala kicked the nearest Demon in the face. Her Titan strength caused him to jolt backwards giving her enough time to leap to the next table.

With only a few inches separating her from Rotoph, Kala slashed the knife forward.

It was enough.

A trickle of blood formed on the side of Rotoph's arm from where Kala nicked him.

Whirling around to see if her idea worked, Kala smiled.

The two Malaks grinned at her triumphantly. Rotoph had no powers now, which meant no control over the Malaks.

The first Malak called out, "We've got it from here. Go. Accomplish your mission."

The Demons snarled at their new opponents while the Malaks finally looked like they were fighting the right enemies.

It sounded like a catfight breaking out as the Demons and Malaks tried to rip each other to pieces.

Kala stayed on the table, watching as if she were witnessing a train wreck.

Demons and Malaks didn't fight elegantly. They fought like animals. They fought to destroy.

Kala filed that away in her arsenal. Always know your opponent. And Kala was pretty sure she would be fighting a lot of Demons in the days to come.

Rotoph reeled on her, furious, yelling over the noise of the destruction of the bar. "I stabbed Talan so that he would listen!"

"Yeah, that's smart, stab the guy you want to talk to. It's too late to explain yourself, jackass. Next time don't look like you enjoyed it." Kala jumped down from the table and stood next to Talan. "Powers up?"

Talan nodded. "Ready to go."

"Take us to Penny. I actually miss her." Kala shrugged.

Rotoph reached out, his face pleading. "Talan, please! Listen to me. I want to free our brothers and sisters! I just did something that could get me killed, but it won't be worth a thing if you don't help me!"

Talan shook his head. "You turned against your own kind and left us in that prison to rot."

"Rot is a strong word," Kala interjected, remembering the beauty of the Grigori pokey.

But Talan and Rotoph ignored her. Talan looked at his brother with a genuinely hurt expression. "Why should I listen to a word you say, Rotoph?"

Before Rotoph could respond, the two Malaks came at him from both sides.

Then Kala noticed what was left of the three Demons laying on the ground. It was as if a bear had broken into the bar and mauled the three of them. Kala figured that was probably what the headlines would read when the bodies were found.

Rotoph had no defenses.

The Malaks ripped into him like savages.

"Is he going to end up like these three?" Kala had a momentary pang of sympathy.

Talan shook his head. "Grigori can't be killed. Even powerless." He turned to her, eyes sad. "Shall we?"

Kala nodded wishing she could say something to make Talan feel better, but her mind came up blank. "Let's go."

Talan reached over and held her hand.

Kala's surroundings blurred for a second. They re-focused sharply moments later when they teleported into Talan's apartment. Kala felt a strange solace being back in Talan's lair. Even though it was a tiny studio with the simplest of décor – a couch, recliner, super-sized flat screen and a small kitchenette – it still felt a little bit like home.

Penny sat on the couch thumbing through her stack of papers. She looked up when hearing them arrive. "What took you so long?" Then she noticed the blood on Talan's shirt. "What happened?" She hurried over to examine Talan.

Talan waved her away. "I'm fine."

"Your shirt is covered in blood and it's slashed. What kind of Demon could get the jump on you like that? Did *she* distract you?" Penny's eyes barely glanced in Kala's direction.

Kala took back reminiscing about Penny. "His brother, Rotoph, had the privilege, thank you very much." Kala pulled out the knife from her jacket. "Using this beauty."

Penny's face turned about three shades of white. "Where did you get that?" She turned to Talan as if Kala had made up the whole thing. "Is that true? Rotoph attacked you?"

Talan apparently didn't feel like confiding in Penny, or maybe he just didn't want to re-live it. "Yes, Rotoph stabbed me." Talan's eyes glanced at Kala.

Kala was shocked that she knew exactly what he was telling her without him saying a word. He didn't want Penny to know that not all the Grigori had escaped. Talan wanted to keep her in the dark, and by telling her that Rotoph needed Talan's help to break out his brethren would reveal too much. Kala had no idea *how* she knew Talan's thoughts, but she didn't question it. Once she decided she could trust someone, Kala stuck by their side to the bitter end.

And in Talan's case, that could be very dangerous.

Penny crossed her arms in annoyance. "Are you going to elaborate?"

Kala stepped in front of her. "Why don't you stop acting like a jealous girlfriend and do something useful. Did you find anything else in your scrolls?" Kala nodded to the stack of papers on the couch.

Penny pursed her lips from anger and walked over to the couch. "No. Just more of the same." She eyed the knife. "That doesn't belong to you. My father made that knife, you should give it to me."

Kala laughed. "Yeah, right."

Penny turned to Talan for support. "You don't honestly trust her with that blade, do you? She could rip your powers from you anytime she wants!"

Talan was livid. He moved so that he was inches from Penny's face. "I trust Kala with my life. The knife stays with her."

Penny didn't argue. She looked positively shocked. Then her face softened as she turned to Kala. "I'm sorry. You've more than proved your loyalty. I'm just not used to everything being so out of control." Penny laughed nervously. "I never thought I'd think of my days with the Atlas as easy, but compared to this?"

Talan eased up on his attitude as well. "That's the nature of prophecies. They come with a lot of destruction."

Penny sighed deeply and said to Kala, "The 5th and Zeus can wait. How can I help you fulfill your mission?"

Her mission. Kala didn't want to think about her mission. She wanted to find Zeus and force him to break the curse. The last thing on the planet Kala wanted to do was find Fortski and destroy his life's work. If the curse was broken and *balance* went back to happening on its own, then Fortski's cure for cancer would somehow be destroyed if that was what the universe wanted. Kala just didn't want to have to be the one to do it. It was hard enough adjusting to the fact that she was a Titan. Without the curse, what would that mean? Maybe Turner would take her back and she'd be some kind of super soldier with her Titan strength.

Kala felt like she deserved to be condemned to this life after what she did to Jack. But if Zeus broke the curse, then killing him would have been for nothing. It would just be murder. It left a gaping empty hole in her chest that was too painful to contemplate. If she continued to do Atlas's job, then at least Jack died for something.

Penny grabbed her attention once more. "Can you tell us your mission?"

Kala snapped out of her reverie. "No. I told you: I'm not ready yet. I want to confront Zeus first. Besides, didn't you say you wanted to save your dad? What exactly are we saving him from?"

Penny couldn't hide her emotion. "Hephaestus is being held against his will by Cronus. He's being forced to make weapons for the Titans and Demons. Rotoph sears the runes into them like he did with that knife. The fact that you managed to steal that blade is a small miracle."

"Not really a miracle, more like bad planning on his part." Kala examined the knife more carefully. "This rune drains the power of the user. Can we get rid of it or something?"

Penny and Kala both looked at Talan for an answer. He gently took the blade from Kala and touched the power-sucking rune. When he pulled his hand away, the rune still remained. Talan shook his head. "Rotoph always had a knack for this kind of thing. Owen might be able to remove it."

Kala took the blade back and tucked it into her jacket. "I don't care if it drains me. I haven't felt anything so far and I've used it twice. I'm thinking the Olympians did a lot more than just a few slices."

Talan's eyes flared with bitterness. He nodded. "My brothers and sisters were hacked into pieces. Only a few of us managed to fight back, but even the injuries I sustained kept me weak enough for Cronus to banish us all. When the dimension sealed shut, there was nothing any of us could do."

Unsure of how to respond, Kala felt for Talan. Her rage grew every time she thought of Cronus and his lackeys hacking up angels. The supernatural were egotistical jerk-offs. Kala didn't want to have anything to do with them. Of course, she was one now, too, and that only made her angrier.

Kala imagined seeing Owen lying in pieces…

"If we have this knife, where are the other eleven?" Kala decided to be tactical instead of emotional. It helped her in life when she didn't want to deal with feelings she wasn't ready to face.

Penny was very sure of herself, "Cronus has them. After the banishment, Cronus sealed the blades away in the 5th Level of Hell. Rotoph and my father have been working for him ever since. I don't think Rotoph knew what he had gotten himself into when he betrayed his kind."

Talan responded thoughtfully, "I don't either."

When he didn't continue, Penny plopped down on the couch. "If we're not going to complete Kala's mission, then she should rest before we go to the 5th."

"Rest? Let's go now." Kala's adrenaline was pumping, and she was raring for a fight.

Talan turned to Kala and looked at her like she was the only one in the room. "Pandora is right. You need to sleep. You may be a Titan now, but you're human as well. Your body is still transitioning."

"I'm not tired," Kala protested. And lame. She had thought that being a god would mean she wouldn't be susceptible to sleeping and eating and *human* things. The thought had been pretty darn exciting. Kala hated that she had to eat and sleep. She often times wished that she could do without. It wasn't that Kala didn't like food and rest; it was just frustrating that it was essential to living. It seemed like such a waste to her. She always thought about how much more she could get done if she didn't have to stop her life for *human fuel*. "What time is it anyway?" Kala looked over at Talan's digital clock.

Kala had almost forgotten that she couldn't see time in a normal way anymore. The countdown startled her momentarily.

3d 11h 13m 45s.

Realizing what time it was startled her even more.

5:47 P.M.

Where had the day gone? "Look, I don't feel like taking a *nap* when I could be breaking this damn curse..."

Talan touched her forehead mid-sentence. Before she could utter a profanity aimed at him, Kala was out cold.

Chapter Eight

Kala awoke to find herself feeling pretty darn good. She hadn't felt that way in a long time. Even before her life had turned to the crazy ride it was, Kala had been a horrible sleeper. Always having to be on alert did that to a person, especially to a sniper. Catnaps were more her thing. Getting rest while she could on a mission or even in life. It was a skill she was proud of, but now?

Pulling the blanket back, Kala slid out of bed feeling more rested than she had ever been in her life. "Was that some kind of Grigori sleeping pill? Holy crap." Kala stretched her arms.

Talan and Penny were on the couch watching television. It was so normal that Kala had to remind herself that the two of them were supernatural beings. Kala grunted when she tried to see what they were watching. She'd never know. The vision of Kala destroying Fortski's cure re-played itself over and over.

"Would you turn that off?" Kala asked.

Talan looked at the TV and it shut off. Apparently, Grigori didn't need remote controls.

Kala looked at the time.

3d 01h 03m 34s.

3:53 A.M.

Kala clutched her chest in panic. "You let me sleep for thirteen hours! Are you insane?!"

Talan was instantly by her side. "You needed it, trust me. Your body is still trying to assimilate to a Titan. You'll thank me later."

As good as Kala felt, she didn't think she would thank Talan anytime soon. So much time lost. Kala was only an hour away from Day Two and that made her stomach drop and churn into a giant stress ball. Sleep was her enemy. It made time pass too quickly. Kala vowed not to sleep again until she made Zeus break the curse. If she had to go through with her vision of destroying the cure for cancer, Kala didn't want it to come sooner than it had to.

"Enough rest. I'm ready to go." Kala stood up and Talan joined her.

Penny walked over to the two of them.

Talan nodded. He reached out and clasped Kala's hand.

Then he turned to Penny. "Sorry, Pandora."

Kala saw a glimpse of shock and betrayal as Penny's face popped out of view.

***

Kala fell to her knees coughing uncontrollably. The air was

filled with the smell of sulfur and rotted flesh. Kala had been around enough dead bodies in her life to recognize the stench. It reminded her of cinnamon, which was why she'd always cringe whenever someone was chewing cinnamon gum or had the nerve to eat Red Hots in front of her.

Talan touched her chest and she could breathe again.

The smells were still there, but at least she wasn't choking on them anymore.

"Lovely," Kala observed.

Her surroundings were oddly beautiful in a terrifying kind of way. Kala oftentimes found beauty in the grotesque, if just for its sheer uniqueness. The ground reminded her of lava, as if she was standing inside a volcano, but with no heat. She and Talan were in some kind of hallway with hundred foot ceilings and walls that were a width of at least that long, all covered in sharp spikes.

It was the sound that set Kala's teeth on edge. It was as if a trillion snakes were slithering around them, hissing and spitting. She kept glancing over her shoulder expecting to see a python coming her way. It threw her instincts off, which kept her guard up even more.

Aside from the two of them, there was no one to be seen. No gods, no Demons, no nothing. If it weren't for the noise, scenery, and stench, Kala would have wondered if they were in the right place.

"We're at the gateway," Talan spoke over the hissing. "I'm going to need your help to enter unseen."

If this was the gateway, Kala wondered what the rest of the joint was like. The quicker they found Zeus, the better.

"How can *I* help?" The fact that Kala wasn't on Earth started to sink in. She figured her ability to cope with the situation was a combination of military training and Atlas's memory of this place. Though she couldn't remember the specifics, a part of her knew that she had been here before.

"You're a Titan now, Kala. And this is a *Titans-only* place." Talan led her down the long hallway.

The uneven ground felt awkward under her feet. "Why didn't you bring Penny?" Kala decided she would broach the topic. She had been certain that Penny was along for the entire ride, but just like that, Talan had left the girl behind.

"I don't trust her to make smart decisions," Talan spoke with a finality that left Kala chilled.

"Ouch. Okay," Kala responded.

Talan stopped and turned to Kala, concern etched in every feature. "Pandora has been trying to rescue her father for several thousand years now. She put Atlas in hiding because he was the only link she had to finding him. She knows Hephaestus is in the 5th. Kala, she'd do *anything* to save him."

"Anything? As in, sell us out?" Kala asked.

Talan nodded.

"The girl bugs me, but I understand her need to rescue her father. I'd do anything for Owen and I would have done anything to save Jack," Kala admitted.

Talan looked away. "I'm sorry."

Kala sighed. She didn't want to discuss it with Talan. It made her angry. "Let's just find Zeus."

Talan walked ahead without another word. There wasn't much to say anyway. After a few minutes trudging down the awkward landscape, Kala was ready to tear her ears off from the sound of hissing and spitting on constant repeat. Motioning Kala to halt at a spot that felt the same as any other, Talan pointed to an area on the sharp spiked wall. He instructed, "Touch here and imagine a doorway."

Kala looked at Talan, incredulous. "Really? Imagine a door and it appears?"

"I'm not sure it will work since technically you're only half Titan, but it's our only option. Only Titans are allowed into the inner sanctum. Any other being needs permission," Talan warned.

"What? You're saying a big powerful Grigori couldn't bust through?" Kala half-teased but was actually curious as to the answer.

"Oh yes, I could break in, but then we'd have every Titan on us in seconds. I could take two maybe three on my own, but all twelve? I'd rather slip in under the radar," Talan confided.

Kala's military training forced her to agree with the guy. "Okay." She placed her hand on the designated spot and closed her eyes. It was easier to play make-believe with her eyes closed. Creativity wasn't her strong suit, unless she was trying to win a fight. Kala could think of all kinds of crazy when she needed an exit during a failed mission. She pictured the door to Owen and Linda's house. It was the only home she had ever known and the easiest for her to visualize. Kala imagined reaching forward and turning the knob.

"We're in," Talan's voice sounded next to her.

Kala opened her eyes and saw the opening before her. It looked like a black hole formed out of the spiked wall. Normally, Kala wouldn't even consider walking through something so sketchy, but when Talan moved forward, she knew she had to follow.

Kala looked down at her watch.

3d 00h 02m 53s.

Day One was almost up.

Kala didn't want to be stuck in Hell when Day Four rolled around. She took a deep breath and entered the blackness. There was a moment of utter darkness as Kala passed through the gateway. When she arrived at the other side, her breath caught in her throat.

An enormous cavern spread out before Kala with stunning brilliance. This was nothing like the hellish hallway she had just left. It felt as if entering into the inside of geode rock. The walls, ceiling, and ground were crystallized purple, each crystal glowing from its own light source. It was as bright as daylight, but with no sun. There were dozens of archways carved into the walls, all leading to different parts of the 5th Level of Hell, Kala assumed. She was utterly speechless as she took in the beauty of the cavern.

Talan's voice broke the silence. "If Zeus is being held anywhere, it would be in The Pit. It's this door over here." Talan headed left toward one of the entryways.

Kala shook her head as she followed Talan. She couldn't wrap her brain around the fact that this was the 5th level of any kind of Hell. It was too beautiful. She had expected more of what she saw when they first arrived: sulfur, hissing, and lava spikes. But this? This was stunning!

She suddenly heard a voice that made her skin crawl.

"Buttercup, you came to save me."

In the corner of the cavern, hidden in the shadow of one of the arched doorways, was someone Kala hadn't expected to see.

Chained to the wall and grinning at Kala like a lion about to pounce on its prey was Asmodeus.

DAY TWO

Chapter Nine

Kala audibly grumbled.

Talan's face lit up with a kind of happiness Kala had never seen before. "I see the Titans punished you for your ineptitude."

Asmodeus ignored Talan completely and focused entirely on Kala. "Are you going to let me down from here or what?" he said with as much charisma as a man chained to a wall could have.

"Actually, no." Kala didn't know how much clearer she could be. "You're much safer tied up."

"I'd much more prefer it if *you* tied me up instead." Asmodeus smiled slyly. "Now, seriously, you're not going to leave me here are you?"

"Yes. Yes, I am." Kala couldn't believe the king of Demons actually expected her to help him escape. She turned to Talan. "Please, lead the way."

Talan had a satisfied expression on his face. "My pleasure."

Talan began walking toward the archway that supposedly led to *The Pit*.

Asmodeus called out, "I know you love following your little Angel-boy there, but Zeus isn't in The Pit."

Kala stopped. She knew she shouldn't. She knew Asmodeus was probably lying. Trying anything to keep her there to help free him. But her gut told her he was telling the truth.

Apparently, Talan felt the same, because he turned to Asmodeus with irritation in his eyes. "Let me guess: you won't tell us where he is unless we unchain you?"

"Grigori were always known for their intelligence." Asmodeus finally acknowledged Talan's presence. "In my experience that was just a rumor."

"Har-de-har-har." Kala had no patience for Asmodeus's quips. "Why should we believe anything you say?"

"Have I ever lied to you before?" Though his tone was light, his eyes were intense. "Besides, when I wiped your brain," he added with a sly smile. "Technically, I never said I was your boyfriend, I just implanted it."

"So you made me lie to myself and therefore it shouldn't count?" Kala rolled her eyes. "If I drastically stretch my imagination, then no, you never lied to me. But there's a first time for everything, and I'll never really trust you."

"I'm not asking you to trust me. I'm asking you to break me out in exchange for the location of Zeus. Why do you want to see him anyway? You think he'll release you from that curse? Only the true Atlas could..." As the words were leaving Asmodeus's mouth, he started to focus on Kala. His eyes widened. "You didn't... How?" He turned to Talan, shocked. "How did she do that?"

Talan shrugged. "She's stronger than you think."

Asmodeus's gaze veered back to Kala with utter surprise and admiration. Kala noticed with annoyance that her joining with a Titan made the Demon even more attracted to her. "*How* did you do it?" he asked, amazed. "I must know."

"You must, huh?" Kala grunted. "I have no freaking clue. But the more memories I have of the guy, the more I realize what a loser he was." Then she added, a little embarrassed, "I ate him." Kala had never talked much about the details of her experience, and confessing to Asmodeus wasn't something she planned to do, but the raise of his eyebrow said it all.

"I knew I had a feeling about you," he said.

Talan stepped in. "Tell us where Zeus is and we let you live." Talan apparently had enough of confession time.

Kala assumed it was because he didn't like her interacting with Asmodeus, but she was relieved not to share anymore. Somehow Asmodeus had the ability to make her spill her guts and she didn't like that about him one bit. It was dangerous. It made her feel weak.

"You can't kill me." Asmodeus didn't look worried at all. "And I do know where Zeus is being held. You need me, Grigori."

"I could snap your soul into pieces," Talan warned.

Kala had never seen Talan look so vicious.

"I may be serving my punishment, but the Titans still protect me," Asmodeus snarled.

Before the Angel/Demon testosterone level reached epic heights, Kala yanked Talan to the side to talk to him privately. "Look. Can you find Zeus or what?"

It took a few moments for Talan to calm himself enough to

focus on Kala. Then he nodded slowly. "Eventually, yes."

"Eventually?"

Asmodeus chimed in making the *private* meeting not so private. "It could take days, weeks, months. The world will have ended by then. What is your task this time anyway?"

"Shut it, Demon," Kala snapped.

"Demon? So impersonal." Asmodeus huffed, but when seeing Kala's disapproving glare, he looked away. "Fine. I'll just stay here, then. Let you two work it out."

Kala focused back on Talan. "Is that true?"

Talan stared at her frustrated. "Yes, but I wouldn't let you fail your mission. We can always jump back here and keep looking."

Kala shook her head and turned to Asmodeus. "Tell us where Zeus is and Talan will zap you back to earth. Deal?"

"Deal," Asmodeus agreed happily.

Talan shook his head. "I can't agree to that, Kala."

Kala should have known Talan would continue to balk at freeing Asmodeus, but Kala needed to talk to Zeus and Asmodeus appeared to be the only one with immediate knowledge of his whereabouts. Asmodeus wasn't trustworthy, but he was familiar. Kala could read him pretty easily. Definitely an evil she knew.

Asmodeus joined in helpfully. "He doesn't have to send me back, just get me out of these chains and I'll do the rest."

Kala was immediately suspicious of Asmodeus's perky nature, but she chalked it off to excitement at being released. She turned to Talan. "Just the chains?"

Talan took a few minutes to think. Finally, he nodded. He walked over to Asmodeus and touched the heavy chains that kept him captive. They disappeared.

Kala kept her guard up as Asmodeus massaged his wrists. "Much better, thank you."

"Zeus." Kala kept Asmodeus on target.

"Ah, yes, Zeus." Asmodeus held his arm out for Kala to take.

"Not happening." Kala deflected Asmodeus's flirting tactics. Even in the 5th Level of Hell, the guy tried to have game.

"No?" He acted mock-offended. "A little privacy perhaps?"

Both Kala and Talan looked at each other, unsure of Asmodeus's intentions.

Asmodeus snapped his fingers.

A ten-foot snarling dog appeared in the giant cavern.

Kala stared at the enormous dog growling in front of her. He looked like a cross between a Doberman pincher and a Pit-bull, except his teeth were black and had razor edges.

"Say hello to Spot, Grigori. Created by the Titans to eat little pesky angels like yourself." Asmodeus was quite pleased with himself.

Kala didn't move for fear of the giant beast gobbling her up, but she was more than livid. "Were you ever going to take me to Zeus?"

"Oh, buttercup, I'm still taking you to Zeus. I just don't want the third wheel tagging along."

Spot apparently didn't feel like waiting around for a conversation: his enormous head lunged toward Talan.

Talan plunged his hands forward and fire flowed out of his body with laser-like precision. The ray of fire engulfed Spot's left eye causing the dog to screech in pain.

Asmodeus tried to grab Kala to get her out of there, but there was no way she was going to leave Talan defenseless.

Kala leapt at Spot and grabbed the dog's head between her hands. It was like holding the front end of Volkswagen Beetle it was so huge. Then she used all her Titan might and threw Spot clear across the cavern. His body smashed against the purple rock and a few shattered pieces fell to the ground.

Spot was up in seconds, but instead of running toward Kala like she wanted, he ran full force toward Talan. Asmodeus was right. This dog was bred to hunt Grigori. She could beat him until he died, but he wouldn't attack her because she was a Titan.

Kala shrugged. She'd have to kill the poor bastard. Kala loved animals, even ten-foot supernatural ones, but if it meant Talan getting hurt or worse, the dog would have to go.

Spot took a running leap straight at Talan, but Talan threw his hands out and water flowed out of his fingers this time. As it touched the dog's body, it turned to ice. In less than a second, Spot had turned into a Popsicle.

"Well, that was disappointing," Asmodeus observed.

Spot shook loose of the ice.

And now he was pissed.

Kala ran full force at the dog and knocked him right into Asmodeus's smug face. It felt pretty good to hear both Asmodeus and the dog yelp from the impact.

Talan took advantage of the moment and sent another wave of fire toward Spot. This time there were large flames designed to burn. The fire engulfed Spot and turned him into a fiery ball of teeth and fur.

The dog quickly rid himself of the burning blaze with a full body shake.

Spot had had enough.

Before Talan or Kala could retaliate, Spot's gigantic head snapped forward and swallowed Talan whole.

As in: no more Talan.

Legs and all.

Kala was too dazed to register what had happened.

One minute they were fighting the Titan's guard dog, the next moment Talan was kibble.

Kala was about to break off a piece of purple rock and slice Spot's stomach open when she felt Asmodeus's hand on her shoulder.

Oh crap! Kala thought to herself as her surroundings blurred from Asmodeus teleporting her away.

Chapter Ten

Apparently, teleporting in Hell was the same as teleporting on earth. It took a few moments for Kala to adjust her eyes, but when she did, she smacked Asmodeus in the chest.

"Take me back!" Kala yelled at the Demon.

Asmodeus looked at her as if she were a child who didn't understand something. "Relax. Your boyfriend will be fine."

"He's not my boyfriend! And I don't believe you. Take me back now or I swear to God…" Kala started in anger.

But Asmodeus cut her off. "You'll what? Punch me with your Titan strength?" He grabbed Kala's hand and kissed it before she could react. "I'd much rather you use that strength for something more fun."

That was it.

Kala punched Asmodeus with as much force as she could. His whole body flew across the room, but before he made impact he used his Demon powers to stop himself and land on his feet. He massaged his jaw with a smile. "Look around you. Familiar?"

Kala did as he asked out of military habit, more than any command from Asmodeus.

Memories from Atlas flooded back to her as she recognized where she stood. It was a chamber made of what looked like shredded steel on the walls and ceiling. The ground was some kind of rusted metal. The combination of old and new only emphasized the contrast between the two metals. There was a single closed door at the end of the rectangular-shaped room and Kala knew where it led:

Zeus's prison.

Her Atlas memory remembered vividly. She knew that when she opened the door, Zeus would be chained inside a cell lined with the same shredded steel that surrounded her out here.

Kala threw up her hands. "Fine. You're a Demon of your word. I'm here. Now take me back."

Asmodeus casually walked over to Kala and put his hand out. "See for yourself." A holographic image hovered above his hand. It was like watching security footage, supernatural-style. Talan was in the cavern they had just left, covered in Spot guts. What was left of the beast coated most of the purple rock. It looked as if there had been a hurricane made of dog entrails and Talan stood in the aftermath.

"How do I know this isn't fake?" Kala asked suspiciously.

"Because you know. Am I wrong?" Asmodeus moved his hand and the image disappeared.

Though Kala couldn't explain why, she *did* know. It gave

her a sense of relief, but also made her furious. "Bring him here right now!" she threatened.

"Now why would I do that?" Asmodeus replied as if Kala wasn't in her right mind. "The only reason I was not put in chains the second Talan freed me is because I turned him in. Turn in a Grigori and apparently all is forgiven." Asmodeus was pleased with himself again.

"Is he with the Titans now?" Kala was incredulous. "We have to save him!"

"Talan won't stay long enough for them to capture him. He's probably teleporting back to earth as we speak." Asmodeus reached toward Kala's head in what she could only assume was to touch her face or hair in some way. She smacked his hand away.

"Just keep your distance." Kala couldn't really argue with Asmodeus's logic. Talan wouldn't stay. He couldn't travel without causing more alarm anyway.

Then a horrible thought struck her. Talan was convinced that the two of them were soul mates. Kala knew he would throw caution to the wind and fight his way to her.

She had to get a message to him somehow. Tell him she was okay. That he *should* leave the 5th.

This would be a good time to find out that Atlas has some kind of telepathy power. Anything? Kala sighed inwardly. She knew Turner's wife Roberta had powers like that. The woman had entered Kala's brain to help her fuse Atlas's essence with hers. Without Roberta, Kala would have died.

Kala? Roberta's voice sounded in Kala's head.

Kala stood very still. Was she crazy? Or did she just hear Roberta in her brain?

Asmodeus was apparently growing impatient. "Look, we'll talk to Zeus, then I'll take you back to earth…"

Kala put her hand up sharply. "Shut it. I'm listening."

Asmodeus looked around the room confused but, to Kala's relief, did as he was told.

Kala tried talking to herself, hoping she wasn't imagining Roberta. *I'm here. I need your help.*

What do you need? Roberta answered fast.

Whoa. Kala thought. *Is this real?*

You and I have a connection now. Anytime you open your mind to me, I can enter and you can do the same to me. Roberta's voice sounded as clearly as if they were in the same room.

Kala wasn't sure if she liked this new development, but she didn't want to lose Talan to the Titans. *The old Voodoo guy that teaches you magic, he's really that angel I brought with me when I became Atlas.* Talan probably wouldn't appreciate her telling Roberta about his disguise, but Kala wanted him safe, so she rolled the dice.

Interesting. Roberta sounded intrigued. *He needs help?*

Yes. How do you normally contact him? Kala asked.

The same way we're communicating now. Remember what I told you the night I taught you the telekinesis spell? About contacting you?

Kala thought back to that night, when she had asked Roberta how to reach her in the future, Roberta had replied *I have my ways.* Kala figured it was a pretty good guess that *this* was the way.

That's how you were going to find me? Kala had wondered how Roberta would track her down.

Helping you assimilate with Atlas made that a lot easier. Roberta confirmed. *Now, what can I do for Pierre?*

Contact him. Tell him you know he's Talan, and that I'm okay. He needs to leave the 5th, Roberta. He'll die or be imprisoned if he doesn't. Just make sure he knows I'm fine and that I have Asmodeus in check. Can you do that?

Of course. Roberta responded. *I'll do it now.*

Before Kala could answer back, she physically felt Roberta's essence leave her mind. It was light, like a small breeze.

"What was that about?" Asmodeus asked.

Kala didn't want to tell him. "Sometimes when I have memories from Atlas's past, I zone out a bit." It wasn't a lie. She did zone out when she experienced Atlas's recollections.

Now that Roberta was hopefully making sure Talan was safe and not playing hero, Kala decided to actually figure out what Atlas could recall about this place. Separating Atlas's memory from the present moment was a little bit more difficult for her after the mind-melding experience with Roberta. Regardless, she tried to focus on what Atlas remembered.

Atlas had come here to make Zeus fulfill his promise after the Titans captured all the Olympians. Atlas still couldn't believe the war was over, not after picking the wrong side for a second time. If he could just talk to Zeus, Zeus could free him of his curse. It wasn't fair that Atlas helped the Olympians and was still being punished. Helping Zeus should be enough to make him break the curse. It wasn't Atlas's fault that the Olympians had lost.

Kala really hated the way Atlas thought. It was such a weasel thing to think. But Atlas was a part of her now and she had to accept it. It was hard enough dealing with her own regret, now she had to deal with Atlas's too?!

The memory became more vivid when Atlas opened the door

to see Zeus chained to the shredded steel wall. The Olympian looked weak, skinny, and pale. Not at all what a powerful god should look like. He barely glanced at Atlas.

"I'm here to help you escape," Atlas lied. He figured if Zeus thought he was going to free him, he might be more likely to break the curse.

Zeus may have appeared weak, but when he spoke, his words were pure power. "You betrayed us!" Zeus accused.

Atlas had not been prepared for that. "I did not! I did everything you asked! How was I to know that Cronus was two steps ahead of you? It's not my fault your father is manipulative and evil!" Atlas felt his chances of Zeus helping him slip away.

Zeus growled, "You were always loyal to my father! I deserve this punishment for being so foolish as to trust you!"

Atlas panicked. "I swear to you, Zeus, I did nothing! Now break this curse! I did everything you asked!"

Zeus laughed. "You are despicable, Atlas. Groveling to me when it's your fault I stand here chained for all eternity. I'll never lift that curse. *Never!*"

The force of Zeus's words jolted Kala out of the memory.

When she blinked her eyes to re-focus on the present, she was suddenly face to face with Asmodeus, his hands cradling her waist as he stared down at her.

Kala pushed him away. "Seriously? You need to find some nice Demon queen to settle down with, because *we're* never going to happen."

"When you've lived as long as I have, never say never." Asmodeus smiled.

That brought Kala back to Zeus's threat of keeping Atlas

cursed forever. "I actually hope you're right about that." Seeing Asmodeus's eyebrows rise in sudden hope, Kala quashed it. "About never saying never, not about hooking up."

Asmodeus seemed pleased by this anyway. "What's the difference?"

Kala didn't want to argue semantics with the guy, so she plowed toward the door.

Once she reached it, Kala wondered if it was locked. If this place was a super prison, shouldn't it be much harder to get to the prisoners? She paused in front of the entrance, not wanting to rush into any potential traps or surprises.

Asmodeus stepped next to her, a little close for her taste, but she was too on guard to do anything about it. "You know it's unlocked, right?" Asmodeus peered down at Kala obviously curious as to why she had paused. "Or are we having another flashback?"

Before Asmodeus could wrap his hand around her waist in hopes she was in spaced-out-memory-lane mode, Kala smacked his hand away. "Why aren't there any guards? What's stopping Zeus from escaping?"

Asmodeus laughed out loud. "Because he's in the same chains I was just in. Only Titans and Grigori can break them. And you saw for yourself: Grigori can't get into the 5th without the help of a Titan."

"But they can transport your ass here." Kala pretty much verbally bitch-slapped Asmodeus. Her foster father, Owen, had banished the king of Demons to the 5th like it was child's play.

Asmodeus lost his smile and shrugged. "True. But look how stupid your boyfriend was to free me."

"Stop calling him my boyfriend," Kala responded, not knowing why she always rose to the bait with the Demon. "Come on, let's see what Zeus has to say for himself."

Kala breathed in deep and opened the door.

The cell was as Atlas had remembered it. Except for one thing.

Zeus was no longer there.

Chapter Eleven

"Well, that's a surprise," Asmodeus observed. "The Elders are not going to like that."

Kala was in shock for all of two seconds then her emotions turned to anger. "Do you think they moved him? Maybe when they realized I was here they took him somewhere else?" Breaking her curse was starting to feel like it was getting farther and farther out of reach.

"Anything is possible, but why move him after 2,000 years? Just because a half-breed – no offense – comes to interrogate Zeus is hardly cause for panic. Really? What could you possibly do?" Asmodeus mused.

"Thanks," Kala retorted sarcastically. Nothing like the Demon King to make her feel completely inadequate. It was a new sensation for her not to be respected as a soldier. She was used to being the elite of the elite, and to be thrown into a world where she was lower than the bottom of the totem pole was very humbling. "If not the Titans then did he escape on his own?"

Asmodeus shook his head. "I told you: only a Titan or Grigori could break that chain."

Kala had a sinking sensation in her stomach. *I just did something that could get me killed, but it won't be worth a thing if you don't help me.* Rotoph's words echoed in Kala's head. She was starting to imagine that Rotoph's *something* had been freeing Zeus. But she wanted to see what Asmodeus would say about her suspicions first. "You don't think a Grigori…"

"How? The Elder alarms would go off if they got anywhere near his cell. No. You were right the first time. They must have moved him. Maybe they're more scared of you than I thought."

"What about Rotoph? Doesn't he work for the Titans? He could have done it." The more Kala thought about it, the more she knew that Rotoph showing up yesterday morning was more than just a Grigori reunion. He had probably released Zeus and ran to the only person he thought would give him the time of day: Talan.

"How do you know about Rotoph? Never mind. Don't tell me. Listen, sweetie," Asmodeus said seriously, "Rotoph is not someone you can trust. He's dangerous."

"Ha! This coming from you?" Kala guffawed. But Asmodeus's concern made her pause. "I stabbed him a couple of times." Kala felt like defending herself.

"Really?" Asmodeus raised his eyebrow, impressed. Then his face turned ashen. "Stabbed him with what?"

Kala pulled out the Grigori blade.

Asmodeus's eyes widened. "Where did you get that?"

"I stole it from Rotoph." Kala was careful as to what she wanted to reveal to Asmodeus. She knew there were certain things she could trust the Demon with, but knowledge of Rotoph's plan to free the Grigori wasn't one of them. If Rotoph had helped Zeus escape, then Kala recognized that he had been sincere in his plea for Talan's help. He really did want to free the other Grigori.

And Kala had left him vulnerable. Oops.

By the way he looked at Kala, Asmodeus was definitely impressed. "You are just full of surprises." He eyed the knife again. "You know that drains your powers, right?"

Kala shrugged. "So far I've used it three times and I haven't noticed anything. Maybe I need to use it excessively to trigger the power-sucking rune," Kala voiced her theory.

"Maybe." Asmodeus looked thoughtfully at Kala. "Or maybe the fact that you're a walking anomaly gives you a certain amount of protection."

Kala had never thought of that possibility. The fact that she was a human who had consumed a god apparently never happened before. Asmodeus might be right. Maybe her *differences* would protect her from things that would normally hurt a god. Only time would tell, but Kala decided to rest on the cautious side for now. "I don't plan on hacking up any Grigori in the near future, so we'll never find out if this knife drains me, will we?"

Asmodeus smirked as if hiding something.

"What was that look?" Kala didn't like a smirking Asmodeus.

"Nothing. Good on you. No more stabbing Grigori." Asmodeus led Kala out of the cell and back into the adjoining room. "We should get you back to earth."

"Oh no, stop right there." Now Kala was certain that

Asmodeus was keeping something from her. "Spill."

"Just tuck that away, and let's get out of here." Asmodeus eyed the knife with disdain.

Kala peered down at the blade. Kala couldn't figure out if Asmodeus didn't like her talking about not killing Grigori or the knife itself. But he was definitely acting squirmy. "If you don't tell me what you're hiding, I'll have to stab you with this myself."

"Is this what our relationship has turned into? Stabbing me if I don't share my most intimate secrets?" Asmodeus smiled mockingly.

But Kala noticed he kept his distance.

It was all she needed.

"Ha!" Kala laughed. "I can read you so easily. This blade hurts *anything* supernatural, doesn't it?"

Asmodeus didn't look upset by Kala's revelation. If anything, the hearts in his eyes appeared to grow even larger. "You *can* read me, can't you?" Asmodeus obviously felt it was worth the risk of a good stabbing because he reached out and pulled Kala to him.

Kala debated whether or not to gut the Demon to escape his grasp, but his hands were loose enough around the small of her back that she could free herself easily. And letting Asmodeus feel like he was getting closer to her only made him reveal more information. There was another teeny part of her that was trying to ignore the tiny thrill that went through her at his touch. Something she wished she could squash from her brain entirely. "Tell me about the blade," Kala said with as much seduction as she could muster.

It worked.

Asmodeus wore the same expression of every other guy Kala

had ever lured into her bed when she wanted a one-night stand. Until she met Jack, Kala only believed in one-night-only deals. They were easy, no emotions, and it got the job done. And no one could deny the thrill of the chase.

Kala let Asmodeus tuck the hair back behind her ear. "You're right. It hurts all supernatural beings."

"Even Titans?" Kala cooed.

Asmodeus leaned in close so that their lips were inches from each other.

If Kala wasn't in interrogation mode, she would have been tempted to have rebound sex with Asmodeus. Talk about no strings attached. At least for her. And the chemistry she was feeling between them was intoxicating. She could almost feel his lips on hers.

Asmodeus's voice was almost a whisper, "Yes, even Titans. It's why they kept the blades under lock and key after the Grigori and Olympians were disposed of. But it doesn't strip them of their power like it does for Grigori. It only makes them weaker."

Though the tension was palpable, this new information brought Kala out of the lust fest she almost dove into. She now had a weapon that she could use against all her enemies. And, hey, a knife worked on human enemies as well.

Kala pulled away from Asmodeus, more to clear her head, than anything else. "All right, let's get back to...earth." That sounded weird. Those weren't words she ever expected to come out of her mouth.

Asmodeus was still half-leaning down for the kiss he expected. It was as if Kala pulling away was particularly torturous for him. "Right." He surveyed the metal room with seeming understanding. "You want to go somewhere more comfortable."

"You keep believing that." Kala turned on the coldness that had propelled her into many fistfights with grown men.

But Asmodeus was different. His face showed that he kind of liked Kala's refusals. It had become a game to him. A game that he apparently was enjoying thoroughly.

"As you wish." He bowed. Asmodeus gently reached out and touched Kala's arm.

Nothing happened.

Asmodeus was just as confused as Kala.

He touched her again.

Nothing.

"Uh, oh." Asmodeus cringed.

Kala's scenery warped and swirled until she stood in the same throne room that had been in Atlas's memory, but this time only one Titan was in the room.

Sitting on the throne with an expression of rage was Cronus.

Chapter Twelve

"**H**ey." Kala lamely nodded her head in greeting.

The room was much bigger to Kala in person. Though her Atlas memories felt as vivid as if she were experiencing them in person, for some reason *actually* being in the same location live felt different. It was almost as if her surroundings were extra sharp.

It was difficult to imagine fighting Cronus, since, of course, that was what Kala was trying to figure out. She had the Grigori blade tucked safely in her jacket. Knowing that it could hurt the Titan was enough for her; it was simply about how to land a hit.

Cronus's voice rumbled as he spoke. "How dare you enter my realm."

"Neat trick with the voice. Is that supposed to intimidate me or something?" It absolutely *did* intimidate Kala, but she wouldn't let Cronus know that. Keep him off guard. It was the only way she could see of having a remote chance to escape.

"It should intimidate you because I could crush you with a mere thought," Cronus bellowed.

Kala was an excellent poker player: she knew a bluff when she saw one. "If that were true, I'd be dead already. So why don't we get to the point. What do you want from me?" Kala hoped the terror that she felt inside didn't show. Unlike Cronus, bluffing was one of her strong suits so she crossed her fingers that he was buying it. And if she could garner information out of the guy, then hey, bonus.

Cronus studied Kala. She knew that look. She had certainly seen it enough when people couldn't figure her out: surprise. She puzzled the Titan. "I see Atlas inside of you, but you are nothing like him." He may have been thrown off by Kala's responses, but his face was still etched with fury. Cronus didn't like being caught off guard any more than he liked intruders. She was the enemy and he was weighing his options. Kala just hoped he didn't pick the *crush her* option.

"I may have devoured your little Titan nephew or whatever, but I'm still me. And Atlas was a *douche*," Kala responded defensively. Sure the superpowers were awesome, but having memories that made her feel like a total wimp were devastating.

"I'm not sure what a douche is, but it seems to describe Atlas accurately." Cronus sat back on his throne, his eyes full of rage. "You are a conundrum."

"Is that good or bad?" Kala tried to gauge if Cronus was preparing to hurt her or not.

"I haven't decided yet," he mused, his voice laced with anger.

"I vote for good." Kala eyed her surroundings, waiting for anything Cronus might throw at her.

Cronus stared at Kala, his eyes fuming. Maybe he always looked like that. Either way, it made Kala nervous. She felt like a very tiny mouse near the maw of a very large cat. "Atlas's blood runs in your veins. I can smell it."

Rub it in.

"That's what happens when you swallow a god, I guess," Kala answered sarcastically. "Why did you bring me here?"

"How did you consume him?" Cronus leaned forward, examining Kala as if she were a lab rat. "HOW?!"

The room shook violently.

Kala stumbled but kept her footing. She tried not to sweat. This was way out of her comfort zone. What she wouldn't give for a sniper rifle and target. Kala had thought her life was hard then. Looking back, that was just child's play.

"I'll never tell you." Probably because Kala had no idea *how* she ate the Titan, but she wasn't about to tell Cronus that. *I don't know* never sounded as good at *I'll never tell.*

Cronus leapt out of his chair and in one swipe of his arm, Kala flew through the air, her body smacking a nearby pillar.

Surprisingly, it didn't hurt as much as she thought it would. All her limbs were still intact despite the crater her body had just created. But Kala knew how to fight better than anyone. And this was just a very odd fistfight.

Kala pretended to be knocked out from the blow. The way she situated her body was strategic. Her legs were bent for an easy stand-and-run while her hand rested on the hilt of the Grigori blade.

"Your human form makes you pathetic," Cronus crowed, overconfident.

Exactly what Kala needed him to be.

Kala heard, then felt, Cronus walking up to her still form.

A slight nudging of her body from Cronus's foot told her that he bought her unconsciousness act.

The Titan leaned down and Kala felt his hand as Cronus turned her head to examine her face.

Right where she wanted him.

Here goes nothing.

Kala flipped her body and thrust the knife hard into Cronus's gut.

The Titan screamed in anguish, reeling back from shock as Kala twisted the Grigori blade for added damage.

Kala knew she had to act fast. Her momentum would be gone in milliseconds. Pulling out the Grigori knife, Kala slid across the floor and slashed Cronus's Achilles tendon on his left foot as she went.

Cronus howled in rage.

He was so much faster than Kala could have imagined.

Cronus's hand was around her neck before Kala could make her next move. He tossed her like a rag doll clear across the giant hall. Remembering how graceful Asmodeus had been when Kala threw him, Kala tried to land with some kind of decorum.

Nope.

She was all limbs as she smashed into the marble wall. Another crater.

Cronus was on her fast. He lifted her up by her hair this time and crashed her down on the floor.

It shocked Kala that she was still alive. Not only alive, but only slightly beat up. The Atlas part of her could apparently take quite a beating. The human part of her wanted to demolish the Titan.

She started to understand why everyone hated Cronus.

He appeared to have healed completely from the wounds Kala inflicted. She knew she had been reaching, but she had to try.

As Cronus made her fly across the room again, Kala had enough sense to survey the chamber at startling speeds. She looked for an exit. Kala had no idea how to get out of the 5th Level of Hell, but she was a resourceful girl. She'd find a way. As her body collided with Cronus's throne, she saw the entrance at the other end of the hall.

Wracking her brain for Atlas's memories of this place, she suddenly recalled that there was a room outside this chamber than led to Iapetus's chambers. Kala knew Atlas's relationship with his father was strained, but she was technically Atlas now, so maybe she could make amends enough to ask Iapetus to teleport her back down to earth.

It was all she had.

Desperate, but Kala had to try.

Cronus charged.

This time Kala used a simple Aikido move on him. Using the momentum of his advance, Kala leaned in, blocked his grasping hand with her arm, and used his own force to throw him into a pillar.

Where Kala's body had left a small dent, Cronus's snapped it in two.

He was utterly surprised at the blow.

When Kala rushed him, she suddenly found she couldn't move.

"That's enough." Cronus dusted himself off as he stood.

No matter how hard she tried to break free, she wasn't budging.

"Afraid of a fight?" Kala couldn't stop herself from taunting even if she wanted to. "You have to use some kind of spell to stop me? You're a bigger 'fraidy cat than I thought." Kala laughed. "Hiding in the 5th? Afraid of Grigori? Afraid of everyone! You're the pathetic one!"

Cronus was all fire.

He stood in front of Kala. Ten feet of raging fury.

"I'm afraid of nothing," Cronus roared.

"Sure, buddy, and I have some swamp land in Florida I can sell you." Kala rolled her eyes.

Chances were the Florida joke went way over his head, but he must have surmised the meaning because he spat, "I could never be afraid of a puny Titan like you. You're not even worthy of my presence."

"Then why am I here? Send me to earth if I annoy this much." Kala decided to make a Hail Mary move. Briar Patch anyone?

Cronus smiled wickedly. "So, you'd abandon your Grigori boyfriend just to get back to earth. Where's the loyalty? Oh yes, I've forgotten to whom I'm speaking. You may have another skin, Atlas, but you're still the same traitor you've always been."

Kala struggled hard at that, but she was still frozen in place. "What did you do to Talan?"

Ignoring the traitor talk, Kala's heart sunk. Roberta must not have been able to reach him. Or worse, Talan had decided to stay and look for Kala despite her assurances.

"What I plan on doing to all Grigori," Cronus snarled.

A pile of what looked like thick logs appeared above Cronus's head. With a flick of his wrist, the logs flew at Kala's still form and dropped at her feet.

Talan.

Hacked.

In pieces.

His head staring at her, lifeless.

His limbs were bloodless, as if they were frozen.

"YOU KILLED HIM!" Rage burned inside Kala like lava.

Cronus laughed. "You're not the only one with a Grigori blade. And I have the other eleven. Speaking of which…" Using his Titan-telekinesis, Cronus pulled the knife from Kala's unmoving hand and into his own.

She barely noticed.

Kala couldn't see straight.

She'd never been this furious before.

Kala stared at the most powerful Titan of them all and felt no fear.

"YOU WILL PAY!" she screamed.

Cronus started to laugh again, but stopped when the whole chamber started to shake violently. His looked around in disbelief. "How are you…"

BOOM!

The invisible bonds that secured Kala in place exploded with a deafening roar.

Cronus was downright mystified and to Kala's delight…

Scared.

The ground shook even harder.

Pillars crashed to the floor.

Cronus's throne shattered into a million pieces.

"NOW YOU WILL DIE!" Kala's voice was not her own. It was like the moment when she had consumed Atlas. Something deep inside her, speaking for her, saying words she didn't understand.

Cronus's eyes filled with terror as part of the ceiling crashed down on him. "The Grigori is still alive. They can't be killed. Another Grigori can put him back together," Cronus sputtered in a panic.

Kala wanted to give into this inner voice. This inner depth that could crush Cronus where he stood, but she knew that it was wrong.

Talan was alive. In pieces but alive.

The bellowing rage disappeared. Whatever was inside her, crawled back down to her subconscious.

But one thing it left her with.

Knowledge.

Knowledge of powers Kala hadn't been aware of.

For one: telekinesis.

"I'll be taking what's mine," Kala said and made the Grigori blade fly back into her hand.

Cronus stared at her, afraid she would destroy him.

And for another: she could teleport.

Kneeling down next to the mound of body parts that were Talan, Kala gave Cronus one last snarky grin. "Later." She saluted.

Kala touched Talan's body and they vanished.

Chapter Thirteen

In a sudden rush, Kala landed in the last place she imagined.

The Compound.

More specifically, General Turner's lab. Kala remembered this room. It was where Turner introduced her to the tranquilizer gun that helped her fight Malaks and Demons. The actual size of the room was huge, almost the size of a football field. There were computers, wires, electronics, and robotic parts covering almost every inch of the place. After teleporting herself for the first time, Kala felt a little dizzy from the onslaught of metal and lights. She was still kneeling with Talan's body parts at her feet.

"Lieutenant Hicks?"

Kala looked up, General Turner stood above her. He appeared more curious than shocked. Something she was getting used to with the man. When he saw Talan's bloodless limbs, he glanced at her with concern. "Is that a person?"

Kala stood up, shaking her head. "It's Talan, the angel you met before. And, apparently he's not dead. He just needs to be put back together."

Turner nodded to two scientists working at their respective stations. They walked over like mindless servants.

Inspecting the room, Kala noticed that aside from the two scientists, there were only three others in the giant space.

"Get a table and put him on it," Turner ordered. As the two men left, he turned to Kala. "This is the angel that you wanted Roberta to contact?"

"Yes." Kala tried to use as few words as possible. Her mind still reeled from what had just happened.

Turner scrutinized *the Talan pile*. "Fascinating. You said this is the same man who appears to my wife as Pierre?"

Kala nodded. Revealing *that* might not have been a great idea, but desperation had made the decision for her. And for no reason it appeared. Kala damned Talan for being stubborn and loyal, traits she normally admired, but now made her feel horribly guilty.

"Pierre taught my wife powerful magic. That's where she learned how to make that ooze that works so well on Demons." Turner seemed quite chipper for someone who stood next to a pile of body parts. He was definitely an odd one. Then he said something that made her pause. "I'm assuming he's actually Dr. Fortski as well?"

Kala laughed, it threw her off so much. Her mission was to destroy Fortski's work, but he was so brilliant Turner thought that the doc had to be supernatural. "Nope. Fortski's the real deal." Kala didn't elaborate because she didn't want to reveal her mission. She also didn't want to divulge any more of Talan's secrets. He'd be mad enough at her for the whole *Pierre* thing. Nice name by the way. Wonder how long it took him to come up with that one.

The two scientists returned with a metal table on wheels and began piecing Talan together. After a few moments, they had loosely connected his body together. They left without a word, returning to their stations.

The current circumstances were bizarre enough, but the two scientists only added to the weirdness factor.

Kala detached herself from the situation to keep her head on straight. Having Talan thrown at her by Cronus awoke something inside her. It terrified Kala. She couldn't admit that to anyone but herself. The supernatural world needed to believe that she was not only unshakeable, but someone to be feared. Her legs shook from the confrontation. Not because of the fight, but because she didn't know where her power came from. Kala had consumed Atlas and if she was honest with herself, she knew that she could have done the same thing with Cronus.

He knew and she knew it.

And he was scared.

…But so was she.

"Clifton can't know I'm here."

Turner threw Kala a look that suggested he wasn't an idiot. "If I can hide Mr. Echolls under Clifton's nose, I think I can hide you. And I'm assuming after you've put Humpty Dumpty back together again you'll be on your way?" Turner examined Talan with fascination.

Derek.

"Is Derek okay?"

Turner kept studying Talan's body parts with fascination as he talked with Kala. "Mr. Echolls is fine. I thought you would make more use out of him."

"Trust me, that wasn't my idea. Talan thought Derek would be safer, and considering what happened to *him* I think it was the right call." Kala's heart squeezed as she stared at Talan.

Turner nodded at the disassembled body. "It appears so."

Kala ran her hand through her hair, observing the room. "I don't even know how I got here. I've just discovered that I apparently have teleportation powers and it was a quick exit. I guess my brain sent me somewhere familiar," Kala rationalized.

"Well, you've only been to this lab once, but I'd say it was a pretty productive trip the last time you were here," Turner observed.

He was right. It was the first time Kala had witnessed a *regular old human* actually hurt Asmodeus. Turner had used the tranq gun filled with Roberta's mojo juice and injected it into the Demon. Asmodeus turned into a crying baby, giving Kala enough time to escape. Kala had felt like she had a fighting chance after that. It made sense that her mind would take her here.

Maybe Turner had some more toys she could use.

Kala couldn't stop staring at Talan's broken form.

Even though she logically told herself that Talan was still alive, part of her doubted Cronus. What if Talan really was dead? It bothered her more than she liked. The guy had been her backup throughout this whole ordeal. She may not share the same feelings for him that he had for her, but Kala cared about him. Talan had helped her when he shouldn't have and saved her when it would have been safer for him to let her die.

Only one person could help Talan now.

Owen.

"I need to get someone here who can help," Kala announced to Turner.

Turner waved to her encouragingly. "By all means. You can come and go as you please apparently."

"I don't think I have to. I think I can bring him here." Kala had no idea how to pinpoint her foster father and teleport to him. She figured that whole mind-speech thing that Roberta did would work better. She just needed to figure out how to use it with someone besides Roberta. "I have to concentrate." Kala turned away from Talan's body.

Now what?

Kala closed her eyes.

Owen? Kala felt like an idiot. Why did she think this would work?

Because it works with Roberta. Kala scolded herself.

And when was talking to herself a good idea?

Kala wanted to scream. She needed Owen and she had no idea how to connect with him, let alone contact him in any other form.

OWEN! Kala screamed in her head.

"I'm here, Kala."

Kala opened her eyes. Standing in front of her was her foster father, Owen. She fell into his arms, relief flooding through every vein. Kala only recently found out that Owen was a Grigori angel like Talan, but it didn't make her look at him any differently. Owen and Linda had saved her life as a foster kid. They were the first two people who ever showed her what it meant to love. Kala might not be related to them by blood, but they were her parents. Period.

Owen's arms felt like the most comfortable place on the planet right then. Kala wished she could stay there forever. But eventually Owen pulled away to look her in the eye.

"What is it, Kala? Are you okay?" His face was all concern.

Kala nodded behind her at Talan.

Owen looked over her shoulder and his eyes widened. He hurried to Talan's body. "Who did this?"

"Cronus," Kala answered. She couldn't help but notice Turner's eyebrow raise at that. Kala admired the fact that Turner knew when to be quiet, not in the sense of being polite, more like he was observing and gathering information. No wonder Talan sought him out. The guy was a sponge.

Owen stared at Kala even more shocked. "How did you escape without Talan to help you?"

Kala turned to Turner. "I'm not sure how much I should say with some of these guys in the room." She gestured toward the handful of scientists. Sure, they seemed pre-occupied, but if just one of them was a spy for Clifton – or worse a Demon – Kala didn't want to say too much.

Turner shrugged, not concerned. "They're loyal only to me. You can say anything you like."

Kala wasn't convinced. "You can't guarantee that."

Owen gave Turner a knowing look. "Yes, he can."

Kala looked at Owen, surprised. "You know something I don't?"

Owen said pointedly, "Let's just say these workers couldn't

say anything even if they wanted to."

"Magic?" Kala asked. Maybe Roberta had put them in some kind of worker-bee spell. It would explain their drone-like behavior.

Owen nodded. "Something like that. The point is you can trust them. Now, tell me what happened with Cronus?"

"I'm not sure." Which was the truth. Kala still wasn't positive what had happened, but she told Owen and Turner everything that took place. Maybe one of them would have some insight.

Turner didn't look fazed at all, probably because all this talk of Titans and angels wasn't in his wheelhouse of experience. Turner was a science guy. Magic and mythology was more his wife's cup of tea. Though from the expression on his face, his curiosity was definitely piqued.

Owen, however, appeared rocked. His eyes didn't seem like they'd ever blink again. "Kala," was all that came out.

"What does it mean?" Kala was afraid of the answer, but she had to ask.

"I can't say for sure." Owen's voice was hoarse as if what Kala had said took the wind out of him. "There are so many things about you that are impossible. We've just added another one to the list." Owen managed a smile. "You still have the blade?" Owen asked. Kala pulled it out and he nodded in approval. "You hold onto that. We may need to use it."

Kala tucked it back into her jacket.

Kala knew Owen's smile was to make her feel better, but she also knew that he was seriously freaked. He turned his attention back to Talan. "Maybe Talan will know. Let's put him back together."

110

Turner asked Owen, "Is there anything you need from me?"

Owen motioned to Talan's shredded clothing. "He's going to need something to wear."

"Of course." Turner motioned to one of his zombie-scientists to fetch some clothes.

Owen suddenly looked self-conscious as he turned to Kala. "We're going to have to strip him down. Maybe you should turn around."

"I've seen a naked man before." Kala shook her head with a smile. It reminded her that Owen was still her dad and she would always be his little girl.

Owen looked embarrassed. "Right. Good to know."

But Kala knew it wasn't really *good to know*. Owen didn't want to discuss Kala's love life any more than she did. He was actually blushing. It was hilarious.

"Let's get this done." Kala took the initiative and ripped off what was left of Talan's clothing. She let Owen take care of the crotch area. No need to mortify him any more than she had to.

In order to cope with the disturbing sight, Kala made herself see Talan as a disassembled mannequin.

At this point, Kala and Turner were just by-standers. Neither one of them could turn away from what was happening.

Owen began at Talan's feet. His hands glowed a warm hue of gold. When Owen touched the gap between Talan's feet and the bottom part of his legs, the two fused together. It was quick work after that: each body part reattached with Owen's glowing hands, until finally all that was left was Talan's head.

It all came down to this moment for Kala. She trusted Owen's abilities implicitly, but part of her doubted that Talan could be saved. The concept of a real person being chopped up into pieces and reassembled without a scratch on them was a thing of fiction to Kala. She knew Talan wasn't *human*, but that was how she saw him.

Kala held her breath as Owen laid his glowing hands on Talan's neck.

Talan shot up to sitting position, gasping for air.

Before Kala could think better of it, she reached over and pulled Talan into a hug. Feeling his arms around her made her feel immense relief. He was okay. He was alive.

He was naked.

Kala pulled away and kept her eyes focused on Talan's. She didn't want her view roaming to… other places.

Talan apparently could care less about his nakedness. His eyes were alight with his feelings for Kala. No matter how many times Kala put him in his place, Talan couldn't hide his emotions for her.

And at that exact second, it felt good. Kala had never thought she'd see him look at her ever again. Let alone with so much affection.

"Clothes." Turner handed Talan a stack of folded attire.

Fatigues and a white t-shirt. It fit perfectly. A little too perfectly. The boy looked good. The shoes were standard issue army boots.

Kala had to admire that a Grigori angel could look like a boot camp grunt.

Talan was on his feet. He embraced Owen and shook hands with Turner.

"We should leave." Talan took charge. To Turner he said,

"Thank you for your hospitality, but this place isn't safe for Kala."

"I couldn't agree more. Three levels above us Clifton is planning an all-out manhunt for Ms. Hicks here. The sooner you leave, the better." Turner was on the same page as Talan.

Kala asked, "Where to?"

Owen responded first. "Your mother wants to see you."

That sounded amazing to Kala. The thought of seeing Linda made Kala feel like her heart might be able to start to mend. There was nothing like the healing embrace of a mother.

Kala and Talan agreed.

Owen reached out and touched the two of them.

Nothing.

Kala was having flashbacks from the 5th. What? Did Cronus stop teleporting in the Compound as well?

Talan touched Owen and Kala, trying to use his teleporting power instead.

Nothing.

"What's happening?" Owen focused on Turner.

Turner was genuinely baffled. "I have no idea."

Before Kala could truly process her situation…

General Clifton and a team of his men marched into the room.

Their guns were raised and they were all pointed at Kala.

Chapter Fourteen

Clifton's smug expression made Kala's skin crawl. "After our last teleporting visitor, I made some changes to our defenses."

Turner looked impressed. "How did you pull that off, Harry?"

Harry didn't even look mad at Turner. Their relationship went beyond Kala's understanding. She could see that she wasn't going to get any help from Turner though, not when Clifton was standing next to him. He had to protect his own neck.

Clifton shrugged. "You have your scientists, I have mine."

"I'd like to meet yours." Turner raised an eyebrow in curiosity.

"I bet you would," Clifton guffawed.

Watching their exchange was fascinating. But Kala didn't want to kill soldiers, she just wanted to get out of there.

"You know you can't hurt us, right?" Kala wanted to wipe the triumphant smirk off Clifton's face.

The smirk didn't go away. He didn't believe her. "I saw the

security footage from yesterday's attack. I know about your shielding technology. And you're not leaving here until we get it from you."

Clifton included Turner in his *we*. The sad part was that Turner knew Talan's *shielding technology* was supernatural.

"Good luck with that. He used magic." Kala loved that it sounded absurd. And she loved that it was true.

Kala couldn't believe she had been scared of Clifton as her superior. He was such a tool. Of course, the fact that she was an immortal Titan helped curb the fear of ten guns being pointed at her, but still. It was nice standing up to him. He reminded Kala of every bully she'd ever encountered in her life.

As her boss, she had to put up with it.

As a god, not so much.

Clifton didn't buy Kala's *magic* comment for a second. He didn't live in that reality. He lived in the reality where rival governments were constantly developing new and cutting edge weapons. Clifton thought she was a smart ass (which she was), and he didn't like it.

"We're leaving." Kala turned to Turner. "Where did you get me out last time?" She knew she shouldn't remind Clifton of the fact that Turner helped her escape, but it was so hard not to want to take him down a few notches.

Turner sighed. "You know I can't tell you that."

Kala saw Turner touch the face of his watch. If she hadn't been staring at him, she wouldn't have noticed. No one else seemed to. Was he giving her a signal? Was he trying to say something about time? Kala was immortal, so she didn't have to worry about dying, but the Compound was miles deep and miles wide. There was no way she was getting out of there without help. Kala had limited knowledge of the layout of the Compound. She had only been allowed into a few designated areas. It was a maze that Kala did not have a key to.

"Enough!" Clifton bellowed. "Take them. If they resist, kill them."

The guy was a fool.

Clifton's men kept their guns raised as they closed the distance between themselves and Kala.

Kala knew they were just doing their job. She also knew that these soldiers weren't about to capture two Grigori and a Titan. In military-mode, Kala loved to use any advantage available to her. And being a god was definitely an advantage.

Owen barely moved his hand: Clifton and his men dropped to the floor.

"Okay," Kala observed. "That was easy."

"They're out cold for a few hours." Owen focused his attention on Turner, who looked quite amused. "A way out?"

"Right." Turner eyed Clifton's unconscious body, contemplating. "I'm afraid the escape route Ms. Hicks left through the last time has been closed off. Harry's security measures. But, since I clearly didn't realize how fast you'd take care of *this* situation, I already called for backup."

As if on cue, Derek entered the room, gun at the ready. Seeing Clifton and his men sprawled on the ground, he lowered his weapon and placed it in its holster. He smiled at Kala. "I knew you had this handled." Derek recognized Owen and saluted. "Sir. Good to see you again."

Owen saluted back. "I know you've been looking out for my

daughter, and I'm eternally grateful."

"I'm not sure how much I've really done to help, but I'll always have Kala's back," Derek responded.

Drawing Derek into a hug, she whispered, "Thank you." As she pulled away she said, "And teleporting you away was not my idea."

"I figured. Can you even do that?" Derek treaded on territory Kala wasn't so sure he wanted to know about.

But she was honest with him. "Apparently so."

Talan was surprised, and Kala responded, "How do you think I got you out of the 5th?"

"I figured Owen answered Roberta's call and rescued you," Talan admitted.

Owen stepped in. "It's far greater than that, Talan. What Kala is capable of…" he didn't finish his thought. Kala could tell it was because he was afraid she couldn't handle it. Such a dad.

"We can discuss my *amazing* powers later." Kala glanced at Derek and Turner. "Get us out of here."

Derek liked orders. He had confided in Kala once that orders made him feel grounded. In their line of work, there was too much chaos in the world and having a chain of command made the terrifying easier to cope with.

Nodding for them to follow, Derek led Kala, Talan, and Owen through the giant research lab to the exit door. Kala remembered coming in through this same door just a few days ago to get away from Asmodeus. She was amazed that Derek knew where he was going since this part of the Compound was a complete labyrinth to her.

Once outside the room, they entered a series of hallways.

The walls used the same black metal that most of the Compound was constructed from. Whatever ingredient was in it supposedly made the entire structure invisible to radar. Being that this place housed devices that most of the public was unaware existed, secrecy was the highest priority.

Kala followed Derek closely, with Talan and Owen trailing. Soldiers' weapons weren't a threat to the three of them, so they walked with confidence. Derek was the only vulnerable member of their party, but Kala and her two Grigori would keep him safe.

No, the real mystery was how Clifton had managed to prevent teleportation out of the Compound. Clifton saw Asmodeus's surprise arrival as a weapon, so somehow he had found a way to block supernatural activity without even knowing it. Kala had to find out how. If she could stop Malaks and Demons from popping in or out any time they felt like wreaking havoc on her, it would be invaluable. Turner would find out. And when he found out, she'd find out.

Turner and Roberta turned out to be strong allies. It shouldn't be surprising, considering Talan had picked the two of them to train. It just surprised Kala because Turner had been so intimidating when he was her boss. It was amazing how becoming a Titan relieved all fears of Clifton and Turner. Power could do that. Before, with a snap of their fingers, Kala could be dead.

Now, they couldn't touch her.

Apparently, the only thing they *could* do was prevent her from leaving.

And after she had just learned to teleport.

Figured.

Several elevator rides and staircases later, Derek steered them deeper into the bowels of the Compound.

"Shouldn't we be going *up*?" Kala asked as they entered yet another elevator going down.

"We have to go down to go up," Derek answered. "Trust me. This is the best way to avoid Clifton and his lackeys."

"I'm not really worried about them," Kala admitted honestly. "I just want to get out of here."

Derek shook his head. "I get that. But I'm still working for Turner and *I* need to get in and out of here on a daily basis."

"You're right, sorry." Kala hadn't thought about that.

"No worries. We're almost there," Derek informed her.

Kala sighed inwardly. She was so involved in what was happening to her, she hadn't even considered how Derek was managing to survive. Working for Turner required being at the Compound – and the Compound was half Clifton's. *Of course* Derek needed a stealthy way of entering and leaving the high-tech structure.

And it was all her fault.

If Kala had never become the next Atlas, then Derek would still be an elite soldier working for Turner *and* Clifton. Not one side against the other. There was nothing she could do about that, but it still hurt. Derek was a better friend than she was.

Kala vowed then and there to keep Derek safe at all costs.

Speaking of *safe*, Kala wondered why the Compound appeared to be deserted. They hadn't run into a single person on their long trek into the depths of the building. It didn't shock Kala, since the whole building was a giant security entity, but a part of her was a little surprised at the lack of people.

Another long hallway and one metal staircase later they

arrived at a steel door. It had a retinal scan security lock. Derek placed his eye in the proper location and the tiny lasers scanned his eyeball.

With a loud KERCHUNK, the door opened.

Derek explained, "This is Turner's private lab. Clifton leaves it alone so it's safe for me. The exit to the surface is in here."

Kala entered with the rest of them.

Her heart stopped.

Kala stood in the lab from her vision.

This was where she was supposed to destroy Fortski's research and his cure for cancer.

"Okay. *Really* need to leave." Kala gulped.

Chapter Fifteen

"**W**hat? Labs freak you out now?" Derek teased.

"Yes. Yes, they do." Kala didn't want to elaborate. She tried to hide the emotions she felt. From the tables to the computers to the experiments, it was identical to her vision. The only thing different was the fact that Fortski's three computers were intact and not destroyed.

The place reminded Kala of the lab in Roberta and Turner's house, where Fortski had injected her with a drug that allowed her to confront Atlas. Of course, it was this confrontation that led to Kala consuming the Titan, but that wasn't Fortski's fault.

As if thinking of the man made him appear, Fortski walked into view. He appeared to be the only person in the room. It had been the same at Roberta and Turner's. Apparently, the guy liked to work alone.

Which was the key factor to making her mission easier. If

Fortski was this private in his working environment, he was most likely even more private when sharing his research. Destroying his computers would be enough.

Just as her vision showed her.

A part of her wanted to do it now. Get it over with. This was only her second Atlas mission, but when she had been a soldier, her missions had never been given to her on a silver platter like now. Derek would think she was crazy, but Talan and Owen could hold him off.

But what would be next?

The clock would reset.

Kala glanced at the clock on one of the walls: 2d 03h 12m 43s

1:48 AM!

Almost to Day Three!

But maybe in those two days she could find Zeus and force him to take this curse away from her. Then she'd never have to ruin the research of the most brilliant man alive that would save millions of lives.

No. Kala couldn't perform her task now.

Not when there was a shred of hope.

It might only be a shred, but it was enough.

Killing Jack had destroyed her in ways she couldn't comprehend yet, and he was only one life.

Destroying the cure for cancer would kill so many innocent people. And she would be responsible. Maybe indirectly, but that was semantics to Kala. She'd feel the weight of every loss of life as if she had shot them herself.

Despite the fact that Jack was supposed to be Atlas's surrogate and not her, Kala had to believe that he would want the universe to be in the hands of the *universe*. Not in one person. The curse shouldn't exist. Zeus was an idiot.

And Kala was going to make the Olympian make amends.

Fortski seemed a little surprised at the unexpected guests, but when he saw Kala and Talan, he managed a friendly smile. "Ms. Hicks, Mr. Talan, good to see you again. I trust all your issues have been resolved?" he asked pointedly at Kala.

Fortski had a front row seat in the battle to integrate Atlas into Kala's human form. As a scientist, he must have found the whole thing fascinating, but at the time, he was at a loss. Kala wasn't even sure he truly understood what had happened. Even if he did, he may not believe it. His work was about curing diseases.

Or was it?

It suddenly occurred to Kala that she had no idea what Fortski's work was about. Sure, she knew he had just found the cure for cancer, but had that been his goal? He was employed by a covert military general. Somehow cancer research didn't seem a likely topic of interest for him.

But Kala could only go on what she knew. And what she knew was that, whether intentional or not, Fortski had found the cure for cancer and Kala's job was to destroy it.

Kala responded to Fortski's greeting with a smile of her own. "Dr. Fortski. Good to see you again. I'm doing fine, thank you."

"Good. Good to hear it," Fortski replied jovially.

There was something about Fortski that Kala really liked. He had an air of discovery about him that showed in his enthusiastic expression. It was almost painful for Kala to see, knowing what she might have to do…

"We really need to leave." Kala's patience was at an end. She couldn't be in this lab a second longer.

Owen glanced at Kala with a look of worry. "There's something here that scares you. What is it, Kala? Is it this man?"

Always the protective father, Owen was misreading Kala's desire to save Fortski's work as being wary of the scientist.

Kala was never very good at hiding her emotions from the people that knew her. "I'm fine. I just want to get away from this place and find Zeus."

Fortski's eyes widened. "As in the god Zeus?"

Kala grasped how ridiculous that would sound to someone like Fortski, but she was surprised to see that he was genuinely asking. Maybe he actually believed her infusion into a Titan god. Working for Turner and Roberta, the guy had to have seen some pretty crazy things.

"I know that sounds insane," Kala began.

But Fortski shook his head. "Not at all. Geoffrey explained everything to me. Some of my research is based on the results we found in your brain scan, Ms. Hicks. That was before you completely integrated with the deity, of course, but the results were quite fascinating nonetheless."

Owen didn't let Kala change the subject. "I know that look, Kala. What's wrong?"

Derek and Talan stared at Kala as well. The more scrutiny, the harder it was to keep up her poker face. "Just leave it alone." To Derek, she pleaded, "Out. Now."

It was Talan who spoke next. "Your mission. It's in this room."

"What!" Kala exclaimed a little too loudly. "You're crazy." To Derek she added urgently, "Seriously, Derek, let's go."

Kala walked ahead even though she had no idea where she was going. She just needed to move. The last thing she wanted to do was to have a blowout with two angels and Derek.

Fortski seemed intrigued by the suggestion. "Mission? In here? What kind of mission?"

Kala spun around, defensive. "There is no mission. Can we drop it, please?"

Owen stepped toward her. "Kala, we can help you. Just tell us what it is."

"I said, drop it!" Kala's temper got the best of her.

Derek knew better than to push Kala. He nodded toward the north side of the room. "This way."

"Thank you!" Kala harrumphed.

Before Kala could follow Derek to the exit, she felt Owen's hand on her arm. "Kala, stop." His voice was calm and steady. "It might be easier with us here."

Kala's panic flared. "I can't!"

"What are the odds that you'd be in the very spot of your mission? How do you expect to get back in here?"

Owen tried to be rational, but Kala didn't want to hear it. "As we know, I can teleport in, I just can't teleport out!" she said with the attitude of an unruly teenager.

Derek stepped in at this point. "I think we should go. She obviously doesn't want to do whatever it is you guys are talking about."

Fortski piped in, "Maybe I can help you?"

His words made Kala even more upset. All she could see was the look of anguish that would be in Fortski's face when she destroyed all his work from her vision.

"You definitely can not help." Kala needed space. She took a few steps back from everyone and ran her hand through her hair nervously.

"Kala…" Talan began.

She cut him off. "Talan, don't." Kala turned to Owen. "I still have two days. Two days to get out of this curse. Please, just give me those two days."

"I'll give you all the time you want. That's not the issue. You have an opportunity to complete your task with people who love you. You're not alone." Owen looked like he wanted to hug her, but Kala kept her distance.

"If you knew what it was…" She shook her head.

"Tell us, then," Owen prodded.

"NO! Just trust me. You don't want me to do this. And if Zeus can release me of this curse, then it won't need to happen and the universe can do its own damn work. Let the chips fall as they may." Kala stared at Owen. "Please don't make me."

Owen nodded. He turned to Derek. "Let's go."

Fortski wasn't ready for them to leave. "I really can help. Anything you need."

Kala turned to the scientist and smiled sadly. "Hopefully, you'll never see me again."

Apparently, the way Kala said it made Fortski's face turn white. "I see."

Kala didn't want to wait for another response from Fortski. She glanced at Derek. He may not know what was going on, but with everything he had seen over the last few days, Derek knew it was something big. And his first priority was to save his friend.

126

"Follow me," Derek directed. He led them across the room, leaving Fortski behind.

Kala hoped she wouldn't have to come back there, but her mission-based side was comforted by the fact that at least she knew where to go if need be. She was less than two hours away from Day Three, but Kala was determined to find Zeus. Forty-eight hours had to be enough. She was running on no sleep, but adrenaline was keeping her alert. Not knowing how long that would last, she concentrated on leaving the Compound.

Derek ushered them out a door that in turn led them up a long staircase. Steps that kept going and going and going. Kala was surprised at the fact that she was hardly winded at all. Granted, she was as in-shape as an elite soldier could be, but even under ideal circumstances this many stairs would exhaust a marathon runner. Kala heard Derek panting, slightly out of breath, and he was the healthiest guy she knew.

Besides Jack.

The thought grabbed her chest and made it tighten.

Jack should be beside her, and he never would be.

Kala compartmentalized before she broke down. Swallowing up her emotions was second nature for her. Being an abandoned child, she learned this skill early on. Facing her feelings was completely new to her and Kala wasn't very good at it. Shoving everything down felt natural, normal. It might be unhealthy, but it was what made her a good soldier.

Looking back at Talan and Owen, they hadn't even broken a sweat. Evidently, Grigori were immune to exertion as well.

Derek informed them in the dark, "About a hundred feet to the surface."

The last set of stairs went quickly. They came to a top hatch with another eye scanner. Derek placed his eye in front of it and the device lit up green. Pushing with his right shoulder, Derek lifted the round door and flopped it onto the concrete above.

Stepping into the early morning air felt more amazing than Kala could describe. From being stuck in the 5th for an entire day to being in the bellows of the Compound, Kala missed fresh air. It felt crisp and chilled her cheeks. She took in a deep breath as Talan and Owen exited the Compound to join her.

Kala knew where they were: about a mile from the main entrance point to the Compound. She could see the dilapidated warehouses in the distance, perfect cover for the military base. Since the underground facility was made of untraceable metal, any enemy flying overhead would see abandoned buildings, nothing more.

Derek shut the top hatch and it blended in perfectly with the ground. "We're exposed out here. Behind that set of trees is my jeep." Derek moved swiftly towards his car.

The landscape was cracked dirt and shrubbery with a few pockets of trees here and there. It had the appearance of a dump. But it was an exit, and that was all that mattered.

Within a few seconds they all arrived at Derek's jeep. It was covered in a camouflage mesh tarp, which he quickly bundled up and tossed in the back.

Before Derek could enter his car, Talan put up his hand for him to halt. "We may not need to drive. Let's see how far Clifton's teleport-shield goes." Talan reached over and touched Derek.

Nothing.

"That's crazy." Kala was shocked. "How can he restrict

teleporting out, but not in? He's not that smart. And if he had any scientists that were that smart, Turner would know about it!"

"He had help," a voice sounded from behind them.

Kala knew that voice.

Turning around, she came face to face with Rotoph.

But what really made her furious was the person standing next to him.

Penny.

Chapter Sixteen

"**W**e leave you behind and you turn to the enemy? Shocker," Kala accused Penny. She had started to like the girl, but Rotoph? Was Penny really that stupid?

Penny kept her eyes on Kala. "Just listen. Rotoph is on *our* side."

Before Kala could utter a hearty laugh, Owen moved faster than Kala would have thought possible. He had Rotoph in a chokehold before anyone could move.

Rotoph teleported out of Owen's grasp, reappearing a few feet away. "Owen! I need to talk to you."

Before Owen could attack a second time, Kala put her hand up to stop him. She pulled out the Grigori blade and nodded toward Rotoph. "Will you agree to let me take your powers away so we can talk?" She decided to be diplomatic since she suspected that Rotoph may have freed Zeus from the 5th. Plus, the sight of her foster father getting into a brawl with another Grigori wasn't something Kala wanted to see.

Rotoph nodded his agreement.

Owen still looked like he was on the verge of pouncing, but he stayed where he was.

Kala carefully walked over to Rotoph with the blade in hand.

Rotoph gave her a small smile. "Not the throat this time."

"If it weren't for the fact that we need you to talk..." Kala gently sliced a nick on Rotoph's wrist. "Okay. You've got five minutes."

Owen went to Kala's side. "We don't need five minutes. Now that his powers are gone we can teleport out of here."

Kala had never thought of that. They could leave right now before Clifton awoke from the Grigori-sleep-bomb and caused them more trouble. If Rotoph was the one helping Clifton, then teleportation was back on the table.

But there was something to the fact that Rotoph let himself be disarmed. Whatever he wanted to say, Rotoph thought they'd want to hear it. And if her suspicions were correct about Rotoph and Zeus...

"Let's just listen," Kala suggested cautiously.

Owen shook his head. "Kala you don't know him. We listened to him before and he betrayed us. He engraved that knife you're holding. A knife like that one that tore Talan into pieces. Trust me, Rotoph is our enemy."

"Owen..." Rotoph began, but Kala stopped him.

"Don't speak. You're not helping your cause." Kala turned to Owen. "You have a personal beef with this guy, I get that, but something tells me we should listen. If we don't like what he has to say, we leave him here. Without his powers, he's not going anywhere."

Owen paused. After a few moments of thinking, he gave a slight nod.

Rotoph looked relieved. He focused his attention on Kala since she appeared to be the only one willing to listen. "I know my brothers will never believe me, but I'm trying to make amends for the mistake I made. I was power hungry, and Cronus offered me the world, and I took it. But he fooled me like he fooled the Olympians. I've been his slave for the past 2,000 years..."

Talan interrupted with anger, "Are we supposed to feel sorry for you? You're not telling us anything we don't already know."

Talan had been so quiet during this whole confrontation Kala had almost forgotten he was there. But apparently, hearing Rotoph complain about being Cronus's bitch was too much for him.

Rotoph was annoyed. "Yeah, because the 5th Heaven was so horrible. I made sure you were banished in paradise!" he shouted the last part.

Kala had to agree. She had seen the Grigori prison and it was spectacularly beautiful. At this very moment though, she didn't want to take Rotoph's side in front of Talan and Owen. "Just continue, please," she prodded Rotoph.

"Prison is prison!" Talan wasn't letting it go. He turned to Owen. "Why are we still listening to him?"

Rotoph forced eye contact with Talan, then Owen. "Because I'm the one who freed you."

Pin drop.

Rotoph took advantage of the silence to continue, "Didn't

you ever wonder how you were able to break out? Did you really think you were powerful enough to escape a prison that strips you of all your powers?" He looked at them as if they were ludicrous to even consider the notion.

His answer was more silence, which indicated to Kala that they hadn't really considered that they'd had help from the outside.

Owen was the first to speak. "Only five of us were able to leave."

Rotoph nodded. "The strongest. Yes, I know. I've kept tabs on all of you for the entire two hundred years you've been out. I need you to free our brothers and sisters, but it's Talan's skills I need most. Please. Help me."

Talan started to soften. "I want to trust you, Rotoph."

"What possible motivation would I have to trick you? There are only five of you. The Titans could crush you if they pooled their resources. I was a fool. Please. Let me prove myself to you," Rotoph begged.

Kala had to admit that Rotoph seemed sincere.

Derek was on a time crunch because he said, "I may be the only *human* here, and I get that you guys could probably stop any military attack, but I really don't want to be around to see it. Can we have this conversation somewhere else?" He air-quoted "human," of course.

It must have been strange for Derek not to consider Kala human, but he was the kind of soldier that took everything in and went with it. Derek's period of adjustment on the *stranger than fiction* table was over and he was on board with anything that came his way. Derek was also practical. As much as he wanted to help Kala's cause, his future safety was at stake. "This is my only way into the Compound and if it's compromised, I'm screwed."

Kala wasn't about to let her friend be in the lurch like that. "Let's go. Now."

All of sudden Penny decided she wanted to be a part of the conversation. "No. We take care of this now." She turned to Rotoph. "You promised!"

Kala could hear Derek groan. He always hated hysterics. Kala had to agree. It was annoying.

Owen was the calm one, though. "Promised what, Pandora?"

Even Owen knew who she truly was. It didn't surprise Kala, but it made her wonder how small a circle this whole gods/angel/demon thing was.

"Tell them!" Penny ordered Rotoph.

Rotoph looked directly at Kala when he said, "I can take you to Zeus. I'm the one who freed him." When Penny continued to stare him down, he added, "And Hephaestus."

Hephaestus was definitely for Penny's sake, but Zeus? Kala could feel the stirrings of hope rise up in her. Her guess had been correct: Rotoph had freed Zeus from the 5th Level of Hell. And now Kala would have a chance to confront him and make him take away her curse.

"When do we leave?" Kala was in full mission-mode.

Rotoph had an apologetic expression on his face. "I'd love to, but someone took away my powers."

Kala wanted to punch something, but she knew there was nothing anyone could do. Only Rotoph knew the location and only *he* could teleport them there. They'd have to wait out the effects of the Grigori blade.

But not there.

"To your place?" Kala asked Talan.

Talan nodded and motioned for the small group to gather around him. "Everyone, grab on."

At the same time, Kala and the others touched Talan's shoulders.

A disorienting moment later, they all stood in Talan's small apartment.

Derek's face showed little of the discomfort Kala was certain he was in.

It was crowded in the tiny space and the situation struck Kala as funny somehow. Three Grigori, Pandora (as in the actual Pandora), a Titan, and Derek all in a Washington D.C. apartment overlooking the Washington Monument. It felt like the beginning of some awful joke.

"How long before we leave?" Kala asked Rotoph.

"An hour, maybe two." Rotoph plopped on the couch before anyone else could.

Kala looked at the time: 2d 01h 20m 12s

3:40 AM.

An hour and twenty minutes until Day Three.

Kala's life was all about time now. Always a race. She hoped Zeus was the key.

Since everyone stood around awkwardly, Kala took Rotoph's cue and sat down beside him. She needed to be off her feet even if it was for just a few seconds. Being a Titan didn't mean she couldn't get tired.

Rotoph looked surprised by Kala's presence right next to him, but seemed pleased at the same time. "I've heard about you," he confided.

"Good for you." Kala didn't feel like talking about herself, least of all to a Grigori traitor. He was a means to an end. Kala's way to Zeus. Being pals wasn't on the agenda.

"Your attitude being the most prominent." Rotoph sounded amused. "I had the same reputation amongst the other Grigori."

"Please don't compare yourself to me." Kala started to feel like she'd made a bad decision sitting next to him.

"No? I had a destiny I didn't want to fulfill so I banished my own people. You have a destiny to fulfill, and you're running to Zeus to get out of it. We're not that different." Rotoph leaned his head back against the couch.

"The difference is I have to do it every four days," Kala complained. She couldn't be mad at Rotoph. He saw things the way he saw things; nothing she said would change his mind. Rotoph needed to connect with someone from this little posse and apparently, he had chosen Kala as his willing victim. "What was your *destiny* that you felt the need to imprison your entire family?" Kala was curious.

"That's a story for another time. I'm surprised Owen or Talan hasn't told you," Rotoph sighed.

"To be honest, I didn't ask." Kala suddenly felt guilty for not trying to know more about Owen and Talan's history, Owen especially. Owen and Linda were the closest people in the world to her. Granted, Kala had no idea Owen was an angel before three days ago, but she chastised herself for being so self-centered. She already felt like a horrible human being for killing Jack, this just added salt to the wound.

Rotoph smiled widely. "We *are* more alike than you'd think."

Kala didn't argue. A part of her figured he was probably right.

"Look, I'm going to close my eyes for a few minutes. Wake me up when it's time to go." Kala didn't wait for a response. She closed her eyes and nodded off.

***

Rotoph gently shook her awake in what felt like a second later. "It's time," he announced.

Owen and Talan stood next to her by the couch. Holding his hand out for Kala to accept, Owen helped her to her feet.

"Where's Derek?" She suddenly noticed his absence.

It was Rotoph who spoke. "No human can go where we're going, and you seemed rather attached to the fellow."

Talan reassured her, "I sent him to his safe house. We'll contact him when we get back."

Kala was tired of her supernatural buddies moving Derek around like he was Kala's teddy bear that she couldn't live without. Derek was a formidable opponent against anyone, supernatural or not, and an asset to any team. It bothered her that it seemed as though they thought Derek was an anchor rather than a strength.

But if he really couldn't go where Zeus was located then she was happy he was safe.

"Let's do it." Kala eyed Rotoph, knowing he was the man in charge of this mission.

Penny positively beamed and even Kala cracked a small smile. Being without her father for thousands of years obviously had taken its toll. Now that Penny was about to see him again, she was radiant. Kala secretly hoped it would improve her personality, but she didn't hold her breath.

Talan and Owen acted as her pillars while Rotoph stood in the middle.

"Everyone grab hold," Rotoph instructed.

As soon as Kala touched Rotoph's arm the room disappeared.

They all stood in a small cavern. It was lit by a red/yellow glow from a few rotating orb-like devices above them. Most of the rock was smooth, but there were a few stalagmites draping from the ceiling here and there.

A gasp from Penny made Kala's head turn.

Behind them, two men were near a stone table.

Kala recognized Hephaestus from Atlas's vision. He looked over parchments and maps, his muscular form obvious even through his heavy armor. The second was Zeus. He had his head in his hands as if he were sleeping. He sat on the floor with his back propped up against the wall.

When Hephaestus saw Penny, his eyes lit up.

In seconds the two were reunited, Penny's small cries of happiness were muffled in his enormous chest.

Kala didn't want to intrude. Seeing Zeus so close, she inched her way around the happy reunion and approached the most powerful Olympian alive. "Zeus?" She felt ridiculous asking.

Zeus peered up at Kala through parted fingers.

And that was when she knew...

He was completely out of his mind.

"Pretty girl stands before me. About to die. About to die," Zeus cackled.

Kala didn't like the sound of that. But part of her didn't feel quite right since they had arrived. Kind of like she had eaten one too many burritos.

"Zeus," Kala tried to reason with the god. "You have to break the curse on Atlas. I'm Atlas."

Zeus laughed hysterically. "Atlas would survive this place, but you won't!" He randomly picked up rocks and mashed them in his hair.

"What does he mean?" Kala turned to ask anyone who'd answer. Then a sharp pain stabbed her in the gut. Kala clasped it with her hand.

Talan was immediately by her side. "Are you okay?"

Kala felt like barfing. "I'm fine." She pushed him away and turned back to Zeus. She couldn't lose this opportunity. "Break the curse! You're the only one who can!" she pleaded desperately.

"Die. Die. Die. Die," Zeus kept repeating creepily.

Kala puked. And it wasn't her last meal that came up.

It was blood.

"Is he killing me?" Kala asked Talan.

Hephaestus stepped forward, pulling himself away from Penny. "A part of you is still human. You have to leave here."

"Not without him!" Kala pointed at the mad god. Then she vomited blood again. The pain was like nothing she'd ever experienced, but her stubbornness wouldn't let her go without an answer from Zeus.

"Kala, I promise you, I will find out everything Zeus knows, but you'll die if you stay. You have to get out of here. Owen will take you," Talan begged.

Kala knew she had to go, but she wanted to grill Zeus more. "I'll leave. Just find me." Kala could barely get the words out as she puked out a piece of her intestines.

Closing her eyes, she couldn't think clearly as she activated her teleportation. She had no idea where she was going to end up, but she needed to get out of there.

When she opened her eyes, Kala was staring at Roberta Turner.

"This is a nice surprise." Roberta smiled warmly.

DAY THREE

Chapter Seventeen

Kala was taken aback that her delirious mind took her directly to Roberta. Her body felt better, as if the torture she had just experienced never happened.

"You have blood all over your mouth and clothes." Roberta stood up from where she sat and headed to the bathroom.

Kala was in Roberta and Turner's bedroom. It was decadent and luxurious with lots of maroons and golds. She felt as if she had walked into a home design magazine, everything in its perfect place. Aside from the four-poster bed that she currently sat on, there was a chaise, a two-seater couch and a recliner. It was so far from any reality Kala had experienced in a long time that she wanted to crawl up in the blankets and never leave.

Instead, she sat waiting for Roberta to return.

Kala didn't have to wait long. Roberta brought in a small tray full of medical supplies.

"I just need the towel and some new clothes. I'm not injured," Kala reassured her. She must have looked like a mess with the amount of blood she chucked up.

Roberta handed her a wet white towel. It was warm against Kala's face. By the time she was done with it though, it was completely red.

"What happened? If you don't mind me asking." Roberta sat down in the recliner across from Kala.

"Apparently, I was in a non-human zone." Kala debated what to do with the soiled towel. It felt rude to throw it away.

Roberta picked up on her dilemma and gently took the towel out of Kala's hand and tossed it in the trash. "Blood never comes out anyway."

"Thanks." Kala attempted a smile.

"I thought you weren't human now?" Roberta was puzzled.

"It looks like there's still a part of me that is. I'm not sure what happened to me," Kala vented.

Roberta tossed Kala a pair of jeans and a light v-neck sweater.

Kala accepted the clothes gratefully. "Do you mind if I shower?"

"Of course." Roberta motioned to the bathroom.

Kala stood up and walked inside. It was just as decadent as the bedroom: all white marble and gold trimmings. Since her clothes were covered in blood, Kala made sure none of it touched the pristine counter.

Stepping into the steaming hot shower was quite possibly the best feeling Kala had experienced in a really long time. In fact, she couldn't remember the last time she had actually taken a shower, which was scary all to itself. The water was hot on her skin, relaxing her muscles instantly. Titan or not, Kala still felt stress and so did her body. Her brain didn't even want to comprehend what was happening to her *physically*. She was never one to have health problems, and panicking wasn't her either, but Kala was a Titan now. That was enough to send anyone around the bend. But part of her was human, too. Now that she wasn't puking up her intestines, Kala was slightly relieved that there was still enough human in her to react to the Grigori hideout.

Kala wasn't a worrier by nature. She was more of a problem solver: find the conundrum, figure out a way to resolve it, and execute. This Atlas business wasn't helping since so much of it was entirely out of her control. That was why she didn't want to leave Zeus. He was a tiny shred of the control that she needed and now she had to rely on others to find out what he knew. Or, more importantly, what he could *do*.

As much as the shower comforted her, Kala reached her ten-minute tolerance. She never understood Jack's ability to stay in a shower for almost an hour. Sometimes she would join him…

Kala turned off the water and her memories at the same time.

Jack was gone.

There was nothing she could do about it.

Kala shrugged off surging emotions and quickly dressed herself. The clothes fit perfectly. Giving her hair a good towel dry, Kala walked out of the bathroom and sat down on the small couch next to Roberta.

Roberta had been on her laptop and closed it when Kala walked in. "Better?"

"Much, thanks." So much so, Kala didn't want to leave. She wanted to stay in Roberta and Turner's house and forget about everything. She had a weight on her chest that wouldn't go away. It twisted and turned and made her feel as if she was gasping for air, but she was breathing just fine.

"What brought you here?" Roberta was calm and patient. Curiosity gleamed in her eyes, but she seemed content to let Kala share *what* she wanted, *when* she wanted.

"It must have been our whole *head* connection. I just got out of there and showed up here." Now that Kala thought about it, she was surprised that she didn't show up at her old apartment or Jack's...

Roberta thankfully interrupted her thoughts. "Makes sense. I'm sure teleportation works similarly to astral projection. Our connection is the closest reference your brain has to the process, so you came to the source." Roberta was excited by the prospect.

"Sure. That's probably it." Kala wasn't that interested in the science of it. "I'm just glad I'm here. I *really* don't want to do my mission."

"I can't imagine it being worse than your last one." Roberta looked genuinely sympathetic.

"It isn't. But it's all relative. You're not going to like it, and neither is your husband." Kala felt the need to confess to someone. Telling Talan or Owen was like telling the parent that was going to make you do your chores no matter what. No excuses. Sympathy, yes. But the answer would always be to complete the task at hand. But Roberta and Turner were more *shades of grey* kind of people. And Kala really needed to hear something besides an *obligation and duty* speech, especially since she still hoped to get rid of the stupid curse before her time was up.

"Tell me," Roberta urged.

Seeing the curiosity and fascination in Roberta's expression, made Kala not want to tell her.

Roberta was not going to be happy.

"I'm supposed to destroy Fortski's cure for cancer," Kala blurted. She would have covered her eyes and peeked through her fingers if she had the choice, but Kala stared at Roberta straight on.

To Kala's surprise, Roberta's response was a simple raise of an eyebrow.

"That's it? You're not going to try and detain me or something?" Kala was a bit taken aback by the utter lack of angry-I'm-going-to-stop-you-if-it's-the-last-thing-I-do reaction.

"Cancer, huh?" Roberta repeated aloud. "He was told to drop that." Her voice was laced with annoyance.

Then Kala noticed something she hadn't noticed before: Roberta looked pissed. And not at the prospect of destroying a cure for the disease: she was mad at the fact that Fortski was working on it in the first place.

"You know a cure is a good thing, right?" Kala felt out of her element. Normally, she thought that any human being would be considerably upset that she planned to destroy the antidote to the most deadly killer on earth.

But Roberta appeared as if she would tear Fortski's head off. She stood up, furious. "If he releases this cure, all his other work will be put on hold!"

This whole conversation wasn't at all what she had expected. "What's more important than saving millions of lives?"

Roberta didn't even pause in her answer, "Saving *billions*."

Kala was confused. "So this other work he's doing will save *more* people?"

Roberta nodded. "Oh yes. It'll change the world. I know Fortski. If he releases the cure, he won't continue his other research." Then she paused, upset. "Not in time, anyway."

"What is he working on?" Kala wondered what could be so much more important. She had thought curing cancer was pretty darn big.

Roberta sat down next to Kala again, eyes filled with determination. "I can't tell you that. But Kala, you must do this mission. You *must*. I see how this curse of yours works. Destroying Fortski's research *is* for the greater good. I want you to trust me on this."

"Not you, too," Kala complained.

"It may not be what you want to hear, but I believe in your work. This will restore the balance." Roberta seemed desperate in her plea.

Kala couldn't take anymore. "I should go."

Roberta's face softened. "You don't have to. I won't push, but just think about what I've said."

"Oh, I will." Kala didn't want to think *at all*. She wanted to run out of this place, find a nice cardboard box and live there for the rest of her life. Maybe if she didn't complete the cycle, Cronus's little spell of protection-loss would never kick in and she truly would be safe.

Except for the fact that the world would end.

Just a minor hiccup.

Ugh.

There Kala went thinking again. She needed to stop that. It wasn't helping anyone.

"You wanted me to tell you not to do it," Roberta deduced.

"Yeah, pretty much." Kala leaned back on the couch and sighed heavily. "I have no doubt that my mission restores some kind of balance or whatever it's designed to do, but I don't want to do it. Who would?"

"I'll do it for you," Roberta volunteered suddenly.

That made Kala sit up. "What?"

"I have the access. I know where he keeps his research. I *know* why it should be done. I have no problems or reservations. I *want* to destroy it." Roberta's eyes were on fire with enthusiasm.

Kala was speechless.

Could someone else perform the Atlas duties? If the deed was done, the deed was done, right?

But if Roberta did it now, then Kala's clock would reset and she'd have to do something else horrible! She definitely was on board with Roberta taking on the burden, but she wanted a chance to break the curse first.

"I'm thinking, yes." Kala could hear the relief in her own voice. "But give me two days. I don't want you to reset the clock."

"You give me the word and I'm on my way." Roberta appeared positively elated.

Kala wasn't sure if it would work, but part of her needed to try. Maybe she could find people who *wanted* to do the horrible task. It would be a win-win for everyone, including the world! Kala didn't even want to tap into her Atlas memories to see if he had already tried this tactic. Somehow, she knew a weasel like Atlas would have thought of this long ago, making her a weasel by default. But after murdering Jack, Kala could handle being a weasel at the moment. The sane part of her mind knew it was too good to be true, but knowing that Roberta would do what

Kala had no desire whatsoever to do lifted a huge weight off her shoulders.

Kala exhaled a large sigh of relief and stood up. "I really should go. I need to get back to my father and Talan, or at least get them to come to me." Her brain felt focused again, like Roberta's volunteering was why she had teleported to her in the first place. A part of a plan she could live with. "Are you sure you're okay doing this?" Kala wanted to make sure that Roberta was on board.

Roberta stood up facing her. "I've never been more certain in my entire life."

Kala knew she meant it.

Really meant it.

It surprised Kala a bit. Delving into other people's motivations and thought processes really wasn't her thing. So she just nodded and tapped her head. "I'll contact you when I want you to do it."

"I'll be here." Roberta leaned forward and embraced Kala.

Kala wasn't much for physical affection, but the hug felt nice. It reminded her that there was still a part of her that was human, as weird as that sounded.

Pulling out first, Kala smiled and gave Roberta a small salute. "Wish me luck."

"Good luck," Roberta replied encouragingly.

Kala concentrated on the location of Zeus. She knew she didn't have much time before she became a fountain of blood, but Kala had to know if Owen or Talan found out anything.

In and out.

Turner's house disappeared.

When her new surroundings came into focus, Kala was not

in the mystical cave that housed the king of the Olympians.

She was in a hotel suite.

And from the neon skyline outside Kala figured out pretty quickly that she was in Las Vegas.

"Well, hello, gorgeous."

Kala turned around to see Asmodeus in a bathrobe holding a glass of champagne.

Really?

Chapter Eighteen

"**I** certainly wasn't expecting *you*." Asmodeus positively beamed.

"I have no idea why I'm here," Kala confessed honestly. "I was trying to get back to Zeus." The last place on earth she wanted to be was with Asmodeus. He was like dealing with a teenager in his constant need for affection and desire to get into her pants.

Asmodeus took a sip of his champagne and sat down on a leather armchair. "Where is the old bird anyway?"

"Wouldn't you like to know?" Kala wasn't about to spill the location of the *Titans Most Wanted* to their number one lackey.

Kala figured she might as well eat something while she was in Vegas, so she plopped down on the matching leather couch across from Asmodeus. "We ordering room service?"

"This is becoming a thing with us." Asmodeus grinned.

"Except the actual eating part. We never ordered last time," Kala reminded him.

The room was spectacular. The thing about Vegas was that they did everything big and gaudy. This suite was no exception. Space-wise, it was huge, well over 3,000 square feet and every inch of it was decorated and furnished. The color theme was brown, tan, and gold. It wasn't tacky like most of the Vegas abodes Kala had visited; the décor was tasteful, classy.

Seeing Asmodeus drinking champagne in a bathrobe started to annoy Kala. "Could you get dressed or something?"

"I can get rid of the robe," Asmodeus suggested.

Kala rolled her eyes. "Something casual will do just fine, thank you."

With a snap of his fingers, Asmodeus looked like a model again, with a black t-shirt and jeans. He still held the champagne glass, of course, but a second later one magically appeared in his other hand. Reaching across the gap between them, he handed her the drink.

Kala took it, thinking she could use a drink right about now. This was the third time she had tried teleportation, and it was the third time she had ended up in a place she hadn't expected.

But Asmodeus?

She couldn't fathom why her brain had sent her to *him*. Kala's only desire was to torture Zeus until he released her of the curse. Why would her mind send her to the one guy who had no idea where Zeus actually was? What could Asmodeus possibly do for her cause? It made no sense.

After ordering room service and pigging out on filet mignon and lobster, Kala felt more herself. Maybe this meal was the reason she had come here. It was almost worth it. She glanced at the clock.

1d 19h 21m 43s: 9:39 AM.

At least it was still morning. Kala was amazed at how much comfort that brought her. It reminded her of nights when she'd wake up thinking it was time to go to work, but really had five more hours to sleep. Kala tried to appreciate the little moments, since she rarely had them nowadays.

"So why are you here?" Asmodeus eyed Kala, suspicious but intrigued.

The guy was so readable. Kala wondered how any girl had ever fallen for his charms. But then she looked at him and shrugged. Because he was ridiculously sexy. It pained her to admit it, but there was no denying the fact that the king of Demons had some serious game. Kala just happened to be the kind of girl that was immune to *bad boy* appeal.

That was why she loved Jack so much. He was so *good*.

Her heart squeezed and she leaned back on the couch, closing her eyes.

Before she could open them, Kala felt Asmodeus sit next to her. "Did I upset you?"

Kala was ready to say something snarky when she opened her eyes to see Asmodeus looking genuinely concerned. It was the last thing she expected. "Aren't you supposed to be a Demon? You know Demons are evil. Why should you care if I'm upset?" Snark won out, she guessed.

"Haven't you figured it out yet? I'm entirely smitten with you, Kala Hicks. And now that you're a Titan... let's just say we aren't limited in our options anymore." His grin almost got her, he was so damn charismatic.

"You wish." Kala could always rely on her big mouth to shoot

153

down a would-be-suitor. In this case, she was happy her attitude was running the show. Forget-all-your-troubles-sex was tempting and Asmodeus would definitely fit the mark, but Kala wasn't interested. Her heart always went back to Jack.

"There's that look again. What are you thinking about?" Asmodeus asked.

He was way too perceptive for his own good.

And Kala was too weak to fight it. She had to confess to someone, it might as well be a Demon. "I'll never forgive myself for killing Jack." Saying it aloud made it real. She wouldn't. The world would thank her if it could, but nothing could make her feel justified in murdering him. Nothing.

"You had to. It was your job. I would have preferred it if you hadn't, but that's because I *want* this world to end. Or at least be in chaos." He shrugged. "I'm a Demon, what can I say?"

"You're not helping."

Asmodeus tucked a piece of Kala's red hair behind her ear. "Did you really think I could? I am *evil* as you say." He smiled.

Kala shook her head at his sarcasm. "I don't know what to think anymore. I have no idea how teleportation works. I seem to always show up in the last place I expect. All I want is to go back to Zeus and make him destroy this curse. I can't even do that!" Her frustration was mounting by the second.

"And where is Zeus again?" Asmodeus asked gently.

"Really? I'm a soldier, Demon boy. I'm not going to slip, no matter how much charm you lay on. I'm the girl that doesn't fall for it, remember?" She appreciated his effort, but seriously.

"How can I forget? It's what makes you so fascinating." Asmodeus leaned in closer.

Kala stood up. "No more touchies." She had no idea where that word came from, but it seemed appropriate.

Asmodeus raised his hands in surrender. "No more touchies." He leaned back on the couch as if he didn't have a care in the world. "You won't tell me where Zeus is, and you don't want any of this." He waved his hand over his body like it was on display. "So, why are you here?"

Kala slumped down on the couch next to Asmodeus. "I told you, I have no idea. I focused on the last location of Zeus and I ended up here."

"I see." Asmodeus looked thoughtful. "Maybe he's in a place you can't go to?"

He phrased it like a question, but it jolted Kala that he might be correctly guessing where the Angel-gang was. Unfortunately, her *jolt* only confirmed Asmodeus's suspicions.

He grinned. "So they're in a place you can't go to?"

"I never said that," Kala defended lamely. "I was there before obviously." That was the only argument she could think of.

"True. But you're not there now, which means " Asmodeus took a sip of his champagne. "It's a place where humans aren't allowed."

"I'm not human, remember?" Kala freaked out. He was way too close to figuring it out.

"Oh, but you are." Asmodeus's eyes lit up. "It's another thing that makes you a walking mystery."

Kala pondered this for a moment. It seemed like Asmodeus knew more about her than she did. She was less worried about Zeus's location in that second than she was in finding out what Asmodeus knew. "What do you mean? What am I?" Kala asked.

Asmodeus leaned in closer and Kala didn't fight him off, she just wanted answers. "It means: you're half-human, half-god. You swallowed Atlas, which is troubling the Titans to no end, by the way, but you're still *you*. No one knows what the consequences of that are yet, but the real question is: how *did* you consume him?"

Kala felt baited. He had designed the conversation to lead back to retrieving information from her, and not the other way around. She'd interrogated enough people in her day to recognize the tactic. Kala moved away from Asmodeus and gave him an exasperated look. "You don't know any more than I do. You're so transparent."

Asmodeus's eyebrows crinkled in utter surprise and disappointment. He wasn't used to people seeing right through him.

"Cronus," he began.

Kala cut him off, nodding. "Cronus wants to know how I almost consumed *him*, doesn't he?" She knew her leverage. "Well, you tell that big boy that if he tries to hurt any of my friends, I'll eat him too." That sounded bad even as it came out of her mouth, and of course, Asmodeus was enticed.

"You can eat me first, if you like?" he suggested.

Kala really hated that he was attractive. He was a Demon! Why couldn't he be butt-ugly with some kind of skin disease?

"We're obviously not going to divulge any of our secrets to one another, so do you want to go gambling?" Kala said, suddenly feeling the urge not to be in her own life anymore, and gambling seemed like the best solution.

Asmodeus shrugged. "Sure."

So a Titan and the king of Demons partied and gambled in Vegas in the early afternoon. It was fun and pathetic all at once.

Asmodeus used his telekinesis at the roulette wheel and Kala used hers at craps. The best part of the whole experience was the fact that casinos had no clocks. No glaring reminder that she was neglecting her duty – and it felt amazing. By the end of it, Kala had over a hundred thousand dollars' worth of chips. She was so adrenalized by the rush of it, she turned to Asmodeus and kissed him.

Kala didn't know who was more shocked, Asmodeus or herself. She almost pulled away. But, dang! The boy could kiss! Apparently, it was so mind-blowing she couldn't think straight! His lips were forceful, but not in a smash-your-teeth kind of way. More like a desperate need to devour her.

When all the warning bells officially chimed their way back into Kala's sanity-center, she yanked herself away.

Asmodeus was positively grinning.

"Wipe that smile off your face. I was just happy I won." Kala tried miserably to play it cool.

"Of course, beautiful." He kissed her forehead and she let him, surprisingly. "It was everything I imagined."

Kala grunted and walked toward the cash out booth. It wasn't as if she needed a hundred thousand dollars, but she wanted it anyway. And frankly, Kala wasn't interested in making eye contact with Asmodeus right then. What had she been thinking? She hadn't. It was that simple. Always impulsive. Always having a mess to clean up. Kala hoped Asmodeus wouldn't get any more ideas. That was a one-time kiss and she *never* planned to repeat it. No matter how good it felt.

"Kala," Asmodeus called from behind.

She wouldn't have responded except for the fact that she couldn't remember a time when Asmodeus had ever called her by name. He always used some kind of pet name for her.

The hairs on the back of her neck raised.

Cronus.

She could feel him.

Kala slowly turned around to face a man in an all-black suit standing next to Asmodeus.

In human form, Cronus looked like he owned the casino. He was a little over six-feet, short black hair, clean-shaven with the famous supernatural bone structure. If Kala were to guess, she'd say he was somewhere in his early forties, not the multi-millennia old fart that he was.

Asmodeus's demeanor was subservient next to the Titan. She couldn't really blame him. She had fought Cronus before and he almost demolished her. Not to mention the fact that he had chopped Talan into pieces. In human form, he might not be as powerful, but Kala had to assume he could still destroy her. She had almost beaten him in the 5th, though. Almost consumed him. But she had no clue as to how she did that, so a repeat of the act wasn't statistically looking so good.

So she decided to be deferent. "What are you doing here? I thought I taught you to leave me alone." Okay. Not so much. Submissiveness wasn't one of her traits.

"You will learn your place, Human," Cronus snarled.

Asmodeus gave her eye signals to shut-the-hell-up, but Kala ignored him. "You want to fight me in a casino?" She looked at him like he was an idiot.

Cronus's eyes glowed blue like Penny's had, but his were a lot more intimidating. "No. I want to *kill* you in a casino."

Great.

Chapter Nineteen

Kala concentrated as hard as she could to teleport herself out of there, but Cronus laughed.

"Not today." He grinned.

Right.

Soldier first.

Get to higher ground.

And hopefully before Cronus attacked.

Kala had no qualms about making a fool of herself as she ran in the opposite direction of the Titan and towards the staircase, poker chips flying everywhere. The last thing she wanted was innocent by-standers to get hurt or worse, killed. And Cronus wouldn't care if he took out most of the casino's inhabitants just to destroy Kala.

People swarmed like locusts, diving after the chips, which to them equated to free money. The crowd blocked Cronus and

Asmodeus from following her right away.

Cronus was probably over-joyed at seeing Kala run, but she wasn't doing it to get away. She was trying to find a more defensible fighting area. The roof seemed like the best option, so Kala was about to see if her "god" side had enough stamina to run up fifty floors of stairs. With all the steps she had climbed with Derek in the Compound, Kala knew she was up for the task.

Here was to hoping, anyway.

Cutting her way through the gamblers, Kala reached the staircase and flew up the steps as fast as her legs could carry her. It felt amazing. Her body ran steadily upwards, but there was no exhaustion, no panting, just speed. It was as if she was the Bionic Woman or some kind of super soldier.

As she made her way up, Kala listened for any signs of pursuit, but she didn't hear anything.

Fine. She figured Cronus knew her end game and was already waiting for her on the roof. She needed the element of surprise to survive this fight. Even though Kala had been reassured that it would be near impossible to kill her, she didn't want to take any chances.

A few minutes later, Kala was at the roof entrance door.

She knew Cronus was behind it. Waiting for her. Smug. Expecting to see her spill out onto the roof and be *shocked* that he had beaten her there.

There was nothing like the present.

Kala kicked the door open and jumped to the right.

BAM!

A crack of lightning barely missed Kala as the doorway lit on fire.

Kala rolled behind an air-conditioner the size of a small car. "Isn't that your son Zeus's trick?" she yelled in the direction the bolt came from.

"It's effective," came Cronus's steady voice.

"Except that your aim is terrible." Why did Kala feel the need to antagonize? It came way too naturally for her.

CRACK!

And the air-conditioner was on fire.

Kala didn't have a plan yet, but flames weren't doing her any favors so she high-tailed it to the next mounted structure. It happened to be the base of a giant satellite dish. Her whole idea of getting to higher ground was feeling kind of fruitless.

What did she think she could do?

Her last fight with Cronus consisted of her being tossed around like a chew toy. It wasn't until the Titan dropped pieces of Talan at her feet that some kind of innate power started to spill out of her. She just needed to tap into that.

But Kala didn't want to.

She was scared that she wouldn't be able to control herself and end up chowing down on the leader of the Titans. If Cronus *integrated* with her brain, Kala was sure she'd turn into a schizoid. It was more terrifying than dying.

Speaking of which...

SNAP!

There went the dish, crashing next to her feet. The base was still intact, so Kala stayed where she was.

"You can't hide forever, Human." Cronus sounded amused.

Kala imagined him standing casually in his perfectly

tailored suit, flipping his hand occasionally to drop lightning bombs on the lame half-breed.

"I'm more than human. You can't kill me," Kala baited. She wanted either confirmation of that or for Cronus to slip up and tell her something else she might not know.

"You are more human than Titan. And I can kill you just fine." Cronus sounded bored. "Now come out and face me."

"I really don't feel like being fried with lightning right now." Kala didn't budge.

BOOM!

Kala felt the metal from the structure she leaned against, push into her back, launching her forward to her knees. Behind her stood a twisted mass of metal. Cronus was going to destroy every piece of cover Kala ran to until there was nothing else to hide behind.

Feeling desperate, Kala ran to another air-conditioning unit.

She could feel the annoyance dripping from Cronus's tone. "Are we going to do this dance all day?"

"Considering it's my life, yes." Kala searched her surroundings. Could she survive jumping off a fifty-story building? Not likely. It was the whole *human* part that was unclear. The Supernatural was making her quite aware of the fact that, even though she was a Titan, there was still a part of her that was fragile.

Kala was about to throw caution to the wind and full on body slam Cronus when Asmodeus popped in next to her.

"I wouldn't do that." He guessed her intentions.

"I have to do *something*!" Kala wanted the confrontation to be over with at this point.

"Let me distract him." Asmodeus smiled.

"You work for him." Kala couldn't fathom why the Demon would help her. She had seen the terror in his eyes when he looked at Cronus.

"What can I say? I'm a sucker for a good kiss." And with that, he kissed Kala briefly on the lips and teleported away.

BAM!

Kala stood up. Her gut told her something was wrong.

And it was.

In the spot where Asmodeus must have teleported in to fight Cronus was a pile of dust.

"Did you *kill* him?" Kala was surprised at how much the thought of Asmodeus dying affected her.

Cronus shrugged. "Asmodeus is fine, but I sent him to a place where he won't be returning anytime soon. I won't tolerate disloyalty, especially not from a Demon."

With Owen sending Asmodeus to the 5th Level of Hell a few days back, the Demon had a nasty habit of being banished by his superiors.

Still.

Something felt off about the whole thing.

It was too easy.

Too *heroic* for Asmodeus.

Kala had an itching suspicion that she was being set up. For what, she had no idea. If she knew Cronus's end game, maybe she could figure it out.

Best to keep him talking rather than attacking. *That*, she knew for sure.

"No lightning?" Great. Provoke him. Half the time Kala wished she could divorce her mouth from her brain. They never seemed to agree with each other.

Cronus stared at Kala as if he were dissecting an insect.

She wondered why there was a sudden *lack* of attacking. He had been trying to roast her five seconds ago, but now that she was out in the open...

Nothing.

"Are you going to kill me or what?" Kala asked in a voice dripping with irritation. Kala was tired of constantly fighting and running and fighting and running. She wanted Cronus to make his move and maybe she could counter it.

"I could." He toyed with her.

"Really? Because you've tried a butt-load of times and I'm still here," Kala responded back.

Cronus paused, staring at her again.

"I really wish you supernatural beings would stop staring at me like I was some kind of unicorn. Has no one ever given you lip before?" Kala surveyed the roof while she kept Cronus distracted. A part of her seriously debated whether or not to jump. Maybe if she were far enough away from him, she'd be able to teleport again. Kala made a mental note to ask Rotoph about it later. If Rotoph was able to block teleportation from the Compound, he must be doing it the same way Cronus was now. She never thought she'd actually want Rotoph by her side, but she could really use him right now.

In the mean time, there were more places to duck and cover, but that wouldn't get Kala anywhere.

Cronus looked like a baller in his black suit, watching Kala like a hawk.

"Seriously, what now?" She shrugged her shoulders. "You

either let me go or try to kill me, but this waiting around is starting to bug me." There was nothing worse than a standstill. One of the reasons Kala became a soldier was because she needed action, the adrenaline rush. The only time she could handle sitting still for long periods of time was when she had a rifle in her hands.

Cronus's hands shot out before Kala could react.

CRACK!

Her body was completely engulfed with lightning.

Everything clenched: jaw, legs, arms, neck.

Kala couldn't move a muscle as the energy surged through her.

This is how I die? Struck by lightning from a Titan?

She couldn't accept that.

Not going to happen.

BOOM!

Not knowing how, Kala pushed the energy from the lightning out of her body like the blast ring of a nuclear bomb.

Cronus was knocked to his feet, shock in his eyes.

After a second or two Kala appreciated what she had just done. She looked up at Cronus. "Is that all you got?" She was definitely not feeling the bravado she spouted, but she figured she'd try to bluff as best she could.

Cronus slowly rose, dusting himself off, his expression full of fear and wonder. "I know what you are," he said.

Kala could see his eyes were welling with... tears? It scared her more than the lightning. "What do you mean?"

Cronus shook his head. "You're on the wrong side, Kala Hicks."

And he was gone.

It took a moment before Kala could move, afraid he'd pop back in and snap her neck. Not that it would kill her, but she didn't imagine it would feel too good either.

After she was sure Cronus was gone, Kala ran her hands through her hair.

What was that?

What did he mean he knew *what* she was? What *was* she? She had consumed Atlas and she had almost consumed Cronus. Was she some kind of God-eater? Did those exist? Where did she get *that* skill? From the dumpster her mother abandoned her in? And what about the skill of taking a lightning strike and turning it into a blast ring? She tried to wrack her brain for any memory of Atlas's that showed he could do this, but Kala knew it was fruitless. She could tell by Cronus's response that he thought she was something different.

But what? He looked so sure! It drove her nuts!

And where was Asmodeus?

Did Cronus really banish him?

Probably. She shrugged. It was for the best. What was she supposed to do with the king of Demons anyway?

Kala felt more alone than she ever had in her entire life. Being a foster kid, that was saying something. Standing on a rooftop in Las Vegas with a crushed air-conditioner and demolished satellite dish behind her, Kala couldn't move.

What had her life become?

Who was she?

What was she?

Talan's face suddenly appeared in her head.

A warmth spread through her that she couldn't explain.

Thinking of him gave her a strange sense of hope.

Of home.

Kala closed her eyes.

When she opened them, Talan stood in front of her.

Completely out of character, she hugged him tightly.

His arms gently wrapped around her. Kala almost cried it felt so good. She didn't even pause to think that she had finally made it back to the hideout. She didn't even care that the human part of her body was probably about to fall apart. Kala just wanted to stay in that embrace for as long as she could make it last.

Talan's voice whispered in her ear. "You can't be here. You'll hurt yourself."

Hearing the pained concern in his voice only made Kala want to stay more. She never realized how much she needed contact until this moment. A part of her had felt it with Jack, but she hadn't been ready to admit it back then. But his ability to make her feel safe and wanted was why he was the first man she had ever loved. Feelings she had always been proud that she never needed.

But she did.

"Kala, what is it?" Owen's voice came from behind.

She pulled away from Talan and faced her foster father. "Did Zeus tell you anything?" She didn't want to talk about Cronus yet.

Talan shook his head. "He just babbles. We can't get anything coherent out of him."

"Let me try." Kala started to move toward Zeus with determination. She planned on taking out all her frustration on the god.

Owen stopped her. "Kala, I know that look on your face.

167

Something happened to you. Tell us."

Kala sighed heavily. "Cronus just attacked me again."

"You went back to the 5th Level of Hell? Why?" Owen asked worriedly.

"I wasn't in the 5th. I was in Vegas," Kala informed them.

Looking around to distract herself, she saw the rambling Zeus in a corner. Rotoph, Hephaestus, and Penny were at some kind of forge, clanking on metal. They barely noticed that she was back, they were so focused on their work. Kala figured it must be some kind of super weapon. Maybe something she could use in the future against Cronus? Her soldier mind wanted to go over and find out.

But the looks on Talan and Owen's faces stopped her.

"What?" Kala couldn't tell if they were upset she'd fought Cronus again, or the fact that it was in Vegas.

"Kala, Cronus hasn't left the 5th since the end of the war. It's been 2,000 years." Owen let that gem simmer.

Kala's head started to spin. It didn't help that Zeus began to repeat the word Cronus over and over again.

"Why would he come down for me?" She didn't want to admit it, but she already knew. Cronus had come to assess some theory he had about her and she had confirmed it for him when she pushed the lightning out of her system.

"To finish what he started in the 5th and destroy you once and for all?" Talan suggested.

"No," Kala sighed. "He was testing me. He said he knew what I was." She peered up into Talan's eyes and then Owen's, looking for some kind of recognition. Hoping beyond hope that they would know what Cronus saw and tell her *something!*

But they both appeared just as confused as she was.

After a moment, Owen nodded slowly. "We know something is different about you. The fact that you were able to destroy Atlas and infuse him into your human body without dying has never happened before."

"And you almost did the same with Cronus," Talan added thoughtfully. "The truth is, we don't know why you were able to do those things. There's nothing about you that makes you different from any other human."

"Thanks," Kala joked sarcastically.

"You know what I mean," Talan said.

Lurching forward, Kala was reminded why she couldn't be there. Blood spurted from her mouth before she could stop it.

"You have to leave." Owen placed his hand on her back to calm her.

Kala gently shrugged him away. "No, wait. I think I got this."

"It's physical, Kala, it's not mental. You may die." Talan seemed adamant to make her leave.

"Just give me a second." Kala moved a few paces off. The lightning incident showed Kala that she had powers she was not aware of. Physical or not, she had to try. Seeing mumbling-crazy-Zeus in the corner only inspired her more. Kala knew she could extract the information she needed from the god. Talan and Owen weren't motivated like she was. They weren't the ones that had to do horrific things every four days.

Wiping the blood dripping from her nose, Kala hid her face from the two worrywarts. After chowing down on Atlas, waking up had been an ordeal similar to this one. She almost didn't survive it, but Roberta had worked her mojo and helped her through it. The secret had been keeping calm and focusing on integrating with the warring sensations in her body. Having Roberta would definitely help right about now, but Kala knew she could do this herself.

Leaning forward, Kala relaxed her chest and head. Back to Yoga 101. Deep breaths, relaxing her mind, relaxing her body. She choked a large splattering of blood on the floor but ignored it.

Kala tuned out Owen and Talan, who were still trying to convince her to leave. Out of the corner of her eye, she noticed that Rotoph had walked over. Kala knew he sensed what she was doing. Even Zeus grew more and more excited saying the words, "tricky, tricky, fixy, fixy."

He was nuts, but it gave Kala a surge of confidence.

Closing her eyes, Kala used the same energy she used to push out the lightning to try to push out the human part of her that rejected the hideout. Another cough of blood threatened to break her concentration and will. She shook it off and kept focusing.

As her body started to collapse in on itself, Kala used the anguish she felt to motivate her. She had never felt such intense pain in her life. Integrating with Atlas hadn't been this painful. It was as if her veins were exploding.

Maybe they were, she thought with horror.

Shaking away the disturbing thoughts, Kala imagined pushing out the pain. Pain equaled death.

Blood puke.

Lovely.

She screamed.

Talan and Owen tried to grab Kala.

They were going to teleport her.

"Stay back!" she yelled as blood poured out of her mouth.

Kala stepped away from them, knowing that they wouldn't listen to her.

She just needed more time. Kala was close. She could feel it.

Kala reached deep within her body and mind. *Integrate. Integrate.* She repeated to herself.

Tuning out Owen's booming voice became harder and harder. Her body grew weak.

She was dying.

Kala was going to die.

No.

She wiped the blood from her mouth and cried out, delving into her power, that secret reserve that allowed her do things that were impossible.

Talan managed to grab her.

Kala physically felt her mind blocking his teleportation.

She was staying and no one would stop her.

Human side be damned, Kala wasn't going anywhere.

CRACK!

The sound reverberated through Kala's form. It hadn't come from outside.

It had come from inside her mind.

With one last spurt of blood, the agony disappeared.

Gone.

Kala wondered if she was dead, or if her plan had worked.

Slowly, Kala straightened herself.

Definitely alive.

She wiped as much of the blood from her mouth as she could.

Everyone stared at her. Even Hephaestus and Penny had stopped their work to watch *the Kala show*.

Their faces all had the same expression: shock.

Only Zeus moved. He acted like an excited baboon, jumping and clawing at the walls, his words nonsense.

"Could someone get me a towel or something?" Kala broke the silence. Yet again, she was covered in her own blood.

Talan was the first to respond as he handed her a small blanket. "This is all we have."

Kala took the proffered blanket and wiped her face, hands and neck as best she could. By the end of it, the material was almost entirely red.

Not wanting to talk about what just happened, Kala turned to Penny. "Do you have an extra shirt?"

Penny couldn't seem to snap out of stare-mode, but eventually she shook her head. "I didn't exactly pack."

"Right. Supernatural hideout. Why would you need clothes?" Kala saw the logic in this, but it still irked her. Wearing her own blood on her chest wasn't how she wanted to spend the day, but at least she was alive.

But Talan quickly came to the rescue by waving his hand over her body. All the blood instantly disappeared from her clothing and skin.

"You couldn't have done that earlier?" Kala glanced at the blood-soaked blanket, but she managed an appreciative smile. "Thanks."

"Can we talk about what just happened here?" Hephaestus still had a stunned look on his face. "This half-breed acclimated her human side to a god's station. *That's impossible.*"

"Now I know where Penny gets it from," Kala observed sarcastically. "You and your *impossibles*."

Rotoph stepped forward. "How did you do that?" His eyes were calculating, as if he could gain some kind of advantage if he knew.

Kala felt like she was surrounded by paparazzi. She placed her hands up for everyone to leave her alone. "Look, I don't know how I did it. I just did. It was the same with Atlas, the same with Cronus and the same with pushing out the lightning."

"What lightning?" Owen asked, his face concerned. Kala remembered seeing that expression growing up when she'd stay out without his permission. She hated it then, she hated it now.

At the word lightning, Zeus's mumbling turned to screeching with glee.

Kala ignored him and told the others what she had done when Cronus attacked her.

Instead of talking to her though, they started talking to each other, as if Kala was some kind of circus monkey that had performed a radical trick.

When she heard Hephaestus say, "We should start testing her and see what she's capable of," Kala had to shut down the whole conversation right there.

"Whoa, whoa, whoa! You guys are supposed to be on my side! There will be no *testing*." Kala had had enough.

She walked away from them all, toward orangutan-Zeus. Time to get some real answers.

But she was surprised when it was Penny who stopped her. "Kala, none of us know what's going on. The supernatural world *doesn't change*, nothing is new, it's always the same

173

ancient battle within the families. So when someone like you comes along, it's scary. If you haven't figured it out yet, we don't like change."

Kala sighed. She appreciated Penny's honesty, but it didn't change the current situation. Only Zeus could do that. "I get it, but one thing at a time. I want to get rid of this damn curse, then we can figure out why I'm different. Deal?" She eyed everyone in the room for confirmation.

Owen nodded first, but added, "Cronus claims to know what you are. That could be very dangerous. We'll back burner this for now but, Kala, in your case, knowledge is power. And Cronus has it all."

"Truer words were never spoken."

Oh no. Kala groaned to herself.

She turned to see Asmodeus standing over Zeus.

"I knew you faked that whole hero act," Kala grumbled in annoyance.

Asmodeus smiled. "I had to find this place somehow, and with your heart broken, I figured it was a good bet you'd jump here next."

"Don't flatter yourself. I could never be interested in a lousy kisser. Too much drool." It wasn't true, but she hoped it would sting.

It didn't.

"Being on the other end of that kiss, you didn't exactly pull away, but I understand. You don't want to upset your Angel-Boy over there," Asmodeus snickered.

Kala didn't want to look at Talan and his butt-hurt face. Kissing the guy who had stranded him in the 5th Level of

Hell to be chopped up by Cronus was pretty awful even on a "friend" level.

"I hope you got everything you needed from Zeus here. I did give you a little extra time. If not, I'm sure the Malaks could help you." Asmodeus shrugged with a grin. "Good-bye, beautiful. We'll meet again."

Before Kala or any of the others could react, Asmodeus and Zeus disappeared.

Chapter Twenty

Kala felt a hand on her shoulder. She was sure it was Owen, since she figured Talan would be upset at finding out about the Asmodeus-kiss. But it was Talan's voice that spoke.

"Zeus wasn't going to help you. He can't. He's too far gone. We'll find another way."

Kala touched his hand softly and squeezed it. "There is no other way." She turned around. "I have to get him back."

Hephaestus stepped forward. "It's better that he's gone. As crazy as Zeus was, Cronus has always had a way of extracting information out of him. We hid our work while we were down here, but if he had been here when we broke the prisoners out? All would have been lost."

Owen nodded. "Our brothers and sisters can help, Kala. There are some among them who can track gods. We'll find Zeus once they are free."

Kala took a moment, then nodded. "Shouldn't we move somewhere else? Cronus knows where you are now."

Penny shook her head. "We can't. We've already established where the portal will open. We can't just move it."

"Then you better hurry." Kala only saw this ending in violence. If Cronus knew where they were, it wouldn't be long before he sent his family after them. She would. There was no way he'd let the Grigori return and, if he really could extract information from Zeus, he'd know what Hephaestus was up to and send the cavalry to stop it.

But the best part of this situation was the fact that Hephaestus told her that Cronus *could* obtain info from Zeus. And Kala intended to use that. Even if it meant swallowing Cronus whole. Heck, even if it meant swallowing Zeus whole and reversing the curse herself. She was too terrified to try either option, but more so with Zeus: because if it didn't work, she'd never break the curse. Then she'd be stuck with a crazoid in her head.

And she was afraid of losing herself.

Kala hadn't lost herself with Atlas, but it had only been two days! If Talan hadn't sectioned off her brain to stop her from passing out every time she had a memory, she probably would have been unconscious most of the last forty-eight hours.

Hephaestus and Penny went back to the forge, which apparently held *the portal*. This was all becoming too sci-fi for Kala. Rotoph and Owen followed to help.

Talan stayed with her.

Then Asmodeus's words echoed back in her head: *If not, I'm sure the Malaks could help you.* It had been such a throwaway line, as if he was mocking her, but maybe he knew something about the Malaks that she didn't. It wasn't beyond the realm of possibility that Asmodeus was throwing her a bone.

"What did Asmodeus mean about the Malaks helping me?" she questioned Talan.

"I'm not sure. They're the least powerful beings besides Demons. Ever since Atlas tricked the first human to take over his duties, they've been hunting the surrogates down trying to take over the job themselves." Talan repeated what Kala already knew.

"Are you sure they wanted to kill the *Atlas-surrogate* to gain the power for themselves?" Kala's mind was spinning. There was something there. She just couldn't seem to formulate it into a coherent thought.

"Why else would they want to be the Atlas? Every Malak I ran across always talked of humans being unworthy. Remember Grautlin?" Talan wasn't trying to shoot her down; he seemed to be rationalizing it through for himself.

"How can I forget? The guy tried to kill me *twice*." Kala recalled that Grautlin was pretty adamant about being the next Atlas. As if it were an honor.

But why would Asmodeus bring it up? Was he trying to distract her? Throw her off Zeus and onto something else? It was so hard to tell with the Demon. One moment he appeared to genuinely care, the next he was pretending to be a hero just so he could steal back Zeus, her only lead.

"I need to talk to one. Do you know any? Maybe someone high up on the food chain?" Kala decided it was better to go to the source.

"Aside from a select few, Malaks and Demons don't know the Grigori are back," Talan replied apologetically.

"You really are clueless, aren't you? Do you honestly think the last week has escaped the notice of the supernatural world? Rotoph roped in Malaks and Demons to attack us in the bar, remember? They didn't seem all that shocked to see him – or you. You underestimate the need to gossip. That's not just a human trait." Kala was surprised Talan actually thought that he was still a secret.

From the look on his face, the realization was dawning on him. "Then releasing as many Grigori as we can is our only defense."

"Defense? No one can touch you without the blades, and I *have* one at least." Kala touched the top of the hilt, making sure Asmodeus hadn't pulled any shenanigans.

Still there.

"There are eleven Titans who have the others, and only three Grigori here. We've managed to keep our three other brothers and sister out of this mess in case we fail." Talan spoke of the Grigori who had escaped with them centuries ago.

Kala had never heard Talan or Owen speak of the other Grigori on earth. "Okay. Well, you guys do your thing and I'm going to find some Malaks." She fully intended to leave.

Talan's eyes stopped her. "Kala. We need you. You can't leave now."

"Ten minutes ago you were telling me to get the heck out, so just pretend my *human* side is killing me and let me go hunt some Malaks."

"Ten minutes ago we didn't know how powerful you were. I didn't *want* you to leave. I wanted you to be safe. I understand your need to rid yourself of this curse, but don't you think it can wait until we get some backup?" Talan sounded irritated.

She had actually managed to piss Talan off. It amused Kala for some reason. He was always spouting his love and loyalty, but her one-track mind finally made him crack. "As soon as the family reunion is over, you're taking me to a Malak," Kala ordered.

Talan nodded. "I promise."

Kala smiled at him. There was an affection there between them that she couldn't deny. It felt as if they had been friends their whole lives. Kala knew Talan had no-no feelings for her, and she was definitely attracted to the guy, but no one could replace Jack. No one ever would. Friendship she could handle though. Friendship was safe. And Talan made her feel safe.

BOOM!

"It's starting! Talan, we need you!" Penny's voice yelled out.

Kala walked straight for the forge, followed by Talan.

It was one of the strangest visuals Kala had ever seen. It looked like a tiny tornado drilling a hole into the air itself, growing bigger every second.

Penny, Talan, Rotoph, and Owen clasped hands, then suddenly Penny and Talan grabbed onto Kala's to complete the circle.

Penny shrugged. "I don't know what kind of abilities you have, but they're powerful and we need as much of it as we can."

Hephaestus stayed out of the ring and chanted some kind of spell.

The tornado grew bigger and louder with each passing second. The noise was so intense Kala wanted to snap her hands away and cover her ears, but she held on to Penny and Talan.

The center of the swirling wind started to open up and Kala

could see the Heaven-prison Talan had shown her before. Even through a small opening, it was a stunning view, as if galaxies had collided in one spectacular moment. Why would Grigori want to come to earth when they could be there? Kala still didn't understand that logic, but she supposed if she had been locked up against her will, she'd want out too.

Penny's eyes widened with anticipation. "They're coming!"

Kala couldn't see anything so she assumed Penny had some sort of connection to the portal that allowed her to sense the Grigori on the other side.

KABOOM!

The swirling hole tilted almost two-feet sideways before it righted itself.

"HOLD ON!" Penny screamed. "DON'T LET GO!"

Hephaestus's voice grew louder as he chanted.

Kala held on with all her strength, but the force of the portal tried to pry their hands apart.

Then a person was visible from the other side: a stunningly beautiful woman with dark skin and pitch-black hair. It was a shocking contrast between the raging storm and the calm beauty of the angel.

"Antel!" Owen shouted. "Come through!"

The Grigori named Antel's eyes lit up when she saw Owen and she stepped through the swirling abyss to land safely inside their circle.

Antel yelled over the noise, "The others are coming!"

Penny screamed, "Join the circle! We need your strength!"

Antel nodded, taking Owen and Talan's hands quickly so the circle wouldn't be broken for long. Once their hands were clasped, Kala felt the power intensify. Surges of invisible energy flowed through her body and out through her hands. Angels and deities might be able to handle opening magical portals to angel prisons, but *half-human Kala* felt like her soul was being shredded.

After Antel passed through, a line of Grigori appeared in front of the growing tornado. It was now the size of a small car. One after another they came through, each one joining the circle, until it was ten strong. Five new Grigori already seemed like a lot to Kala; she wondered how many more there were. She tried to count the line of them waiting to pass through, but there seemed to be no end.

The next Grigori started to walk into the portal…

SLASH! SLASH! SLASH!

The portal closed with a loud CLAP!

The energy flow, dead.

Kala looked up and saw Owen, Antel and Rotoph drop to the floor from the blades that slashed their throats.

Three Titans stood behind them: Iapetus, Theia and Hyperion.

Kala saw red.

Even though she logically knew that Owen wasn't dead, seeing his throat cut sent her into a rage.

Deep within her being, Kala let the power that had consumed Atlas and almost consumed Cronus take over. It scared her, but her rage was stronger. It was as if she was awakening something ancient inside her that had always been there, but she'd never known how to connect with it – until Atlas.

Like before, Kala had no control over the words that came

out of her mouth, "YOU WILL BE PUNISHED!"

The Grigori blades flew out of the Titan's hands to land hilt first into Talan, Hephaestus and Penny's hands.

Shock registered on every being in the room. Then Talan responded. He slashed his blade at Hyperion.

The Titans didn't need the blades to attack, they were powerful enough all on their own.

Penny tried to attack Theia, but the Titan threw her across the room. It didn't stop Penny though. She used her ability to disappear from view and popped back in to surprise Theia with a stab to her chest. Theia screamed in pain, but still had enough power to backhand Penny to the floor.

Hephaestus was the most at home in battle. He'd been doing this a long time and it looked like he was enjoying himself as he stabbed Theia again in protection of his daughter. Being locked away to make weapons for the Titans for thousands of years had given him all the anger he needed to use the blade that *he* made.

Kala fought inside herself, trying to stem the power she had no control over. She had no idea what it was or where it came from and as a soldier, Kala's first rule was to always know what her weapon could do. A part of her wanted to use it, but the other part of her warned against it. Last time she let it have free reign, she had devoured a god.

Iapetus was suddenly in front of Kala his eyes curious. "Son, are you still in there?"

He was referring to Atlas, Kala assumed. "He's dead. I have all his memories, but his soul is gone. It's only me." Kala pulled out her own Grigori blade and stabbed Iapetus in the stomach. "You're not my father." She nodded to Owen's still form. "*He* is."

183

Then she slashed Iapetus's throat. "Doesn't feel so great, does it?"

Kala started to feel normal again. Fighting like a human brought her back to herself.

Iapetus mended a lot faster than the Grigori, his gut and neck healing before her eyes. And he didn't even appear mad at Kala, only interested. "The Grigori is not your father no matter how many times you tell yourself that he is." He backed up before Kala could stab him again. "Whether Atlas's soul is inside you or not, he *is* inside you, which makes you a Titan. *My* son."

"Reality check, I'm a girl." Kala feigned an attack to the right. When Iapetus moved left to avoid it, she stabbed him in the heart. "It may not kill you, but it'll make you weak enough to imprison." She cut his ribs for measure. "I'll find my answers and take down every one of you to get them."

Though Iapetus's wound healed quickly, his body showed that the blows were slowing him down.

Seeing the gravity of his situation, Iapetus called out to his sister and brother. "Now!"

A second later, the Titans were gone.

But so was Hephaestus.

They couldn't re-open the portal.

"Well, that sucked," Kala groaned.

Chapter Twenty-One

It took a few hours for Owen and the other two Grigori to regain their strength. Kala didn't leave Owen's side. Seeing her only real dad have his neck sliced in front of her was something she never wanted to repeat.

The five new Grigori eyed her warily, not sure what to make of her. They didn't know her like Owen and Talan did, so Kala understood: they didn't have a reason to trust her. Seeing her rob the blades from the Titans had surprised everyone in the room, including Kala. She wanted to know where her strange wellspring of power came from, but at the same time, she wanted nothing to do with it.

Talan turned to Kala. "I'll take you to Lotun. She's the leader of the Malaks."

Kala was relieved to hear that Talan was willing to take her so soon. Especially since the portal was closed with no way to re-open it without Hephaestus. There wasn't much Kala could do for anyone there anyway. Talan had kept his promise by asking the other Grigori if they could track down Zeus, but none of them had that particular skill, so Kala was back to the Malaks, her only lead. This news made Penny a wreck. She could care less about Zeus, and had hoped they could find her father. She tried to convince anyone who would listen that their first priority should be getting Hephaestus back. Most of the Grigori seemed to be on the same page as Penny, feeling that their numbers were still too small to take on the Titans.

That was where this whole thing was headed: another war between gods and angels. And probably Demons. Seven days ago, Kala had no idea any of *this* existed and now she was a major part of it. She was a Titan. At least partially.

And something else.

Something that scared the most powerful of the gods.

The most powerful of the Grigori.

What was she?

Maybe the Malaks *could* help. It was a stretch, but Kala was running out of options. Asmodeus was a dick, but Kala knew as warped as his feelings were for her, they were real to a degree. To what degree she had no idea, but she didn't believe he'd mention the Malaks if they didn't have something to offer her.

And Talan? He claimed that only a few knew he was back. Kala knew that was a joke, now that the Titans and Asmodeus knew. They'd tell the whole supernatural world just to keep the feelers out so they could wrangle the Grigori back to their prison. But maybe this Lotun Malak knew Talan was around. Maybe they had some kind of a relationship or past. Kala found that she didn't like that so much. She didn't want Talan, but she didn't want anyone else to have him either. It made no sense, but Kala was okay with that. Most of what she felt didn't make sense.

"Let me say goodbye to Owen before we go," Kala said to Talan.

She walked over to her foster dad and placed a hand on his arm. He turned and hugged her. "You leaving with Talan?" he asked as he pulled away.

Kala nodded. "He's taking me to Lotun." She watched Owen's face for a reaction.

He didn't seem surprised. "If any of the Malaks can help you, she can. She'll know if Asmodeus was trying to trick you or not. She knows him better than anyone."

"Really?" Kala mused. Interesting. "Were they friends? Lovers? Enemies? What?"

"I'll let her tell you. I try not to think of Asmodeus," Owen stated flatly.

She felt a pang of guilt. Owen knew she kissed the Demon and she didn't want him to think less of her for it. But the gleam in his eyes when he looked at her told her that Owen would love her forever. "Tell *Mom* that I love her." She had only called her foster mother mom once and that was four days ago, but she wanted to get used to it. And the 'L' word was getting easier to say, at least when talking about her parents. Owen and Linda were her mom and dad no matter what Iapetus said. And the expression on Owen's face made it all worth it.

He squeezed her tight. "I will. I love you, Kala."

"I love you, too." She pulled away and headed to Talan.

Before she reached him, Antel stepped in front of her. She

was truly a stunning woman, her dark skin and eyes to match. "May I have a word?" she asked politely.

"Sure." Kala wanted to leave, but was curious what Antel wanted.

"Owen told me some of the things you've been able to do," Antel started.

When there were at least ten seconds of awkward silence Kala prodded, "And?"

Antel smiled which made her even more beautiful. "And...I want you to be careful using your gifts. Atlas may have given you strength, but he was weak. A more powerful soul could kill you or worse, take over your body. I can see Atlas in you, but I also see something else... *someone* else."

"Who do you see?" Kala's interest was piqued.

Antel shook her head. "I don't know, but there is something very special about you, Kala. You are Owen's daughter and Talan's soul mate, so I will protect you with my life."

Soul mate? Kala didn't feel like arguing the matter, though. Disagreeing with Grigori never ended with convincing them of anything. Once they believed something, that was it. Kala thought she was stubborn, but Grigori were ten times worse. She simply said, "Thanks." Not knowing what else to say.

Did she swallow someone else, too, when she consumed Atlas? Or was the power that allowed her to swallow him in the first place from *somewhere* else? She needed answers. All she had was more questions.

She joined Talan's side.

"Ready?" he asked.

"As I'll ever be," she responded.

Talan's hand wrapped in hers and Kala felt the tingling sensation she always felt when Talan touched her. Which was why she had a *no touching* rule. But he was teleporting her, so they had to have contact. She shrugged inwardly. The Grigori may believe that she and Talan were soul mates, but she still knew that she had lost her true soul mate when she killed Jack.

Taking a deep breath, her surroundings turned to swirls of light as Talan teleported her away.

They arrived in the middle of a forest. Kala hated nature. Sure, it was beautiful, but it was full of bugs and creatures she wanted nothing to do with.

"Where are we?"

"Somewhere in France," Talan answered. "Lotun doesn't like cities. She prefers the forest."

"Of course she does," Kala grunted. It figured the one Malak that could potentially help her lived in the one place that Kala couldn't stand.

The ground was a thick layer of pine needles making it feel spongy as they walked.

After twenty minutes of trudging past endless amounts of trees, Kala grew restless. "Are we going to have to search the entire forest for Malak-girl?"

"You are the most impatient person I know." Talan appeared amused.

"Because you know so many people," Kala retorted.

"More than you think," he smiled.

Kala figured he was right. She knew practically nothing about Talan. Only that he was a Grigori who taught Turner and Roberta in disguise.

And that he had saved her... a lot.

Talan had showed her some of his past in a vision, but it didn't really tell her anything about him personally. What did he do in his spare time? Did he have a hobby? Owen was Grigori and he had seemed so normal. Owen being in the Navy was the reason Kala had joined herself. He loved Linda and they did what human couples did: eat, sleep, shop, watch TV, and go to the movies. Owen was a bit of a gun enthusiast, which in turn, influenced Kala to be one as well. So if her foster father had interests and hobbies it made sense that Talan would have them too. She just couldn't imagine him doing anything but stand there, teaching some kind of super-science-magic-trick or beating up Malaks or Demons.

She was about to ask Talan what his favorite color was, when a woman stepped out from behind a tree in front of them.

Damn these angels and their good looks, Kala eyed the woman who she knew was Lotun. Though her clothing made her look like an ordinary camper with dark brown khakis and long sleeve, fitted t-shirt, there was nothing ordinary about her. Her eyes were overly large in contrast to her small nose and lips. Everything about her was delicate from her lithe figure to her tiny hands. Kala guessed that Lotun was five foot two at the most. Being only five foot six herself, Kala still felt like a giant looming over a child.

Lotun's hair was long and pale blonde. It lay in perfect waves as if she had just stepped out of a shampoo commercial. Kala unconsciously touched her own auburn hair that she had tied up in a messy ponytail, feeling self-conscious in front of the Malak. She was over it in about a second when she realized she didn't care.

Lotun spoke, first addressing Talan with bedroom eyes. "My

Grigori has brought me a toy?" She eyed Kala with a smile.

Talan went straight to business ignoring her flirtations. "Hello, Lotun. We need your help."

The Malak dismissed Talan's plea for help as she stepped up to him, tracing her finger over his jawbone seductively.

That was it.

Kala couldn't watch this a moment longer.

"Asmodeus sent us." She thought she'd tell a half-truth, just to see what Lotun would do. And, more importantly, so she'd stop touching Talan.

Lotun finally turned to Kala with interest. "Did he?" But her interest in Kala was fleeting; she turned her attention to Talan. "Everyone knows you've been back, you know."

"I told you." Kala couldn't resist. She loved being right.

Lotun focused on her. "Who are you?" Then she stared at Kala, really stared. Her eyes widened. "Atlas?"

At the sound of Atlas's name, Kala was transported to another memory. This one was a doozy, and she began to lose consciousness. Feeling Talan's hands hold her up felt as if it were happening to someone else. Kala was aware of his presence, but could do nothing to signal that she knew he was there.

The memory took over and flooded Kala's vision.

She stood in the same forest, which only added to the surrealness of being in two places at once. It was almost as if someone had projected two movies on top of each other.

Different stories, but identical location.

Lotun was there and she appeared very angry with Atlas. Honestly, it didn't feel all that different than the situation she was in now with Lotun. And Kala wasn't surprised that Atlas pissed off

191

another being of power. The guy was seriously annoying.

Before the memory version of Lotun could speak, Kala heard the real Lotun's voice. "Interesting. She's having a memory about me. Can you bring her back?"

Talan spoke. "Atlas shows her what she needs to see. She'll return to us when it's done."

Kala's mind reeled. *Atlas shows her what she needs to see? Atlas?* As if he was swimming around in her head, alive and well. She tried to tune Talan and Lotun and concentrate on the vision.

If a part of her subconscious was Atlas, then her brain was trying to show her information that could be valuable. Kala knew in the depths of her soul that Atlas was dead and not lurking in her head, but it was interesting that Talan wasn't so sure. He really had no idea what was going on. It made Kala feel a little better that she wasn't the only one in the dark. But at least she knew some things that no one else did. She liked secrets. It was one of the reasons she'd taken the job with Turner. Secrets usually kept you safe. The person that knew the most would often be the person with all the power.

The memory of Lotun screamed at Atlas. "This curse is a plague on us all!"

"Don't be so dramatic. I'm the one who has to do it." Atlas crossed his arms defensively. "Why did you bring me to this horrible place?"

On that Kala and Atlas could agree. Nature was pretty on TV and in coffee table books, but not in real life.

"Because I can break the curse of balance." Lotun's voice was full of determination.

That had both Kala and Atlas's attention.

Inside, Atlas's pulse raced a mile a minute and he was beyond excited, but his voice was steady as he asked, "How?"

Lotun wore a look on her face that Kala didn't like, but she could tell Atlas was clueless. She had seen that expression before a thousand times on the field when facing her enemies. It said: *I'm going to have to kill you now.* So she wasn't surprised when the Malak admitted, "The only way to break it is ancient magic. I know the ritual and *it will* release what Zeus did to you and return the fates to their natural order. But Atlas, you'll have to make the sacrifice."

Atlas was too self-involved to understand what she was telling him. "I'll make a sacrifice. What do you want? My children? Pleiades or Kalypso? Take them. They never did me any favors."

What a prick.

Kala almost wished Lotun *had* killed him at that moment, but then… But then her life would have been perfect! She would have been with Jack because he never would have trained to be the *Atlas-surrogate*, and she never would have shot the President.

Yeah, she wished Lotun had killed him then and there.

But this was only a memory.

Lotun set him straight. "No, Atlas, your children are safe whether you care or not. The sacrifice is *you*. You have to die for the ritual to work."

Atlas paused for a few moments before he spoke. He grew angrier and angrier the longer he stared at Lotun. "You want me to *die?*" he asked incredulously.

"To bring order back to the world, yes," Lotun spoke confidently.

"But I do that perfectly well *alive.*" Atlas could not see how under any circumstances Lotun would ever imagine he'd agree to her idea.

"It's not about your job. It's about Zeus tearing balance from the universe itself and turning it into a curse. It's not natural. It needs to stop." Lotun wasn't leaving room for argument. "I'm going to do this, with or without your permission," she added.

Atlas teleported away before Lotun could grab him. Kala could feel his terror. It dawned on her that this memory took place right after the Titans had betrayed the Olympians and then Zeus had refused to free Atlas from the curse. Penny had kept Atlas in hiding, showing him how to trick humans into doing his job. Lotun's plan couldn't happen because she never found Atlas. Tricking humans really *was* his witness protection program.

Before Kala could read anymore of Atlas's thoughts, she was back in the present with Talan and Lotun.

She was on guard. "Look, before you try and perform that ritual on me, I'm trying to break this curse as well."

Lotun eyed her carefully. "You came to me. I *can* break this curse. And now you know how."

Talan's face showed his confusion, so Kala filled him in. "She has to kill me to do it."

Talan was all fury and fire. The Grigori equivalent of *puffing up*.

Even Kala was a little scared. He didn't look any different, but he radiated power like he was a nuclear warhead.

"If you touch her…" he began to threaten.

"Relax. I don't even know if it would work. She's part human and that may throw the whole thing off. I'll have to research it." Lotun didn't like Talan's *puffing* at all. It made her view Kala like competition.

Then something occurred to Kala. "Could you kill Atlas inside of me? I'd gladly sacrifice him to break the curse." If she could get rid of both at the same time… her heart surged with hope. She'd lose her superpowers, but that didn't concern her. She just wanted out of this struggle between gods, angels and Demons.

Lotun sighed. "Possibly. I'll see what I can find."

If this was possible, it was bittersweet. Only Atlas had known about Lotun's ritual, and he didn't tell Kala when she had begged him to get out of killing Jack. If Kala had known, she felt like she could have forced Atlas to do the ritual rather than swallowing him. Jack could have lived if Atlas hadn't been such a coward.

Kala didn't want to die either, but she would if it meant saving the planet.

She just wasn't there yet. Doing the job herself kept the world safe. If the ritual meant they had to kill her, the *universe* would take over her job. So, it didn't make the situation better, it simply shifted the responsibility back to the *fabric of space* as opposed to Atlas.

"You do that and get back to,.," Kala's vision went wonky.

Everything blurred and she stumbled to catch her balance.

She felt Talan's hand propping her up, his voice etched with concern, "Kala, what is it?"

"I don't know," Kala answered.

She could see it now.

Lotun was inside her head.

Reaching, searching, reading her thoughts.

Kala lost her motor functions. She tried to warn Talan, but he obviously thought she was having another memory.

Trying to push Lotun out of her mind was impossible. She

felt helpless as she heard Lotun's voice inside her body. "The cure for cancer, huh? Interesting. It could save so many lives, why would destroying it keep the balance?"

Lotun sounded like a scientist trying to figure out a formula that had been giving her trouble.

"What's this?" Lotun was like a kid in a candy store picking through Kala's brain. "Oh, how tragic. Killing the love of your life." Then her voice turned frightened. "The prophecy..."

It was too much.

It didn't bother Kala that Lotun found out about her mission, or even that she was the Fated One. It was the way she dismissed Jack, as if it were nothing.

But it was *everything*.

This time it was easy. Kala tapped into her hidden power and grabbed the very essence of Lotun crawling around inside her.

Lotun screamed. Not just in Kala's head, but outside as well.

Talan held onto Kala tighter and she could hear him asking Lotun, "What's happening?"

But Lotun kept screaming.

Kala squeezed the part of Lotun that was inside of her with all of her might until she heard a pop.

In an instant, Kala's motor functions were back in working order.

She was on her knees with Talan beside her.

Lying in front of her was Lotun, eyes wide in terror, staring at Kala like she was some kind of monster.

Lotun's voice cracked as she uttered, "You're the Fated One."

"Duh."

Chapter Twenty-Two

"**W**e know this already." Kala quickly rose to her feet with a little help from Talan.

Lotun carefully stood up as well, her eyes never leaving Kala's.

"What happened?" Talan was completely at a loss.

"Such power," was all Lotun could say.

Kala had felt it too, but she had no idea where it came from. She explained to Talan, "I bumped her out of my head. Maybe it was something that I picked up from Roberta?" *Maybe it was,* Kala rationalized. Or at least, that was what she wanted to believe. Having an untapped power source wasn't what it was cracked up to be. It was like having an atom bomb stuck inside you without any idea when it would go off.

With a withering expression, Lotun asked, "Roberta Turner? Are you still teaching her your tricks, Grigori?"

Grigori. So impersonal. Guess she was mad at Talan now.

Talan ignored her, his attention never leaving Kala. "Are you sure you're okay?"

Kala nodded. "I'm fine."

A desperation filled Lotun's eyes. "I have to see more. I'm sorry I have to!"

SLAM!

Kala wasn't prepared for Lotun to smash into her brain a second time. She tried to tap into her wellspring of power again, but was too off balance.

Lotun's voice echoed in her head. "It *is* you. I'm sorry. I'm so sorry."

Kala had no idea what she was talking about. She only wanted Lotun to leave.

She heard Talan's voice. "I come in an act of peace and this is how you treat me? Invading Kala's head like she was yours to play with?"

SWOOSH!

Kala gasped for breath as Lotun left her mind.

When she looked up, she saw why.

Lotun was engulfed in green fire, sent from Talan's outstretched hands.

She screamed in anguish. "I'm sorry! I couldn't stop myself! I had to see! I had to!"

He twisted his hands and the green flames roared louder and touched the trees with their height, though the pine needles didn't ignite.

Lotun's skin wasn't burning, but her face was wracked in terrible agony. Her screams turned silent.

It was horrifying.

"STOP!" Kala yelled at Talan.

He glanced at Kala. Whatever he saw there made him extinguish the fire.

She ran over to Lotun's crumpled form and helped her to her feet. Kala looked at Talan, angry now herself. "We need information from her, not roast her like a marshmallow."

He was taken aback and she could see he was a little ashamed as well. "She was hurting you. She tried to read your most private thoughts. You couldn't seem to push her out. These things can't go unpunished, Kala. Not in our world."

Kala knew he was right. She hadn't been able to shove the Malak out the second time. "So you leap to burning her alive? Couldn't you have just knocked her on the head or something?" It was the extremity that bothered Kala. Seeing Lotun covered in flames... It wasn't something she wanted to see again. Ever.

"I'm sorry," Talan replied quietly.

Lotun's face went from pain to shock. "Grigori don't apologize." She was genuinely perplexed.

"Well, he did, so get on your feet." Kala helped the Malak stand. "What can you tell us about... me?" She hoped Lotun wouldn't clam up in resentment at the two people who'd just tortured her.

Lotun shook her head, not wanting to re-live the memory. "I've never seen power like hers before." She peered up at Talan. "She's more powerful than a Grigori. More powerful than *anything*. I..." The girl was reeling. "Of course she is... she's..." She shook her head, unable to comprehend her own words.

Kala didn't like where this was going. "I'm what? I'm just a human."

"A human that swallowed a god!" Lotun's eyes wouldn't stop widening as she gawked at her.

It irritated Kala. "Stop looking so shocked. That happened days ago."

Lotun turned back to Talan. "She's the Fated One, Talan."

"We know that already, Lotun. We've read the prophecies and it only talks about the person who will take this curse away. *The one who knows death*. Do you know who that would be?" Talan spoke carefully.

Lotun shook her head. The crazed glaze in her eyes worsened. "Pandora only has half of the prophecy. The Malaks have kept it hidden. There's more! The Fated One isn't just a person. Talan, the Fated One is…"

And she was gone.

Popped out of the forest like she was never there.

Kala and Talan stared at each other in surprise. He walked over to Kala and examined where Lotun had been.

"Did she teleport out mid-sentence, because that's really low." Kala was beyond frustrated.

"No. Someone teleported her out." Talan sighed. "Only one being has that kind of power."

"Let me guess. Cronus?" Kala could feel her eyes rolling.

"The master of time and space himself," Talan confirmed. His expression turned regretful. "I'm sorry if I disappointed you with my behavior. I don't like seeing you hurt. Especially by a Malak."

Kala sensed some angel prejudice going on, but she decided to let it go. "How are we going to find the other part of the prophecy? Would some other Malak have it?" Because Kala wasn't interested in having another brawl with Cronus. Now he had two prisoners Kala needed: Zeus and Lotun. He was starting a collection. Was he going to kidnap everyone who tried to give Kala information? Probably.

"I didn't even know more of the prophecy existed. I'll have to tell Pandora." Talan barely hid his worry.

"It sounds like the prophecy says who the *Fated One* is, but it's me. So what was Lotun talking about?" Kala hated having more questions. She hated having questions at all, but the more she delved into this new world of hers, the more out of her depth she felt. Words like *Fated One* belonged in fantasies not real life. Not her life.

Not knowing what to say, Talan stared at Kala sympathetically. Finally, he said, "Whatever she was going to tell us, Cronus didn't want you to hear. It must be what he concluded himself. The prophecy only confirmed it for him."

"You don't think he knew of the prophecy beforehand?" Kala wondered.

"No. If a prophecy doesn't involve him directly, he doesn't pay much attention to it. There are too many to know all of them. If Lotun kept the prophecies about Atlas hidden, then only the Malaks knew of it. And probably only a select few. We just have to figure out *which* few and track them down." Talan surveyed the forest. "You want to get out of here and go somewhere less... rural."

For some reason, Kala didn't. As much as she despised being outdoors, at that moment it felt good. She could tune out the rest of the world and not have to deal with any of her problems. "Can we just sit here for a bit?" Kala plopped down on the ground and lay on her back. The sun filtered through the tight branches, letting small pockets of light touch her face. Despite the dry ground and sharp needles poking through her clothing, it felt amazing. "What time is it anyway?"

Talan lay down next to her but made sure he didn't make physical contact.

Their arms were less than an inch apart, but Kala was aware of the heat radiating off his body. It made her feel connected to him. More connected than if they were actually touching.

"Before you react, everything is going to be fine," Talan began.

She didn't like the sound of that. "It's Day Four isn't it?" The sun looked high in the sky, but she was in France. Her countdown clock was tied to the time zone where she became Atlas, which meant east coast time. France was five hours ahead.

Talan sounded surprised to hear how calm Kala appeared. "Not quite. You have about an hour. It's 4:03 AM your time."

Instead of picturing a clock with the time on it, Kala only saw the countdown.

1d 00h 57m 00s.

A little over twenty-four hours before she'd have to destroy Fortski's research. Or before Roberta would. Her heart desperately wanted to believe that Roberta *could*.

"Talan?" Kala spoke his name softly. "My mission is to destroy the cure for cancer." It felt good to admit it, especially to someone who would support her no matter what she did.

He was silent for a moment, then said, "Why would it be to destroy something that would help so many?"

Relief flooded through her. "Right? That's what I thought. It doesn't matter anyway. I'm not going to do it."

Talan paused. "Do you want to see what will happen if you *don't* do it?"

Kala briefly thought about telling Talan that Roberta would do the deed for her if she ran out of time, but she decided she'd take a look through his *future eyes* first. "Yes."

Talan reached his hand over and clasped Kala's. The familiar tingle sent a shiver through her body. It also made her feel safe. She relied more and more on Talan and his unending support. It went beyond physical chemistry and the fact that he was beautiful to look at. Only Jack, Derek and her foster parents had ever made her feel as protected as Talan did. Kala had relied on herself her whole life. It was difficult for her to trust anyone. But she trusted Talan. She trusted him with her life.

"Ready?" he asked.

She nodded.

The branches above her shifted and swirled as the familiar sensation of *Grigori vision* commenced. She saw the scene that had repeated on every TV or screen where she was about to demolish Fortski's computers. Instead of destroying them, the Kala in the vision started to walk away. On the wall was a digital clock. Five seconds until the end of Day Four. She waited to see what would happen.

Kala's stomach turned when the ground jolted beneath Fortski and vision-Kala. The building started to collapse as giant cracks split the walls.

Not again.

She knew then that it didn't matter what her task was.

It would always end the same.

The world would implode on itself.

The nature of the curse was built that way. If Atlas didn't do the horrible act, the planet would collapse.

"Take me out," Kala instructed Talan.

He broke their connection by releasing his hand from hers. She wanted to hold it for support, but she appreciated his respectfulness.

"I'm sorry," Talan said softly.

"It's okay. It makes sense, I guess. If the world didn't end every time, Atlas would have slacked any chance he could. I don't know what else I expected to see." Kala stared at the branches above. As much as the pine needles beneath her itched and scratched, it was a peaceful moment. Reality wasn't something she wanted to face. "I don't think I can do it," she confessed again. "But it needs to be done." Kala sighed. "Talan." She needed to own up to her plan. "I'm going to have someone else do it."

"What do you mean?" Talan turned to her.

"Roberta said she'd do it."

Talan's eyes said it all. He was trying to think of a way to let her down easy.

"Don't tell me it's impossible. She's going to try. She *wants* to do it. I don't. It's the perfect arrangement."

"Kala, if Atlas could have made people do his dirty work, he would have. Tricking humans into taking his place was the closest he ever came. Roberta won't be able to," he told her kindly.

She stood up angrily, brushing pine needles off her jeans. Her hatred of nature came back in a rush as she pricked her finger on one of them. "Can we get out of here now?"

Talan stood up next to her. "Kala, I'm sorry, but you're missing the point here."

"And what's the point?" She crossed her arms.

"*Why* does Roberta want to help?"

Kala hadn't thought about that.

It suddenly made her stomach turn.

"Because she's helpful?" Kala volunteered.

"I've been teaching Roberta and Turner for years now, and the woman can be kind at times, but she never does anything without a reason. The one thing I don't have access to is Fortski's secret project. He doesn't share it with anyone, not even his most trusted assistant, namely me."

"You know what? I don't care why she wants to do it. She'll do it. In the meantime, let's try and figure out how I can break out of this curse in the first place. I need to find Zeus." Kala was so angry and so frustrated she didn't want to think about Roberta and what her reasons were. All she could think about was Zeus, Zeus, Zeus! Why would he create something so stupid?! Why did he have to be crazy?! Why couldn't anything be easy?! She wanted to punch the Olympian in the face so bad it made her heart squeeze.

A tree would do nicely. Kala swung as hard as she could.

PUNCH!

"Ouch. You do realize you just attacked an invalid?" Asmodeus's voice grated on Kala's last nerve.

She had just punched Zeus in the face.

It took her a second to figure out where she was.

Kala stood in front of Zeus in Asmodeus's hideout.

Score.

DAY FOUR

Chapter Twenty-Three

Kala saw Asmodeus sitting at a small wooden table drinking a cappuccino. He smiled. "Guess you're tuned into me. I'm flattered."

"Don't be." Kala didn't like the implication. "I was imagining punching Zeus in the face and I guess the universe agreed with me."

"You keep leaving that Grigori for me. He's going to take it personally someday." He took another sip. "But I don't mind. I never liked that guy anyway."

"I hardly noticed." Kala rolled her eyes.

The place was a decent-sized room in what appeared to be some sort of mansion, or at least a very nice house. The décor consisted of Victorian era antiques, from the ornate table and chair that Asmodeus currently had his rump parked in, to the floral couch, wooden roll-top desk, and the heavy curtains framing a window overlooking fields of green grass.

Kala decided she had had enough with Asmodeus. Grabbing onto Zeus, she tried to teleport out of there.

Nope.

Asmodeus smiled. "The boss man put a no-teleport spell on the guy. Sorry." He stood up and walked over to her. "Cronus wouldn't like it that you're here, either, but I have a soft spot for you."

He reached out to touch her cheek, but Kala swatted his hand away. "You go sit over there. I'm going to talk to Zeus-man for a bit."

Asmodeus did as he was told, adding, "I hear that you actually took my suggestion and talked to Lotun."

"Yeah, and your *boss* took her away just before she could tell me the good stuff," she complained.

"He tends to do that." Asmodeus pretended to sympathize.

"You wouldn't happen to know what Cronus figured out about me, would you?" Kala thought she'd try.

"Why do you think Ms. Lotun isn't here with Zeus? Because Cronus doesn't trust me when it comes to you. He knows I have a weakness for you." Asmodeus shrugged.

She had no idea why Asmodeus felt the way he did about her, but she wasn't above using it against him. The problem was he kissed like a pro. It was too damn tempting. She really didn't want to do the walk of shame because she had made out with the king of Demons. It would be too humiliating.

"Lotun has another piece of the prophecy about me. She was about to tell me what being the Fated One means," Kala admitted. The whole thing was frustrating.

Zeus rubbed his sore nose, but he perked up his head at the mention of prophecy.

"Prophecy, prophecy, prophecy," he cackled. "The one who knows death; she'll be the one who breaks the curse."

Kala focused her attention on Zeus. "Do you know *the one who knows death*? It's a she? Who is she?" Question him while he was making slight sense, she figured.

Zeus cackled and cackled to the point where Kala wanted to punch him again to shut him up. Instead, she spoke as calmly as she could. "Please, Zeus, who is she?"

His eyes grew wide and he stopped laughing. "The daughter of the man who will sacrifice his life and his gift to save her. She is the one who knows death." He started to giggle again. "You don't have to wait long. She'll be born in three hundred years!" Zeus roared with laughter and began to babble incoherently again.

Kala froze.

Three hundred years?

"He's just messing with me." Kala spun around to Asmodeus. "Right?"

The Demon shrugged. "Could be, but to beings like us, three hundred years isn't that long."

Her heart dropped. "I'm in my twenties and I feel like I've lived a thousand years. I can't do this every four days for three hundred years! I can't!" Kala's mind felt like it was going to explode.

"Calm down, buttercup. Zeus is insane after all. He might be confusing prophecies or people or anything. No need to have a heart attack based on the word of a looney." He took another sip of his espresso.

Kala nodded. She knew Asmodeus was right, but Zeus's words felt true. Her deepest darkest fear was that she'd have to do horrible things forever. And three hundred years might as well be forever to her. As a human, she might have, at least, had some other Atlas wannabe kill her and take over. Morbid, but true. But since she was the full-blown Atlas now, she was stuck with the gig. For as long as the curse lasted.

"Even if it is true, at least you know the curse will be broken someday. That's positive, right?" Asmodeus shrugged his shoulders as if he was giving words of encouragement.

"But three hundred years?!" Kala tried to do the math in her head, but it was never her favorite subject. "That's... I need a calculator."

Asmodeus answered for her though, "It's 27,375 times if you wait the full four days every time."

Kala was stunned. "27,375 *acts of atrocity*!"

"See? That's not so bad." Asmodeus acted like this was proof that Kala was overreacting.

"Not so bad?! I'm going to go insane. There's no way. I'll be straight up evil by the end of it." Kala was beside herself at the mere thought. Every four days doing some vile, horrible thing. Sure, it saved the planet – but what about her? What about her soul? There was no way she wouldn't be destroyed by it. She couldn't even do her second mission, and if the world hadn't been crumbling beneath her feet, she would never have done the first.

"Evil is a bit strong. Jaded, maybe, but who isn't a little bit jaded?"

"You're not helping." She was tired of his positive spin on the whole thing. Especially coming from a Demon!

Kala took a deep breath.

She had listened to Zeus rattle on and on about nonsense. She was reading way too much into what he said. The god was crazy. Prophecy be damned, Kala wasn't one to abide by the rules anyway. Besides, she still was unclear as to what *the one who knows death* meant. Did the girl have some kind of relationship with the Grim Reaper? If all these gods, angels, and Demons existed, why couldn't there be a King of Death?

No more supposition. Kala reminded herself. *Think like a soldier. What's in front of me? What do I need to do right now?*

"I need to sit." Kala sat down on the old-fashioned couch. The cushion was hard but comfortable.

"Would you like an espresso? They're really quite tasty," Asmodeus offered.

She shook her head. "They remind me too much of my first encounter with Atlas."

Asmodeus snapped his fingers and a shot of tequila appeared in Kala's hand. "Your favorite."

She didn't argue. She drank it in one delicious gulp. It made her miss Derek terribly. He was always her drinking buddy in between missions. She wondered if he was okay and what he was doing. "Thanks." Kala placed the shot glass down on the ground next to her foot.

"Wow. A thank you. Wonders never cease." Asmodeus laughed.

"Don't let it go to your head." She smiled, despite herself.

"Never." He put his hands up in supplication.

"What am I supposed to do now?" Kala didn't expect an answer. She merely needed to speak her worries aloud.

"Interrogate crazy-pants here some more?"

"You're the one so desperate to track Zeus down. If Cronus knew you were here, he'd have me move him immediately, so I'd ask him while you can." Asmodeus nodded his head in Zeus's direction.

He was right. Kala had been a broken record claiming that all she needed to do was find Zeus, the god who was dumb enough to create her curse. And now he sat in front of her and he might as well be drooling. What did she hope to pull out of Zeus? What she *had* pulled out of him she didn't like very much. Kala just wanted him to get his brains back in order and reverse the damn spell!

The fact that Asmodeus had let her have this much time with Zeus was a testament to how much the Demon liked her. She had to admit, he was growing on her as well, in an annoying-brother kind of way. An annoying brother that happened to be ridiculously beautiful and a mind-blowing kisser. She didn't want to think about it. Kala was just grateful that Asmodeus allowed her to stay.

No time like the present.

Kala stood up and then kneeled in front of Zeus.

"Zeus?" She tried to stop his ranting.

After repeating his name a few times, the god finally went silent. Zeus stared at Kala with wide, child-like eyes. "I'll tell you something, but we have to be alone."

She looked over at Asmodeus, but he shook his head. "You know I can't do that."

"He can turn around, turn around, turn around," Zeus sang as if these were the words to his favorite song.

Kala pleaded to Asmodeus. "I'm not sure how long he's going to be coherent. Could you just turn your back or something?"

"Fine," Asmodeus sighed. He flipped his chair around and sat with his back to Kala and Zeus.

She focused back on Zeus. "Okay, he's turned around. Now what can you tell me? Can you break this curse?" She still didn't think she was above consuming him if she felt it necessary. Kala didn't want an insane Olympian stuck in her brain, but if it meant breaking the curse, she had to consider it.

Zeus motioned her forward. "Come closer. Secrets. Secrets."

Kala leaned in, her face only inches from his.

He whispered, "The prophecy. I know the rest of it. *He* can't know." Zeus nodded toward Asmodeus. "*He* doesn't want you to know. Neither does Daddy." He giggled. "But Daddy knows. He knows what you are."

Kala carefully took his hands in hers and their eyes met. "What is the prophecy? What am I?"

Zeus stared down at their touching hands. When he looked back up at Kala, his eyes were crazed. "Fix me now."

The words sounded strange to Kala's ears. She was about to ask him to repeat it when she felt an excruciating pain flood through her hands and to the rest of her body. She tried to move, but found that she was paralyzed. Not even her voice would work. With all her strength, Kala tried to scream out to Asmodeus, but Zeus had her locked in place.

His voice was barely above a whisper, "This won't kill you."

Small comfort.

The pain intensified. Kala tried to tap into the power inside her. To swallow him, to fight him, anything to stop the agony.

She found it right away. The spot where she had pulled her strength from before. But Kala couldn't touch it, couldn't use it, couldn't do anything with it.

Because Zeus was draining it dry.

The silent horror of what was happening made Kala feel completely useless. The pain started to wane, but so did her energy. She was losing consciousness. It was as if Zeus had tapped into her life-source. He was recharging. Healing himself. Kala could see it in his face. His eyes cleared up, his skin de-aged until he looked about thirty-something, his hair turned from white to brown.

And then Zeus had apparently taken what he needed, because he dropped Kala's hands. All of her functions returned to her, but she was so exhausted she could barely move a finger. She struggled to keep her eyes open. She wanted to stay awake. Zeus had used her. Sapped her. She was going to lose him.

Zeus cleared his throat to grab Asmodeus's attention. When Asmodeus didn't turn Zeus replied. "You really do have an affection for the girl. Such loyalty."

Asmodeus turned around at that.

Kala could see the terror and shock in Asmodeus's face at seeing Zeus fully restored and capable. Then worry and anger at Kala flopped out on the floor.

But Asmodeus was smart. He put his hands up in peace. "What did you do to her?"

Zeus laughed. Not the crazy-insane laugh like before, but an honest mirth at Asmodeus's words. "Nothing Ms. Hicks can't handle. She'll be back as new in a few hours."

Somehow that didn't make Kala feel any better. She could barely stay conscious.

"Asmodeus, you must choose. Me or my father?" Zeus put it to him candidly.

"Can't I be Switzerland?" The Demon raised an eyebrow with a hopeful smile.

"I don't understand that reference, but I'm assuming you don't want to decide just yet. I'll give you a few days to think it over, weigh your options. But know this: I plan on uniting everyone and everything against my father and if you don't stand with me, you will pay the consequences." Zeus's words were filled with power.

Kala tried to slap herself awake, but it was no good. Her body was completely depleted. She wanted to speak. To ask him questions. If he was at full strength he could break the curse. The obvious war that was coming didn't faze her. She didn't care about any of it.

Kala just didn't want to do horrible things anymore.

As if Zeus had heard, he peered down at her. "I'm sorry, little one. I'll need you on my side, so don't take what I did personally. My father will try and convince you to side with him, but you mustn't listen. He should not rule. He should never have ruled in the first place."

It took every ounce of strength for Kala to speak. "What... did you... do... to me?"

Zeus leaned down. Though his eyes were full of hope and kindness, Kala still wanted to punch him again if she were capable. "I'll let you discover that on your own. I'm sure my father will tell you as a way to gain your trust. You have something very old and very powerful inside you, Kala Hicks. Even before you consumed Atlas no supernatural being would have been able to harm you."

He sighed and smiled warmly. "The Fated One. I never thought I'd see the day."

"What… about the curse?" she croaked out.

His face turned sad and he shook his head. "As crazy as I was, I was telling the truth. A girl born three hundred years from now will be the one who breaks it. I would if I could but, if truth be told, I don't know how I created it in the first place. It was born of anger and madness. I had no control. But this girl. She will be very special. Like you."

Kala wanted to cry. She didn't want to believe the Olympian. She wanted him to be lying. Three hundred years of doing the unthinkable. It hurt her so deeply she couldn't stay awake any longer.

She just wanted to be unconscious so she wouldn't feel the pain anymore.

So she wouldn't feel anything.

Kala closed her eyes and fell asleep.

Chapter Twenty-Four

That didn't work.

Kala woke up encased in dirt.

She could breathe, though, which quashed her initial panic. Figuring it was because of her Atlas-side, Kala tried to find a way out.

Maneuvering her hands and arms was easier than she thought it would be. The dirt was loose so she was able to dig in an upward motion. Even though her nose, mouth, and eyes were caked in soil, for some reason it didn't bother her.

Normally, the mere thought of being buried alive would have terrified her, but for reasons she couldn't explain Kala felt comforted. It was as if the earth was blanketing her from all the horror she had faced her whole life.

After a few minutes of digging, Kala stopped. She wasn't making any headway and the longer she stayed in the dirt, the more at home she felt. For someone who despised nature, this sensation was completely foreign. Breathing made all the difference. It made her understand that the real fear was suffocating to death.

Kala didn't have that.

She knew she couldn't die like this.

Kala had no proof, but deep down, she just knew.

The longer she stayed, the stronger she felt.

She was recharging.

It was such a strange notion that she almost dismissed it entirely, yet the more she thought about it, the more she knew it was true. She could feel it. Literally, feel the part of herself that Zeus had drained gaining strength, pulling energy from the earth, from the life within it.

Was this a skill that Atlas had? But her secret-power-source was the part of her that devoured Atlas, so it had nothing to do with him.

Why would lying inside the dirt heal her?

Kala hated dirt.

She hated bugs. She hated camping. She hated all of it.

Give her a city and the girl was happy. Take her out to the woods and she was miserable. It had always been that way.

Now, she was buried alive and… loving it.

A part of her wanted to stay down there. If the world ended, she doubted she'd feel anything. She could just sleep. It would be so nice to rest. Really rest.

But like all good fantasies, Kala awoke from hers as two hands yanked her out of the earth.

She could barely see because of the cake of dirt covering

her face. The sun was so bright she had to squint to focus on anything. When her vision finally adjusted, she stared up at the man who pulled her from the ground.

Cronus.

Fantastic.

Kala replied warily, "Could you not electrocute me right now? I've had a very hard day."

"I'm not going to hurt you. I'm the one who buried you. To heal you." Cronus's voice was calm and what was worse... nice.

"Zeus said you'd be sucking up." Kala always used to feel jealous of powerful people because of the way everyone would always swoon and give them what they wanted. Now that the head Titan and the head Olympian were both vying for her favor: it felt gross. Fake. Annoying.

"You do feel better, don't you?" Cronus prodded.

She did.

Kala didn't want to give him the satisfaction though, so she cut to the chase. "What do you want?"

"Don't you want to know *why* you feel better?" Cronus watched Kala's reaction carefully.

Yes, she did, but she really hated it when people "fished." Lali used to do that. Of course now Kala knew her former team member was a Demon, so maybe it had been Lali's way of irritating Kala. Lali would always leave voice mails, such as *I have huge news, call me* or *You'll never guess what? Call me.* So the only way Kala could find out what happened is if she phoned back and asked. It was a serious pet peeve of hers.

Kala viewed her surroundings. An enormous mansion towered behind them. It looked like it was built hundreds of years ago, definitely European in its architecture. It reminded Kala of a BBC mini-series for a Jane Austen or Dickens novel. She had been buried in the back yard of this gigantic estate. The place where Cronus had pulled her up out of the earth ruined the perfectly manicured lawn.

"Well, don't you want to know?" Cronus lost his patience.

"You obviously want to tell me and I'm not going to beg." Kala shook her head. "I'm sick of being pulled back and forth between sides. I don't care what you people do to yourselves, just leave me out of it."

Cronus examined her with an unreadable expression.

Kala could tell he still wasn't used to her giving him attitude. She just hoped he wouldn't throw another lightning bolt in her chest.

"It makes sense, you know. Your attitude, your power, your abilities. I don't give much thought to prophecies unless they involve me, but I should have paid attention to yours," Cronus began. Then he motioned toward the house and a small garden area with table and chairs. "Would you like to sit?"

Kala glanced down at herself and comprehended how crazy she looked. She had a thick layer of mud and dirt over every inch of her body. "I think I need to wash up."

Cronus snapped his fingers. She was clean from head to toe.

"Nice," she approved. "Look, I've been dicked around since I met you and your little family. Just tell me what you know about me and the prophecy." She was tired of waiting. Tired of these *superbeings* lording over their knowledge. Knowledge about *her*.

Cronus nodded slowly. "Very well. I'll show you the prophecy and we'll see what you make of it." He waved his hand slightly and an old parchment appeared. Handing it to Kala, he said, "The complete prophecy."

Kala carefully took the parchment paper from him. The prophecy wasn't that much longer than Penny's, maybe a paragraph. But the last sentence that referred directly to her didn't make sense to Kala. It only confused her more:

One cannot live while the other one exists. A new Atlas shall reign and the potential must die. A beginning to the end and an end to the beginning. A new paradise shall be born. The Fated One will be the last.

The cost will be great, and the immortals will reign. The one that knows death will release the curse of balance. She will be born from the man with the power of death. He will sacrifice his life and his gift to save the balancer.

The Fated One is the first. The first of us all. The mother of us all, born into a human.

"What does it mean?" Kala peered up at Cronus.

Cronus smiled gently. "It means you were born with the power of Gaia."

Crickets.

"Who?"

Irritated, he accused, "You really don't know anything, do you?"

"I'm sorry if I'm not a history major. Just tell me who the hell Gaia is and why she's stuck inside me?" Kala felt a flood of relief, finally hearing some answers, but it was rapidly morphing into stress because she had more questions.

"Gaia is my mother," Cronus answered. "She's the Earth. As in *Mother Earth.*"

Kala could see that she had stretched Cronus's every last nerve. "And I'm her?" This was going nutzoid fast.

"A part of you, yes. But my mother has been sleeping for thousands of years. She is still very much alive. So, no, it's not like when you devoured Atlas. She simply placed a part of her power inside of you. But it was enough to consume Atlas, and it would be enough to consume any of us. Gaia's powers are endless, even a small piece of it. But, Kala, she gave you her power so that you could save the world from the Grigori." Cronus was dead serious.

Kala shook her head. "Oh, no. You're not going to rope me into this little battle of yours. Owen is my dad and Talan is my… well he's my… friend. And he doesn't attack me with lightning bolts!" Cronus was a professional manipulator. Zeus had warned her and he was right. Cronus was trying to twist the prophecy so he could get her to do what he wanted her to do. It aggravated her immensely. "AND…the prophecy doesn't say anything about stopping the Grigori, so you're full of it!"

"It may not say it directly, but *it's implied*," Cronus argued. He didn't like the fact that Kala didn't automatically fall in line. She could see that he expected it of her.

"You haven't been around humans in a really long time. You need to brush up on your persuasion skills. It's *implied*?! That's ridiculous. There was nothing about the Grigori implied or otherwise in that prophecy. You're scared they're going to take your power away and you want them sent back to their prison. Just be straight with me, I'd respect you a lot more." Kala wasn't going to put up with Cronus's bull for a second. If he thought she'd turn against the only father she had ever known, or the one being who had her back at every turn? Forget it. "You're delusional," she added for measure.

"I'm delusional?" Cronus was taken aback. "*The immortals will reign*," he quoted back to her. "Who do you think makes the immortals?"

"What are you talking about?" Kala wanted to slap some sense into this guy. "*You're* the immortals, all of you freakazoids, including me now that I wolfed down one of you. Grigori can't *make* immortals."

"Can't they? Let me show you what will happen if you *do* complete your mission." Cronus's eyes were full of fury and intensity.

It made Kala take a step back. "I don't want to see..." That was a lie. Kala desperately wanted to see *why* destroying the cure for cancer was a good thing.

Cronus cut her off. "You do. I can see it in your eyes. That pet of Talan's, John Fortski, invents something much more dangerous than a cancer cure. Because his research is destroyed, he has to start from scratch. It's because of that act that he discovers the formula that he's been working his whole life to make." Cronus's eyes were wide with dread. "Kala. He gives humans *immortality*."

Kala knew this was supposed to horrify her, but it gave her a sense of relief. If humans were immortal then they'd be cured of *all* diseases. "That's kind of cool," was her honest answer.

"Kind of cool? That could be the end to true immortal beings, including yourself, and you think it's *kind of cool!*" Cronus was furious.

"Don't get your panties in a bunch. I'm pretty sure you'll be just fine. Zeus said I'd be doing my job for another three hundred years. Yay. So, I think we're all going to be okay." Kala felt like she was dealing with a serious drama queen. A suit-in-tie-Titan drama queen, but a drama queen all the same. So what if humans found immortality? They'd certainly been looking for it for a long time. And it made Kala feel a lot better about her job. She still hoped Roberta could do it for her, but if she had to do it, now she knew Fortski would invent something even better. Balance. It was finally making sense.

"Do you want to see this wonderful future you think you're going to be living in?" Cronus had a look on his face that pretty much told Kala she couldn't refuse him.

Kala had seen what would happen if she didn't wipe out the cure: mayhem and destruction. There wasn't anything that Cronus could show her that would be worse than that. But she hadn't seen the future of what would happen if she *did* destroy it. Her curiosity could never say no to a *future vision*, so it made it easy for her to say, "Sure."

Cronus held out his hands and Kala tentatively took them. Trusting the Titan didn't feel natural. Considering the only time she'd had contact with guy ended up in some kind of super-battle, she felt pretty justified in her wariness.

But he held onto Kala without zapping or attacking her.

As with Talan, the vision flooded over her like she was watching a holographic movie. As the years flew by it was like watching humanity on fast-forward. And Kala saw the real problem with immortality.

There were too many, more and more people, to the point where it almost made her feel claustrophobic. On the ground, in malls, in the sky with lane upon lane of flying cars, humans were everywhere. No one died. People kept reproducing. How long could the earth sustain it? What was the point of immortality if the planet you lived on wasn't big enough?

Apparently someone else had the same idea, because the rest of the images that flew by her were a horrifying blur: men in hazmat suits exterminating people as if they were cockroaches, serial killers with free reign to kill, executions, staged natural disasters, all in poorer areas, all people who the rich wouldn't miss or even knew were gone.

Population control.

She felt Cronus's hands slide away. The vision stopped.

He looked at her with a sad expression on his face. "Your precious Grigori are teaching the man who is responsible for all of that chaos. He will rule the world someday if you don't stop them."

Kala couldn't imagine anyone killing that many people, even if it was for the greater good. Whoever this man was, he needed to be stopped. "Who?"

"Who do you think? General Geoffrey Turner," Cronus spat.

Turner? How? Why? What could possibly turn the man she admired so much into a mass murderer? It didn't make sense. It couldn't be real. She needed to talk to Talan. She needed answers from someone other than Cronus.

The Titan shook his head. "I won't let you complete your mission," he added with determination.

"But then the world will end."

"I'd rather end it all than see the future we saw come to pass," Cronus said.

"What are you going to do?" she asked, not wanting to hear the answer.

"I'll stop you by any means necessary."

Ominous.

Great.

Kala grumbled.

Chapter Twenty-Five

In a blink of an eye, Cronus disappeared and Kala was alone on the manicured lawn. She had no idea where she was. It could have been anywhere really. This whole teleportation power was pretty handy when she could control it.

Kala figured she'd better concentrate on Angel-Boy since she had a flood of questions to ask him, the first of which was how on earth Turner could be responsible for what Cronus had shown her. Knowing the man and working for his elite military team had given her special insight into Turner's character. She knew him to be fair, and honestly, a very helpful human being. Kala never would have survived her ordeal with Atlas without Turner and Roberta. Even if what she saw was true, maybe it really was to save the planet. Look at what *she* was being forced to do to stop the world from ending. As terrifying and horrible as the vision was, Kala knew the wisdom of never judging unless you'd walked in the other person's shoes. And Turner had never judged her. Neither had Roberta. Kala couldn't imagine that they'd kill so many innocent people. Maybe Cronus was lying, trying to turn her against them so that she would join his side.

She just didn't know.

Talan.

A second later, Kala was back in Talan's D.C. apartment.

At this point, it felt like home.

Talan was alone and sitting on his couch. When she popped in, he looked up, his face filled with concern. He stood up and met her from a respectable distance of about a foot. It felt like a mile. That was the problem with chemistry: you didn't have to be touching to feel it. Sometimes being across the room could be more torturous than holding hands.

Kala shoved her feelings aside. "I was with Cronus." Then she told him everything, from Zeus recharging his batteries, to the whole *Gaia* thing, to the future vision, to Cronus's threat to stop her from completing the mission.

Speaking of her mission made Kala glance at the clock.

0d 10h 33m 15s.

7:27 PM!

PM!

Before Talan could respond to her lowdown, Kala gasped. "I only have ten hours! What happened?!"

Talan gently touched her arm. He tried to hide his shock over everything Kala had told him. "You were probably in the earth for hours. Cronus was right, you needed to recharge after Zeus drained you."

It blew Kala's mind that she had rested comfortably in dirt

for what must have been at least thirteen hours. Her life now was so foreign to her, Kala was surprised she could function properly. It had to be her training as a soldier. Take one step at a time and only focus on what was in front of you. Without it, she would have been bonkers by now.

"It explains so much." Talan shook his head. "Gaia." Apparently, this made him awestruck.

"I'm still not sure what all this means. Talan, the future I saw…" Kala began.

His far-off look turned back into super-focus. "If Fortski does invent a cure to mortality, then over-population is the natural order. But mass murder? I've seen Turner make sacrifices most people would never consider just to save *one* soldier. It would have to be a pretty desperate situation for him to resort to killing innocents."

"Is there any way we could see? Maybe Cronus altered the vision to make me side with him." Kala didn't want to believe Turner was capable of what she saw. "Or maybe it wasn't Turner at all. I never saw him in the vision."

"One way to find out." He held out his hand.

Kala took it gladly. She needed to feel their connection. The energy that always passed between them. It invigorated her as much as it comforted her. She closed her eyes and waited for the vision to start.

Colors swirled and took form. It was the same future that Cronus had shown her: humans multiplying like rabbits. But before seeing the mass murders, though, she saw roads being replaced by grass and trees, water recycling plants, paper and packaging laws – so many things that improved the world it made her dizzy. But the people kept coming. Growing in number, taking over every inch of unpopulated land.

Turner was there. He was a leader, in charge of population control. He appeared to be very powerful. He was being told that the trees and grass weren't enough: the world was running out of oxygen. He had to think of something. He was in charge of keeping the human race alive. Him. Only him.

She'd seen enough.

Kala took her hands away from Talan's to make the vision stop.

"I know what happens next. I don't need to see it again." Kala didn't want to watch the killings. Cronus had been right, but he'd only shown her the worst parts. Whether his goal was to manipulate her or not, Kala knew that the murders were true. Kill in small amounts to save the many. As a soldier, she knew that mantra well. It was something that Jack believed in more than anyone she knew. It was why he'd begged her to kill him.

To save the world.

"It doesn't look like he'll have a choice." Talan seemed to be processing what he had witnessed as well.

"Is this what we want for human kind? Sacrificing innocent people just so the rest can live forever? Is immortality worth that? This doesn't seem like balance at all." Kala's anger rose steadily. "Curing cancer sounds way better!" She was venting now. "But because of this stupid curse, I don't even have a choice! If I don't destroy it, the world will end anyway! It's like the universe is blackmailing me!"

Talan carefully touched her arm, trying to stay within his bounds. "You can't control what the world sees as balance, Kala.

No one can. We may not like it, but that future is the one destined for mankind. If your curse didn't exist, the powers-that-be would have destroyed the cure for cancer some other way. It's destiny."

Kala shrugged away from his touch. "The Grigori are the ones that brought people into this new age. Maybe Cronus was right to imprison you."

She regretted saying it as soon as the words left her lips. Talan's face fell.

"I'm sorry," she started.

Talan cut her off. "No. You're right. We helped shape this future to come. But as horrible as some of it is, the marvels you humans have created and are going to create are miraculous. I don't regret what we did, I'm proud of it."

Kala didn't argue with him. She was simply upset by what she had seen. But she couldn't completely agree with Talan, either. Maybe Cronus was right; maybe the Grigori were too dangerous.

It didn't matter.

Kala was loyal to a fault.

Owen and Talan could be the devil themselves and she would still die for them. That was Cronus's big mistake, because he'd never be able to convince her to betray them. Having a childhood without any strong connections to anyone made Kala overly loyal to those she considered family. What could she expect from a Titan who would turn on his own father and then his own son? He'd rather let the world die than have a future where humans could potentially out-power him.

"You know I'll never turn against you, right?" Kala needed to say it aloud.

She could see from the expression on his face that Talan didn't know the extent of her loyalty.

She felt an overwhelming desire to comfort him. It was so strong she found her hand reaching out to touch his face before she could stop herself. "I know I can seem cold at times, and that I don't appreciate everything you've done for me, but I do. I really care about you, Talan." Expressing emotions was more difficult for Kala than being Atlas, but she wanted Talan to know she didn't take him for granted.

Talan reached up and held the hand that touched his cheek. Kala felt a thrill at his touch. Normally, she'd jump the guy and take out all her stress and aggression in wild, amazing sex, but she genuinely had feelings for Talan and she didn't want to ruin what they had. He already thought they were soul mates; having sex with him would just confuse things. Kala's heart belonged to Jack. She knew he was dead, but the emotional wound was still raw and fresh with pain.

But the longer he held her hand, the more she wanted him. It may have been pure chemistry and hormones, but Kala wasn't the poster child for restraint. Look at her kiss with Asmodeus.

Before she could think better of it, Kala leaned in and kissed him. Electricity raced through her as his lips answered her back in the most passionate kiss Kala had ever experienced. She could feel her brain turning to mushy-mush-mush as Talan pulled her in tight from the small of her back. Their bodies pressed against each other, Kala felt the heat between them like a living fire.

She didn't think she could stop.

She didn't want to.

Kala wanted to hold onto this sensation. It made her forget everything. It made her feel amazing. It made her feel alive.

232

She had thought Asmodeus was a good kisser, but Talan… It was so intense Kala's brain turned to jelly. Her mind could think of nothing else but his hands on her body, his lips on her mouth, and the ache in her chest only had her wanting more.

Kala could barely breathe it was so overwhelming. She took control and threw Talan on the couch so that she was on top. This only excited Talan more as he pulled her in close, grabbing on to her thighs as if he would devour her whole. His need for Kala fueled her passion.

As if coming to his senses, Talan pulled away slightly. "Kala, maybe we shouldn't…"

She shut him up by kissing him hungrily. She didn't want to hear logic or should we- shouldn't-we. Kala just wanted to lose herself in the physical pleasure she was experiencing. To forget everything and just be in this moment with someone that cared about her.

Deep inside Kala, she knew what she was doing was wrong. She cared about him, but she didn't love him. She only loved Jack. And he was gone forever.

To wipe the thought from her mind, Kala peeled off her shirt so she was only in her bra. She started to unzip Talan's pants.

Talan's hand gently stopped her. "You're not ready," he said breathlessly.

"You don't know what I'm ready for." She continued trying to take off his pants, but it was too late.

His words took over and jolted her into reality.

It hurt.

The pain in her chest squeezed and Kala couldn't stop it.

What was she doing?

So much had happened in the last four days, Kala hadn't had time to mourn Jack. Instead of dealing with it, she was trying to avoid it by using Talan and his feelings for her.

She didn't think she could feel any lower.

Kala was grateful that Talan had stopped them. Being with him would have made things so much more complicated. It was going to be bad enough from this make-out session alone. Was he going to turn all stalker-puppy on her?

Looking into Talan's eyes, she knew he wouldn't. She saw something in him that she had only seen in Jack.

He loved her.

It struck her like a bullet to the heart and she cracked.

"Don't look at me like that!" she yelled. But it was too late. She could feel the tears threatening to take over. Kala hardly ever cried. Only when she had killed Jack had she truly lost it. She learned early on that crying only led to more pain and never did her any good. Being a Titan – fighting gods, angels and Demons – those were close enough to being a soldier that Kala could deal. But *her feelings*? The flood of emotion threatened to drown her.

"I can't help how I see you." Talan reached out his hand and touched her cheek. "I know you don't feel the same, but I love you, even if you never love me back."

"Please, don't. I can't hear that. I..." Kala desperately tried to push down her emotions. "I miss him," her voice choked.

Talan held her and she fell into his chest. He stroked her hair as she took comfort in his arms. "I'm so sorry, Kala."

Normally, Kala would fight being held by any man, but she was tired. Tired of fighting, tired of her walls. As much as sex would have given her a momentary ounce of satisfaction, being with Talan and feeling him hold her close ended up being so much more fulfilling.

I've been waiting for your go-ahead, but time was running out and I happened to be in Fortski's lab... Anyway, I couldn't do it. I tried to smash his computers, but it was as if some kind of force field protected them. I thought they were Fortski's invention, but he looked just as shocked as I did... Hello?... Kala? Are you there?

It was such a shocking moment, having Roberta jump into her brain just then, that Kala forgot how to respond back. But Roberta's words started to sink in.

Kala sighed heavily.

Roberta couldn't do it.

Of course she couldn't.

Kala knew this from the beginning. She merely enjoyed living in denial for a while.

Where are you now? Kala asked.

Oh, thank God, I thought Clifton had found some way to shut down our communication. Kala, I'm in trouble. You're going to have to find Geoffrey.

A knot twisted in Kala's stomach. *What happened?* She asked with dread.

Fortski flipped out as you can imagine... Kala... Clifton has me in the Compound, and I don't think he plans on letting me out. Ever.

Kala's head hurt. This was all her fault.

I'm on my way.

Chapter Twenty-Six

Quickly dressing herself, Kala pulled away from Talan, a spring in her step. Missions. She liked those. At least the kind that meant saving someone and not doing something unconscionable.

Talan was alert. "What is it?"

"Roberta just *mind-melded* me and she's in trouble. Clifton has her prisoner for trying to destroy Fortski's lab."

"Did it work? Was she able to do it?" Talan seemed genuinely curious.

"No, Mr. Smarty Pants, you were right. She said it was like some sort of force field."

"Only the Atlas can perform the Atlas duty." He nodded as if this news confirmed everything he had ever thought.

Kala wasn't up for a round of I-told-you-so, so she laid out her plan. "Let's teleport inside the Compound, grab Roberta, then take her to Turner. I can worry about the mission in…" She glanced at the clock. "Nine hours, really?" The countdown began to crush her soul yet again, but focusing on Roberta's rescue helped.

"I'm with you." Talan clasped her hand.

Together they focused on the Compound.

Nothing.

Kala concentrated as hard as she could.

Still nothing.

Talan took his hand away. "Something's wrong. You don't think Rotoph is blocking teleportation again?"

A sinking sensation roiled in Kala's gut.

I'll stop you by any means necessary. The words repeated over and over in her head.

"Cronus," she said aloud.

Talan nodded. "He's blocking us from teleporting in."

"I'll have to do it the old-fashioned way, I guess." Kala shrugged. "Time to talk to Turner and Derek."

Talan was on board. He gripped her hand.

***

The next second they were in Turner's house. His living room, to be precise.

Kala eyes met Derek's.

A surge of warmth spread through her body and she felt as if her heart would explode where she stood. Seeing his beautiful brown eyes and dazzling smile made her happy beyond measure.

Derek ran over to her and picked her up off her feet in a giant bear hug. Kala enjoyed the moment as long as she could, which lasted until Derek put her down.

"I was worried about you," he said. His face radiated relief at seeing her alive and well.

"I'm kind of hard to kill nowadays." Kala bumped up against him playfully.

Turner stepped into view, seemingly amused at finding Kala and Talan in his living room. "What brings you two here?"

Kala didn't want to be the one to tell him, but she needed his help. "Clifton is holding Roberta in the Compound."

Turner's face turned pale. "Why would Harry detain my wife?"

She could see the anger starting to boil inside Turner and she didn't want to admit the situation was her fault, but she needed him to know everything. "She was doing me a favor…"

Turner cut her off with his hand. "Is this about the cancer thing?"

Kala nodded. "I didn't know…" What didn't she know? She knew it was dangerous. She knew Roberta was risking herself. She knew it probably wouldn't work. But did she stop Roberta? Did she ever consider the consequences? She was ashamed to admit that the answer was *no*.

Turner was dialing his cell phone. He put it on speakerphone.

"Hello?" General Clifton's voice came through the cell phone in a casual tone.

"Harry? What on earth are you doing with my wife?" Turner accused abrasively.

"Excuse me? What are you talking about? What would I want with Roberta?" Clifton sounded irritated.

He put on a good show. If Kala hadn't known for certain that he had taken Roberta, she might have believed him.

Turner shook his head. "I know you have her, Harry. Let her go and I'll forget this ever happened."

"Where is this coming from? Why would Roberta be at the Compound anyway? I'm telling you the truth. I don't know where she is." Clifton's sincerity was flawless.

This guy was good.

Turner wasn't easily fooled though. "You're honestly going to sit there and lie to me?" He paused, not sure how to proceed. Then his anger erupted, "Deny it all you want, but I have my sources and I know you've taken her. If you harm one hair on her head, they'll never find your body." He hung up.

The fire in his expression was something Kala had never seen in Turner. It was murderous. He'd rip Clifton from limb-to-limb to save Roberta and wouldn't think twice about it. Seeing that look made Kala grasp that his love for his wife was the only motivation he needed to kill innocents in the future she'd witnessed. If Roberta's life was on the line, there was nothing Turner wouldn't do, of that Kala was certain. He had said as much when she asked him what he would have done if his mission had been to kill Roberta. *I'd let it burn.*

And he would.

Right now, Turner looked like he was going to burn Clifton to the ground.

"You're positive Harry has her?" Turner already knew the answer, but he needed to hear it.

"Roberta told me herself." Kala tapped her head.

"Well, you heard him. He's denying the whole thing. He's always been jealous and he's always wanted her for himself. He's

239

going to try and keep her like a possession. The man is insane."

Kala wondered why Turner would have worked with Clifton for so long if he really felt that way, but power created odd bedfellows. Time could build up resentments, destroying the strongest of friendships. If Clifton really did have feelings for Roberta before Turner came along, it must have been pretty painful to watch another man swoop in and marry her whether it was his best friend or not.

"Can't you teleport in there?" Turner asked, his anger intensifying.

"We're being blocked again," Talan informed him.

"That's why we came to you," Kala replied. "We're going to have to break her out. Without magic."

Turner didn't seem fazed by this in the least. "I've got a bag of tricks Clifton knows nothing about." Focusing on Kala, his expression left no room for argument. "Roberta is the mission. I don't care about your *Atlas* thing, understand? Once Roberta is safe, I'll give you access to Fortski's lab and you do what you need to. Are we agreed?"

Being a Titan, Kala shouldn't have felt intimidated in the least, but the man radiated more power than Cronus. He really would rule the world. Kala envied the love Turner and Roberta had for each other. She had chosen the world instead of Jack. If Turner had been in her place, the earth would have crumbled by now. The thought stung in a way she never expected. Kala shook it from her mind and didn't bat an eye as she said, "Roberta's mission one. Agreed." Going after Roberta somehow made her feel better. As if doing this would make what she did to Jack hurt less.

"I'll let Mr. Echolls take you to my own personal Cog." Turner motioned for the two of them to go.

Kala's heart jumped in her throat. The Cog in the Compound was full of insanely advanced technological inventions designed solely for combat. If Turner had a Cog of his own, she was excited to see what toys he had.

Turner nodded to Talan. "You. I need your eyes. I have my own security cameras stationed around the Compound. If there are any of your angels or Titans around, you'll be able to recognize them, correct?"

Talan's eyes lit up. "Yes." He looked at Kala. "I'll gather the Grigori that passed through the portal and we'll take care of Cronus."

Kala was worried about whether or not the Grigori could do much to Cronus. Maybe their combined powers could at least distract him long enough for her to complete her mission and get the hell out of the Compound. Breaking in would be hard enough, but escaping would be so much easier if she could teleport Roberta and Derek to safety. "Be careful," she said.

"You too." Talan smiled, then walked with Turner to another room.

Kala turned back to Derek. He was grinning. "What's that look for?"

"That guy is in love!" He laughed.

"Shut up." Kala punched him in the arm.

"Have you beat him up yet? It seems to be a pattern with you," Derek teased.

"You seriously suck so hard right now. Can you just take me to Turner's Cog?" Kala smiled, but she wanted to change the subject. Even joking about Talan's feelings for her made her uncomfortable.

Derek picked up on her mood change right away because he observed, "I get it. I never thought I'd see the day when Kala Hicks actually had feelings for someone other than friendship."

Apparently, Kala's face was an open book. A thought struck her: Derek never knew about her and Jack. She had never told him and he had never picked up on it. Of course, after the rollercoaster ride of the last eight days, the subject of her love life never came up. Did Derek even know that Jack was dead?

Kala stopped him in the hallway. "Derek."

Seeing Kala's seriousness made Derek pause. "It's none of my business I was just teasing you…"

She shook her head. "Jack's dead."

He stared at her for a few moments, then nodded in acceptance. "These supernatural freaks take him out? Is that why you're so protective of me?"

"I'm protective of you because you're my family, but Derek…" Kala didn't want to tell him, she wanted to blame anyone else for Jack's murder. She couldn't bear to see the look of disgust on Derek's face when she admitted her guilt. Taking a deep breath, she charged forward, "*I'm* the supernatural freak that killed him." The catch in her voice was unavoidable. Saying it aloud to Derek hurt her more than she could have imagined.

"Was he *evil?*"

It was obvious that Derek had complete faith in Kala. He trusted her judgment and if Jack needed to be killed, then he needed to be killed. It made it all the more painful for her.

"No. It was my Atlas mission. If I didn't kill him the world would collapse. That earthquake you felt a few days ago? That was me not wanting to go through with it. I almost let the world end to keep him alive, Derek." Kala shoved down her tears as much as she could. "I loved him."

Instead of the hate and disappointment Kala expected to see in Derek's eyes, she saw recognition and understanding. He could have condemned her right there, and she would have understood completely, but instead…

He hugged her.

It was the last thing Kala expected.

She clung to him, sapping out every ounce of comfort she could.

"You saved us all, Kala. Jack would be proud."

The words were meant to reassure her, but they slashed her heart in two. The image of Jack's lifeless body collapsing to the floor from *her* bullet would stay with Kala forever. And the hardest part to come to terms with was the fact that Derek was right: Jack *would* be proud of her. For some reason, that made it worse.

She pulled away, regaining her composure. Kala needed to keep her emotions bottled up if they were going to rescue Roberta.

But Derek wasn't ready to let Kala off that easy. "I'm sorry about Jack." He paused then shook his head. "I can't believe I never saw it."

"Lali saw it and she was a Demon." Kala's way of squeezing out of intense moments was with humor.

"She's a Demon?" That took Derek by surprise.

"*Was.*" Kala understood he had no idea that Lali was dead either.

Derek's smile faded and Kala felt a swarm of guilt rush over her. In the span of two minutes she had told him that the other two members of their tight-knit crew were gone. Whether Lali was a Demon or not didn't matter. They had spent enough time together that the four of them were inseparable.

Derek was all she had left.

"I didn't mean to make light of it..." Kala was at a loss.

Derek processed his emotions the way Kala did. He took a few moments, then nodded. Slowly he cracked a small smile. "I can see the Demon thing. Lali wasn't exactly friendly."

Kala smiled back. "We're okay, right?"

His expression was serious. "We're more than okay. We're family. You're never getting rid of me."

Kala didn't bother to hide her relief as she sighed, "Good. Now, can we start this mission or not?"

Derek grinned as he led the way to Turner's Cog. "You're the one spilling her guts."

"Shut up." Kala couldn't help but feel happy. Derek always knew her moods – when to push and when to pull back. She rubbed her hands together, readying herself for the Cog. "Let's do this."

After a few more hallways, they arrived at a steel metal door with a DNA scanner next to it. Derek stuck his thumb in and with a KERPLUNK, the door slowly swung open. He turned to Kala before they entered. "This stuff is insane."

She was ready to see what toys they could use. Derek opened the door the rest of the way and motioned Kala inside.

The room was big and cluttered, not at all like the Cog in the Compound. Of course, that one was neat and orderly for secrecy, with every door sealed up, hiding what was behind it. Here, it was a free-for-all for gadgets and gizmos. The actual space was about the size and shape of a semi-truck, long and narrow. The more Kala examined the area, the more she noticed that what had seemed like a mess of wires and metal was actually a structured workspace.

"Do you know what all this stuff does?" she asked, a little jealous that Derek had free rein of Turner's personal technology.

"About a tenth of it. A lot of these devices are still in progress, but some of them would blow your mind." Derek smiled, then thought better of his statement. "Although with your *super powers* maybe it wouldn't." He shrugged.

Kala said playfully. "Ha, ha. Trust me, I'd rather deal with technology than my spotty teleportation skills. I kind of suck at all this stuff. I miss being a soldier."

Derek looked thoughtful. "You'll always be a soldier, Kala. Now you're just a soldier in a more powerful army."

"I guess, but I miss the days when everything was a little more black and white."

He sighed with a laugh. "So do I. Demons, angels, gods, Titans... seriously? And *you*. You're freaking *Atlas*. Now I know why you kept asking me if you were hallucinating. That's how I feel all the time lately."

"Well, I'm still not ruling out that possibility." She shook her head. "I'm glad we're together though."

"Me, too."

Derek knew his way around and led Kala directly to a metal workbench that had three pairs of goggles lying on it. The goggles were a spectacle unto themselves, they had so many tiny levers and buttons attached to them. It reminded

Kala of the night vision goggles she'd used in the past, but more complicated and smaller. Next to each pair was an egg-shaped metal device the size of a thimble.

"Say hello to our eyes." Derek grabbed a pair of the goggles and handed them to Kala. "Put them on. Let me show you."

Kala placed them on, but all she saw was Derek standing in front of her. There was nothing special about the view through the lenses. "Should I press some buttons or something?"

"Hold on, Miss Impatience." Derek picked up one of the metal eggs, pressing a button that opened it up.

The egg appeared empty inside which made Kala want to say something, but she waited for Derek to show her what the device did.

"Okay, now..." Derek reached over and flipped a lever on the side of Kala's goggles.

Tiny pinpricks of red dots flowed out of the small egg.

"Nanobots." Kala recognized.

"Phase-nanobots." He grinned.

Kala looked up at Derek with surprise. "Like the suits?" If the nanobots were like phase-suits they'd be able to move through any wall, and being so small, no one would ever know it. She hated phase-suits with a passion. Walking through walls wasn't a great experience; her propensity for motion sickness didn't help much, either.

He nodded. "Those goggles not only control the bots, they're equipped with cameras as well."

"That's great for seeing what we need to see, but how are we going to break in?" Kala was thrilled with having eyes in the Compound, but without teleportation, she needed some way to get inside.

Derek gave her an apologetic shrug, motioning to the wall behind them.

Hanging off two hangers were the dreaded phase-suits.

"Fantastic."

Chapter Twenty-Seven

After changing into the phase-suits, Kala remembered the last time she wore one. The night she shot the President, who happened to be the current *Atlas surrogate*. It wasn't a pleasant memory, so she tried to focus on what lay ahead instead. The suit was a tight fit and every inch of her body needed to be covered. Body parts could be left behind if they were exposed, and Kala wasn't about to let that happen. She kept the hood off for the time being so she could see better. The thin mesh that covered the face allowed for vision, but it was still a bit cloudy. Her new goggles hung loosely around her neck. If anyone saw them, they'd think they were about to go swimming, since the outfits resembled wet suits, a detail that had saved their cover many-a-times before.

Kala and Derek joined Turner and Talan in Turner's surveillance room. The fact that this room existed in his personal residence showed Kala how paranoid the man was. Or, at least, how well-informed he was, depending on which way one looked at it. There were wall-to-wall screens, showing almost every angle of the Compound both inside and out. A long metal table with a single swivel chair was the only furniture in sight. Everywhere Kala looked, there was a different screen. With thousands of screens surrounding her, it felt as if she was inside a fly's eye.

"Why do we need the bots if we have all this?" Kala motioned to the mass of monitors.

Turner responded, "This is only half of the Compound. There are hundreds of rooms I haven't managed to slip a camera in. Clifton pretends not to know what I'm up to, but he's just as duplicitous. It's a game we play, and this time it's to my disadvantage. He has Roberta in one of his private rooms and we need the bots to figure out which one."

"What about Cronus? Did you spot him on the cameras?" Kala found it hard to fathom that, with all the screens she was staring at, it only showed half the Compound. She never knew how big the structure actually was.

Talan indicated one of the monitors. Sure enough, there was Cronus, dressed as a security guard, with no one giving him the time of day.

Turner pointed out, "I tried having him removed, but as you can guess, anytime anyone came near him they turned away, completely forgetting their task. Some even forgot who they were, so getting the Titans to leave won't be easy."

"Titans?" Kala didn't like the sound of that.

Talan specified three more screens showing Hyperion, Themis, and Kala's favorite, Iapetus. The three of them were spread out around the outside of the Compound. Though they were clearly visible on screen, their powers kept humans away from them. "Cronus is the strongest, so he's staying inside in case his brothers and sister fail. The Grigori will try and lure them to one place and attack. The Titans carry the sacred blades, but thanks to you we have three plus yours."

"And you outnumber them," Kala reminded him.

Talan conceded her point. "True, but they've been gaining power for the last 2,000 years while we've been imprisoned. I don't know how well we're matched anymore." Talan appeared worried. "We won't have to fight long in any case. The Titans are only here to stop you from completing your mission. If they can stall long enough for you to fail..."

"I won't fail," Kala interrupted, then faced Turner. "Roberta first, but as soon as she's safe I have to destroy Fortski's research."

Turner nodded. "You do what you please. I'm not interested in the world ending, so I'll give you as much leeway as I can after Roberta is safe and sound in my arms."

"I'm more worried about Cronus than Clifton and his men, but they are going to be a pain," Kala complained. She eyed the clock.

0d 2h 55m 33s: 2:05 AM.

"Less than three hours. We'd better get a move on." Kala's adrenaline was on overdrive. As horrible as destroying the cure was, it felt like any other operation at this point. It was nothing like killing Jack. Nothing ever would be.

Talan teleported away, back to Owen and the others. Turner gave Kala and Derek the rendezvous point where they were to deliver Roberta. Less than two weeks ago Turner was Kala's boss, now they were working together as equals. It was a surreal moment, but at least part of it felt familiar. It was nice performing a mission for Turner again. It almost felt like old times, except for the fact that she was about to break into her own headquarters and fight men she had worked beside for the last few years.

Derek seemed a lot less fazed by that particular aspect. After working solely for Turner, she noticed he had no problem fighting Clifton's men. Kala couldn't really blame him. There was always a bit of a divide between Turner's favorites and Clifton's favorites. Clifton surrounded himself with arrogant a-holes, while Turner gravitated towards the unique or the intelligent. Even through kidnapping Roberta and lying about it, she'd bet her life that the two of them would act as if it never happened once Roberta was safe. It was such a strange and demented relationship. It made Kala grateful for her own healthy friendships. Of course, most of hers were with non-humans, but she was grateful anyway.

Loading up in a Compound Jeep, Kala made sure she had two handguns strapped underneath her suit. Cronus had stopped anyone from teleporting in, but he may have put some kind of *no magic zone* in as well. She didn't even know if he could do that, but Kala wanted to have a way to defend herself. Prepare for all possibilities. It was her way of life before becoming Atlas. Now it was more vital than ever. Dealing with humans was one thing, but dealing with the supernatural? Best to be ready for anything.

They were silent as Derek drove toward their destination. He was taking back roads to avoid any contact with the public and more importantly, surveillance. Clifton utilized anything and everything, including traffic cameras, so they didn't want to take the chance of alerting him of their approach. Although covered by the darkness of morning and driving with no lights, made it easier to stay hidden.

After thirty minutes, Derek parked under an outcropping of trees about a mile from the Compound's warehouse front. Turner assured them that the phase-suits were capable of passing through the special black metal of the Compound, but Kala was a little apprehensive.

Derek went around to the back of the car and pulled out a round piece of metal two inches thick and about thirty inches in diameter. Kala wanted to ask what it was, but she figured she'd find out soon enough. With her phase-suit and goggles, what was another gadget to add to the undertaking? At least all these things were grounded in science. Magic and powers were still hard for Kala to wrap her head around. It probably explained her lousy success rate at teleporting. Tangible inventions were much easier to swallow.

"We have to stay low to the ground. There's some tree cover that will hide us." Derek didn't wait for a response as he led Kala forward toward the warehouses, holding the large metal circle under his arm.

Kala figured the device had something to do with reaching the walls of the Compound itself. Since there was about a half a mile of dirt between her and the first wall, the biggest problem would be getting down. Derek and Turner seemed positive that their way in wouldn't alert Clifton. She didn't know what a metal circle would do, but at this point Kala had to rely on trust. She had no choice. There was no other way. She really wanted to send a lightning bolt up Cronus's arse for being such a baby. The fact that the Titan was doing all this to make the world end because he was too scared of human immortality was such a pouty-toddler move.

But she couldn't think about that now. She needed to focus on finding and freeing Roberta. The Atlas mission was always lingering on the outskirts of her thoughts, but it wasn't something Kala wanted to think about. It was priority number two and as a soldier, she had to complete her tasks in order of importance. Roberta was number one. It occurred to her how stupid that sounded, since saving Roberta accomplished nothing in the big scheme of things, whereas destroying Fortski's cure would *save the world*.

It was amazing though, how her brain could rationalize why rescuing Roberta was more important. Atlas missions were too painful. Kala needed to feel the rush of doing something good. Something right. And saving Roberta would accomplish that. The woman had saved her life. She had taught Kala how to fight Demons and Malaks when she was a vulnerable human. Kala owed Roberta, and she wasn't about to desert her. Not now. Not ever.

"Here it is." Derek stopped about a quarter mile from the first building. They were in a section of trees that weren't as dense as the others were, but Kala still felt safe behind the large trunks, especially in the darkness. Derek had picked this location because it was one of the few blind spots of the main camera system that Clifton had access to.

He dropped the metal disc on the ground. Kneeling down, Derek touched its surface; a small keypad lit up. He punched in a code and the circle started to spin, making almost no noise. Then it dropped, fast, through the dirt like a silent missile.

Derek explained, "It has a sensor for the type of metal the Compound is made of, so it won't make a sound to alert anyone. The area we're above is mainly for maintenance, but we still have to be on our toes."

Within seconds, the device hovered back up to the surface and Derek pulled it aside, revealing a perfect thirty-inch diameter tunnel with a small cloud of smoke coming out, drifting into the wind. Kala could only assume that the dust was what was left of the dirt that had magically disappeared. Technology that could dissolve soil was pretty darn cool in Kala's book.

She was definitely impressed, but it still didn't answer the question. "How are we going to get down a 2,600 foot shaft?"

"Oh, ye of little faith," Derek teased as he threw her a black metal box.

"Ah, got it." Kala grabbed the box. She had used one once before, on a mission overseas, when she had to rappel down a castle wall. It was a dangerous escape and without this little gadget, Kala probably wouldn't have made it. It was small in size, only three inches tall on each side, housing a cable the circumference of dental floss inside. The box could attach to any solid surface and hold up to five hundred pounds of weight.

Kala turned to the nearest tree and placed the apparatus on the bark. Like superglue on metal, the invention stuck to the tree with no chance of pulling it off. The thin cable popped out with a tiny half-inch carabiner attached to it. She secured it to her phase-suit and was ready to rappel down.

Derek was already equipped and on the lip of the tunnel by

the time Kala joined him. "Me first." He smiled.

"If you recall, I'm the one who has better recovery time with phase-suits." Then she smiled back. "And I am kind of a god now."

He moved aside and Kala started the lengthy trek down the rabbit hole.

It wasn't long before Kala's feet touched the smooth black metal of the Compound's roof. Never in a million years did she imagine she'd be breaking into this place. She honestly didn't think it was possible, not by mundane means anyway.

Being down in the cylinder of dirt, Kala felt the raw energy. At first, she thought it was her adrenaline pumping for the task at hand, but it was the earth itself.

Gaia.

She hadn't processed the whole Gaia-being-a-part-of-her revelation just yet. The only perk seemed to be shocking the hell out of all the big guns like Cronus, the Grigori, and... Zeus.

Thinking of him made her cringe. He was back and at full power. The god had drained her like a battery then left to do who-knows-what. Nothing good, of that, Kala was sure.

Derek hung above her head. The two of them couldn't stand next to each other in the small circumference, so she'd have to go in first.

Activating her phase-suit, Kala felt the familiar sensation of passing through a solid surface as if it were made of liquid. Teleportation was easy compared to this. Talk about something not being natural. The wall was thicker than she expected, well over four feet, so at one point most of her body was encased in the ceiling. Kala remembered to stay still and let gravity pull her the rest of the way through. It was more claustrophobic than being buried in the dirt by Cronus.

Finally, Kala dropped to the floor. She pulled back her hood, taking deep breaths to relieve herself of the side effects of phasing. A moment later Derek was by her side.

No one was in sight.

So far so good, Kala thought.

She just hoped she wasn't jinxing herself.

Chapter Twenty-Eight

Kala made a quick rundown of the space they were in. It was definitely some kind of storage area. The doors were closed, but marked with signs indicating what was inside. Mainly cleaning supplies and science equipment. Nothing that required surveillance or sentries. Turner certainly knew the Compound inside and out to drop them into one of the few areas that didn't have security. She was still on guard, though, never underestimating Clifton or her circumstances.

Derek wasted no time as he popped open the small metal egg filled with the nanobots and let them loose. "You can contact Mrs. Turner with your mind, right?"

Kala nodded, but internally she wasn't so confident. Head-jumping was still new to her and she didn't feel she could rely on it.

Roberta? Kala called out in her head. She felt like some kind of crazy person talking to her imaginary friend.

Waiting was also strange, as if a phone was ringing and no one was picking up.

Relief washed through her when Roberta's voice answered, *Are you in the Compound?*

Yes. We're on the west side. Do you know where Clifton has you?

No. I've never been here before. Harry is acting like he's keeping me for my own protection. He told me that Geoffrey is on a mission and may not make it out alive. I can tell he's lying, but I have to know: is Geoffrey safe? Roberta tried to hide the worry from her voice.

Kala remembered Turner saying that Clifton secretly wanted Roberta for himself. Maybe this was some kind of ruse to convince her that Turner was dead so she'd be with him. How pathetic.

He's completely safe. He's at your house watching from his surveillance room. The room where Clifton is holding you isn't on his radar though. Can you tell me anything about where you are? Kala knew the Compound as well as any soldier, which meant about a quarter of it. But anything could help.

Let me think. Roberta paused. *After his men took me from Fortski's lab, we went up at least one, maybe two flights of stairs, then we walked for at about ten minutes. I just don't know in which direction. I'm sorry I can't be more useful.*

No, that's a good start. We'll be there soon. Kala tried to comfort her.

Harry is treating me well. Tell Geoffrey not to worry about me.

And then Roberta was out.

Derek had waited patiently while setting up the nanos and adjusting his goggles accordingly. "Where we headed?"

He reached over to Kala and flipped a couple of levers on her goggles. She saw the tiny pricks of red light. They looked like microscopic ants, all legs, ready to invade.

"She's either one or two floors up from the lab. She said she walked for about ten minutes, but she doesn't know which direction. Any ideas?" Kala surveyed their area, making sure no one was coming.

All clear.

"There are only two ways they could go on the second and third floor. We'll have to divide the nanos." Derek placed his thumb on the opened egg and a small holographic screen popped up.

"Whoa." Kala was fascinated. She had thought holo-technology was off in the future, but seeing now that Turner already utilized it made her understand just how advanced his research was.

"Pretty cool, huh?" Derek was amazed as well. He punched in a couple of numbers and the holograph turned into a flat map of the Compound. "We'll send them through these spaces here... and here." He pointed to a long line of rooms to the north and south of Fortski's lab on the second and third floor. "These are the areas Turner doesn't have eyes on. She has to be in one of them." Derek traced a line over the two sets of rooms.

Before Kala could react, the nanobots were off, moving faster than she expected. She could see both her perspective and theirs. Kala had to close her eyes because she was seeing double and it made her sick. It almost felt as if she was in an Atlas memory.

Derek apparently could see her discomfort; he leaned over and adjusted a lever on her goggles. "You can lower the opacity on the image. It won't be so disconcerting. I know you and your motion sickness." He smiled.

The image faded and now appeared as a light overlay. Kala's head cleared after a few moments of deep breaths. "I'm good."

More than good. The whole thing was fascinating. The nanobots traveled straight through every wall as if the surface was made of liquid. Kala watched what looked like a faded movie as the nanos raced through each room. She could see scientists, guards, soldiers, all working, none of them the wiser. If they only knew there were tiny robots crawling above their heads and flying through the walls.

"They're about to split. Keep your eyes out for Roberta," Derek instructed.

Kala and Derek stayed off to the side of the hallway so they'd be out of view from anyone who happened to pass by. Kala knew that once they found Roberta they'd be on the move. When the nanos moved in different directions, the screen in Kala's goggles divided in two so she could see both views. Staring straight ahead helped her to see both nano aspects objectively.

"Got her," Derek announced.

Kala saw Roberta a second later. She sat on a couch in a small room on the south side, two guards stood at the door.

Derek controlled the nanos through the metal egg device. He made both teams of bots join back together to survey the entire area.

Kala had to blink hard a few times to keep herself from succumbing to nausea. Being Atlas and having the use of teleportation was actually a boon to Kala, who had always turned a bit green when travelling by conventional methods.

Derek made the nanos seek out every possible way into Roberta's prison. The path of least resistance was through a couple of empty storage rooms coming in through the west wall, which meant at least ten more phases.

Kala had never done that many in one mission. Usually it was one wall and she was in. Being a Titan, Kala knew her body could take it, but she was more worried about Derek. "Maybe I should go alone. I don't want the phase-suit to wreck you," Kala volunteered.

"I'll be fine. They've been rated for twenty entries. This is ten." Derek left no room for argument.

So Kala didn't bother.

"Roberta doesn't have a phase-suit, so we can't go back the way we come in. Also, there are twenty soldiers between her room and the lab." Kala pointed out the obvious.

"That's why we're phasing into her room. There are *two* guards." Derek looked at her with a smile, but he might as well have said, *duh.*

"But we'll be recognized." Kala saw the genius in having the soldiers on the inside of the room so no one would suspect a switcheroo, but at some point somebody would identify two of Clifton's Most Wanted. They didn't exactly blend.

Derek tapped his chest. "I have another toy from Turner. It'll make us look like the soldiers we swap with. If anyone stops us, we'll just claim that we're moving the prisoner."

"Right. I'll just shut up now." Kala wished he had told her earlier about the magic-disguise gadget, but right now she was just relieved he had it. "Couldn't we just use it now and disguise ourselves?" Kala tried to think of all possibilities.

"Kala, seriously. You don't think I've thought of all this? We need to scan their faces and these two soldiers are Clifton's main guys. It's why they are personally guarding her. We couldn't get in pretending to be anyone else, except Clifton himself, and we don't know where he is." Derek's patience was wearing thin.

"Fine. You could have told me all this before we left, you know," Kala muttered defensively.

"I thought you'd trust me, Kala. I know I betrayed you, but I thought I'd proven myself by now. Think of how many times since then that I've blindly trusted you. I got this." Derek shook his head.

"I do trust you." Kala's pang of guilt was spreading rapidly. Yes, Derek had turned her in to Clifton and Turner, but he had thought he was doing the right thing. She had more than forgiven him. Derek had been through a lot because of her and had to *believe* a lot because of her. Questioning each other wasn't a part of their modus operandi. "I'm ready." No more questions. Whatever happened, happened. Kala vowed to be prepared for it and protect Derek at all costs.

Derek steadied the nanos like surveillance cameras, forming them into one group in each area where they were headed, creating thirty small screens in Kala's goggles. It was faded enough that she could still see well enough to move freely and comfortably. She kept the mesh covering of the phase-suit pulled back until they actually had to pass through a wall.

Pocketing the controlling metal egg, Derek led Kala through the belly of the Compound.

The path the nanos found was the path of least resistance, which Kala was grateful for. She didn't like hurting her fellow soldiers.

They were only following orders, and if the situation had been reversed, Kala would do the same thing. As far as Clifton's men were concerned, the two of them were enemy invaders. If only they knew what was really going on. Kala barely believed it – and she was an actual Titan – so the possibility of explaining themselves was out of the question.

The first two phases went off without a hitch. Sneaking into empty rooms and avoiding hallways was the only reason why alarms hadn't gone off. It amazed Kala at how much of the Compound didn't have cameras. It only proved to her the distrust between Turner and Clifton. If anything happened to Roberta, Turner would obliterate Clifton. Saving her would only delay the inevitable, though. At some point, the Turner/Clifton relationship would come to a head. Kala just hoped she wouldn't be around to see it.

After the third phase Derek pulled back the mesh covering on his face and puked. It was so out of character for him, Kala didn't react right away. Then her protective instinct kicked in. "You're staying here. I'll get Roberta."

Derek wiped his mouth and shook his head. "I'm good." He placed the mesh back over his head and walked through the fourth wall before Kala could stop him.

Kala sighed in frustration, following close behind. She knew Derek long enough to know the guy wasn't going to back down.

After the eighth wall, Derek dropped to the floor. This time he puked up blood.

Kala rushed to his side, but by the time she arrived, he was already half-way to standing. "Derek, this is ridiculous. You're going to die. Stay here and I'll come for you when I can teleport back in here," Kala pleaded.

263

Derek shrugged her off with his hand. "No. I can do this."

"The blood-vomit on the floor disagrees with you." Kala was tempted to knock him out and come back for him later, but she was afraid it would injure Derek more. This must have been how Owen and Talan felt about her when she was in the god hideout.

Then she remembered when she first encountered Asmodeus and the Malak, Grautlin, had shot her. Asmodeus had healed her. He was a Demon, not a Titan, but maybe Kala had similar powers. She had to at least try. "Let me try and heal you." She motioned Derek to come to her.

Derek's face was skeptical. "You can do that?"

"Honestly? I have no idea, but before your guts come out of your mouth, I suggest you let me try."

He nodded and moved next to her. Derek always appreciated Kala's bluntness and, by the greenish pallor of his dark skin, he would be willing to try anything.

She mimicked what Asmodeus had done to her, placing her hands on his body, one on Derek's chest and one on his stomach. Then Kala concentrated as hard as she could. She imagined healing Derek from the inside out. Since there wasn't an actual *wound* to focus on, she had to center her thoughts on his entire body.

"Anything?" she asked hopefully.

"I still feel like shit," Derek said weakly.

Kala felt like an idiot, standing there with her hands on Derek. She always used to make fun of faith healers she'd seen on TV. It made her wonder if they were really Demons using their powers to squeeze money out of people. She guessed, if they were curing people of their ailments, it wasn't a bad trade-off. But if those people knew they were being healed by Demons it might screw up their whole *faith* thing.

Kala was about to write-off her attempt to fix Derek as impossible when she began to feel warmth under his skin.

He responded in turn. "I definitely feel that."

A surge of motivation flowed through her and Kala concentrated harder. The heat grew in intensity and her hands began to burn. A part of her questioned if she should continue since she had no idea what she was doing, but the other part of her wanted to fix her friend.

"Kala." Derek's voice was small and choked. Something was wrong.

She tried to pull her hands away...

But they were stuck.

The burning grew more and more intense.

"Kala!" Derek screamed.

She yanked and yanked, but it was as if her hands were glued to his chest.

In a bright burst of white light, Kala was thrown backwards, finally separating her from Derek. Quickly rising to her feet, she raced over to him.

He stood in the same spot where she'd left him... and he was smiling.

"Are you okay?" Kala was terrified that she had caused him permanent damage.

Derek slowly nodded, then flexed his hands open and shut as if he had just injected himself with adrenaline. "I feel... amazing."

Relieved, Kala examined him more thoroughly, but there was nothing really to examine. "You really feel fine?"

"Better than fine. I feel like I could run up Mt. Everest barefoot. Whatever you did, it worked. A lot."

The last time Kala had seen Derek like this was when he drank ten espresso shots on a dare from Lali. "Well, I guess it worked." Kala was happy, though part of her knew she had done more than heal Derek. Burning hands and bright flashes of white light were never good, especially when she had been making it up as she went. She glanced at the clock in the room.

0d 01h 02m 43s: 3:58 AM.

An hour and two minutes. Her heart sank. "Let's get Roberta and get out of here."

Derek was so full of energy he saluted and leapt into the ninth wall. Kala followed and they were in the final room before Roberta's. The phase hadn't effected Derek at all this time. Even as a Titan, Kala experienced some disorientation from phasing, granted a lot less than she had as a human, but still. He appeared as if running through walls revitalized him. She couldn't worry about what she might have done or not done to Derek, they needed to figure out what their next move was going to be.

Derek's eyes were wide with drive. "We won't have much time before Ron and Jim try to signal the alarm. Do you have any crazy powers that could help us?" He seemed juiced to see more of what Kala could do.

She wished she could appease him, but Cronus may have put her other powers on lock-down as well. "We should rush them. You seem pretty amped up. If you run through the phase like you just did, I think we should be able to catch them completely off guard. I'll try and use the whole telekinesis thing, but I'm kind of hit or miss with my new skill sets."

This was good enough for Derek. "On my mark. One, two… three." He ran like a bull through the wall. His body even made a popping noise, he moved so fast.

Kala ran after him. The phase jolted her insides and she almost barfed when she entered the room.

Derek already had Ron in a headlock.

Jim reached for the alarm. Kala sucked up her feelings of discomfort and jumped at Jim's feet, tackling him to the floor before his hand could reach the alarm. She was about to punch him out with her Titan strength when a lamp smashed over his head.

Roberta stood over the two of them, a satisfied grin on her face.

Derek made quick work of Ron and the two guards were now unconscious lumps on the floor.

Roberta held out her hand to help Kala to her feet. "I'm glad you could make it."

Derek pulled out two small disks the size of pennies from inside his suit. Activating them made a beam of light shoot out of each disk. With Ron and Jim side by side, Derek scanned their bodies with the devices, then tossed one to Kala. "Keep it on you and press the red circle."

He pressed down on the disk he was holding. With a flicker of light, Derek's body transformed into Jim's. Kala did the same and she was now Ron. When she looked down at her own hands, she saw the exact same hands that were lying on the ground in front of her.

Derek and Kala tied up Ron and Jim's unconscious forms and left them on the couch.

"We move quickly." Derek opened the door and the trio was off.

The plan was to go to Fortski's lab. Derek knew a secret way out from there and he would lead Roberta to safety. Kala would stay behind to complete her mission.

Simple.

She just hoped it actually would be.

By the time they reached the last hallway leading to the lab, they had passed fifteen of Clifton's men. They were questioned every time, but everyone bought the story that they were moving Roberta to a safer location.

Kala thought they had almost made it when they turned the last corner and came face-to-face with General Clifton.

His eyes widened in shock at seeing his most trusted men moving Roberta from her prison. "I gave you strict orders!" he screamed. "Take her back to her room!" His eyes met Roberta's and he stumbled a bit in his speech. "I promise I'll send word as soon as I find out Geoffrey's status."

Kala made a quick surveillance of the hallway to make sure no one was there. With one Titan-packed punch, Clifton's body hit the ground hard. "He should be out for a while."

Even as Jim, Derek's smile was his own. "Nice. I only wish I could have done it."

"Me, too," Roberta echoed.

Derek was amused by that, but they were running out of time. He led them down the hallway and into Fortski's lab.

It appeared empty, just like the last time Kala had been through there.

Derek deactivated his disguise, Kala following suit.

"You take Roberta back to Turner. I have to stay here," Kala instructed him.

Before Derek could respond, Cronus teleported in behind him.

"You shouldn't be here. Now for your punishment," he scolded Kala.

Cronus snapped Derek's neck.

Chapter Twenty-Nine

For a moment everything froze.

In slow motion, Kala watched her best friend in the entire world fall to the floor, lifeless.

Out of the corner of her eye, Kala saw Roberta's eyes turn black. Then she began to speak, and the words that came out her mouth were ancient and powerful.

Cronus reached over and touched Roberta's arm; she collapsed onto the ground. "She's not dead, but she will be soon enough. She and her husband would have been key players in the future I'll never let happen."

Kala stared at Derek lying on the floor, his head twisted in the wrong direction.

She was in shock.

She couldn't move or speak.

And Cronus kept acting as if they were having a casual conversation.

As if he needed to teach her a lesson.

As if he could justify killing Derek.

Fury pumped through her like fire. She stared at Cronus and deep within the well of her being, she cried, "YOU KILLED HIM!"

Cronus withered in fear. "Now, don't blow this out of proportion. Your friend is fine…"

Rage and wrath consumed Kala's soul. "I WILL SWALLOW YOU WHOLE!"

Cronus took a step back. "He's alive! Remember the white light? Instead of healing his wounds, you healed him *forever*. He can't die!"

Kala heard him, but his words weren't enough to calm her ferocity. Seeing Derek dead in front of her was too much for Kala to comprehend. She needed to end Cronus once and for all.

Cronus appeared to sense this as well, but instead of moving away from her, he shifted toward her. "I can't let you complete your mission no matter what you do to me. I'm taking you to the 5th."

He touched her arm and Kala felt the familiar sensation of teleporting. It only enraged her more. There was no way she was going to the 5th Level of Hell. And there was no way she was going to let Cronus dictate whether or not she would complete her job.

When their surroundings came into focus, they weren't in the 5th.

They were above ground, almost a mile from the main entrance of the Compound. It was where Derek had taken them when they had escaped the structure days before.

It was enough of a shock that Kala was jolted out of the intense anger that threatened to overwhelm her. She peered up at Cronus, whose face betrayed his own surprise as well.

Kala could tell they were both thinking the same thing: that she was responsible. How else could the leader of the Titans fail to teleport the two of them to his desired destination? In her fury, her powers always grew stronger, so it made sense. But, now that she had calmed down a bit, there was nothing stopping Cronus from taking her to the 5th.

He seemed to have the same thought because he reached over to touch her arm again.

Nothing.

Cronus grabbed her tighter.

Nothing.

Kala removed his hand forcefully. "Sucks, doesn't it?"

Cronus tried to reach for her again, outrage and shock visible in every expression line on his face. "How are you doing that? You're not stronger than me! No one is!" His temper was palpable.

"I AM." A large booming voice reverberated in the air.

Before their eyes, Zeus materialized.

"Hello, Father." Zeus smiled. He wore a suit like his dad, but his tie was loose around the neck. Being a few inches taller and wider than Cronus, Zeus was a lot more daunting.

The father-son duo radiated power, staring at each other. Kala suddenly wanted to duck out of their line of fire.

The big *uh-oh* moment for Cronus happened next.

In a line behind Zeus were Penny, Talan, Rotoph, Owen, Antel and the other four Grigori whose names Kala didn't remember. But the one who sealed the deal, and made even Kala take a step back was Hephaestus.

Somehow, Zeus had managed to find and rescue his son. Kala knew with certainty what they planned on doing next.

Open the Grigori portal.

Kala knew who the winning side of this battle was going to be.

Cronus didn't flinch. "You'll be dead before that portal opens," he sneered.

The Titans: Hyperion, Themis, and Iapetus teleported in behind Cronus.

"Now, Hephaestus!" Zeus roared.

In response, the Grigori, Penny, and Hephaestus formed a circle and Hephaestus began the chant that would open the gateway.

Cronus and his Titans stormed past Kala, charging Zeus and the ring of power behind him.

With an audible CRACK, the Titans slapped against an invisible wall protecting Zeus.

The Olympian laughed at his father. "I've been renewed with the power of Gaia! Your days are done, Father! Even as we speak, I have my Olympians taking over your precious 5th and destroying every molecule of that decrepit place! You tortured and imprisoned me for thousands of years, now I intend to do the same to you!" His eyes glowed purple with power and rage.

The *Gaia* part of that conversation left Kala feeling a little responsible. She was the one that had fallen for Zeus's little battery-suck tactic. But the expression on Cronus's face said it all.

He was torn. Torn over whether to stay and fight, or to go to the 5th and save his home.

As an observer, Kala made a few realizations about Cronus over the last few days. He loved power and he loved being feared. He was always trying to assert his authority by *punishing* the beings that *wronged* him. Throwing pieces of Talan's body at Kala's feet, snapping Derek's neck: they were all moves designed to exert his dominance. But as soon as he saw that Kala would kick his butt, he'd backtracked and tried to make nice. He liked being safe. He wanted to be the bully from the next room, unless he was assured of a win, then he'd confront his victims directly.

She could tell Cronus wouldn't stoop to sucking up to his son, so Kala wondered what his next move would be.

When he spoke, his voice dripped with force and intimidation. "I am the god of time itself. Your puny barriers can't stop me, Son." Cronus threw his hand out at the barrier.

BOOM!

Iapetus was the first to react, throwing himself at Zeus and tackling him to the ground.

Hephaestus's chant grew louder and louder.

The portal began to open.

Kala felt out of place. She watched as this crazy supernatural battle unfolded in front of her, with no idea what to do. She wasn't a part of the circle so she couldn't just join in the middle. And something held her back from using her Grigori blade against the Titans. It was almost as if Kala was witnessing a family squabble and she wanted to stay out of it. Granted, the family was made up of super-powered gods and angels, but the maturity level was about the same as any normal human family. Meaning nil to none.

The ground shook violently beneath her feet.

Zeus held back all four Titans as they clawed and scratched to reach past him and pull even just one person from the circle.

Kala was impressed and she knew she should give him some help, but her feet remained locked in place. Why couldn't she move? Zeus was alone and helping the ones she loved. It was something deep inside her. Remembering the future Cronus had shown her. A dark, bleak future full of murder and secrets. He claimed the Grigori were responsible.

And this was the moment.

The moment where she could either stop it or help its coming.

She wanted to do neither.

The ground shook again.

Kala watched in fascination as the portal opened to eight times as large as the previous gateway. Good or bad, Grigori flooded out of the gates and swarmed at Cronus and the other Titans.

Cronus knew the battle was lost.

He briefly made eye contact with Kala, his voice speaking into her head, *Don't let this future come to pass.*

Then he was gone.

The other Titans disappeared with him.

There was still chaos as hundreds of Grigori poured through the portal. Zeus joined the circle and the gateway grew to the size of a house.

Kala had seen enough.

The ground shook once more.

That was when she knew it wasn't the opening that caused the shaking.

It was the end of the world.

Kala hadn't been paying attention to the time.

If she didn't complete her mission, this new future wouldn't exist.

A part of her was tempted to let it burn.

But, if she did that, Jack would have died for nothing.

Kala knew then that she'd never refuse an Atlas mission, no matter how horrible. She couldn't do that to his memory. He'd died to save the world. Kala had murdered him. She needed to hold onto the shred of justification that she had.

Cronus was gone.

She could teleport again.

Kala left the mayhem in front of her and arrived in Fortski's lab.

Derek sat on a stool next to Roberta while Fortski took a sampling of blood from his arm.

Kala nearly cried in relief. She raced over to him and practically shoved Fortski out of the way, hugging Derek fiercely.

"I'm okay. I don't know how, but I'm okay," Derek assured her.

Roberta added, "His neck cracked back into place right in front of us. John is taking a sample of his blood to analyze."

Cronus had been right.

"Congrats, Derek. You're officially death-proof." Kala didn't want to let him go.

When the earth shook again, she knew she was running out of time. Glancing at the clock, she shuddered.

0d 0h 01m 04s.

One minute left.

"Derek, take Roberta out of here." He saw the determination in Kala's eyes and nodded.

When they were gone, Kala turned to Fortski. She didn't have to ask which computers held the answers to a cancer cure. She recognized them from her vision.

"I'm going to destroy all your research on cancer," she told him.

Fortski appeared more surprised that she knew what he was working on rather than the threat. "How did you... I haven't even told Geoffrey... What do you mean?"

The ground shook.

"You feel that? If I don't do it, the world ends." Kala only had thirty seconds left.

Fortski stepped toward her threateningly. Kala pulled out her gun and held it level, but she wasn't aiming at Fortski, she was aiming at the computers.

She shot the three computers containing the cure, destroying the hard drives, and pretty much turning them into a pile of mechanical mush.

Fortski grabbed a pile of papers off the desk and held them in front of him as if they were the Holy Grail.

The papers from her vision.

Kala played her part.

She leapt forward and grabbed the papers from his hand.

Fortski screamed, "Please! You can't! That's the only copy."

"I know. I destroyed all the hard drives," Kala reminded him. "I have to do this. Trust me. It's for the best."

"No, please!" Fortski pleaded. "Do you know how many lives I can save with that? Thousands! Millions even!"

Kala shook her head. "I have to."

"Didn't you ever know anyone with cancer? You can save them! You'll be destroying the cure! Do you understand?! You're destroying the only copy I have! I can't memorize equations like this! Turner will kill you for this!" Fortski was in a total panic. Just like she remembered.

Kala finally felt the calm that she saw in her face when she witnessed the vision. "No, he won't." Kala took her lighter and set the papers on fire.

Fortski shrieked and jumped at her. Kala pushed him away with ease. She had almost forgotten that the push would make Fortski soar clear across the room and crash against the wall. His cries tore her up, but she also knew he'd be inventing something far greater in the future. Something that would cure humans of more than just cancer.

It would make them immortal.

The prophecy repeated in her head over and over for better or worse.

The immortals will reign.

03d 23h 59m 59s.

OTHER BOOKS

THE RISER SAGA
RISER
REAPER
RIPPER

THE ATLAS SERIES
ATLAS
GRIGORI RETURNED
THE UNDERWORLD

RISER SAGA/ATLAS SERIES FINALE:
ATLAS RISING

THE DREAM DIARIES
THE DREAM DIARIES
THE DREAM DIARIES: BLOOD TIES

THE ALEXIS TAPPENDORF SERIES
ALEXIS TAPPENDORF AND THE SEARCH FOR BEALE'S TREASURE
ALEXIS TAPPENDORF AND THE SEARCH FOR ATLANTIS

JERALINE'S ALLEY

LOVE & DARK SERIES (WRITTEN WITH HINA MC-CORD)
VESSEL
FIRST BORN
GUTIAN CODE

Bio

Becca fell in love with storytelling at an early age. The first book she read was The Lion, The Witch and The Wardrobe and she's been looking for the door to Narnia ever since! Becca is a passionate reader, consuming anything sci-fi or fantasy. Mix it in with YA and she is a fan for life. So it's no surprise that she writes in these genres as well. When Becca isn't writing, she loves to sew. From Mortal Instruments rune pillows, to elaborate Firefly/Serenity bags, Becca loves to create!